The One You Call Sister

© Paula Martinac 1989

First published in Ireland in 1990 by
Attic Press,
44 East Essex Street,
Dublin 2.

First published in the United States of America by
Cleis Press, PO Box 8933, Pittsburgh, PA 15221, and
PO Box 14684, San Francisco, CA 94114.

British Library Cataloguing in Publication Data
The one you call sister.
   1. Short stories in English - Anthologies
   I. Martinac, Paula
   823.0108 [FS]

ISBN 0-946211-11-6

Cover Design: Paula Nolan
Typesetting: CaliCo Graphics
Made and printed in Great Britain by
The Guernsey Press Co. Ltd., Guernsey, Channel Islands.

The One You Call Sister

edited by
Paula Martinac

Attic Press
Dublin

Acknowledgments

My special thanks to: the many friends who talked with me or wrote to me about sisters and were on the lookout for stories; E.M. Broner and the members of my writing group—Barbara Ball, Elisabeth Burger, Edith Chevat, Melissa Mishcon, Elizabeth Neuhoff, Tricia Tunstall, and Nancy Woodruff—for their critiques of "Kay, Grown Up" and for their encouragement of my writing about family; Joanne O'Hare for her thoughts on the final selection of stories; Suzanne Seay for her help with and many laughs over the introduction; and Frédérique Delacoste and Felice Newman of Cleis Press for their invaluable editorial suggestions and particularly for their trust.

Finally, this book is for my literal sisters, Carol and Mary Lou, and for my metaphoric ones, especially Suzanne, Catherine, Fran, Nancy K. and Louise.

Grateful acknowledgment is made for permission to reprint previously published material: The title *The One You Call Sister* from the poem "The Mirror in Which Two Are Seen as One" in *The Fact of a Doorframe, Poems Selected and New, 1950-1984*, by Adrienne Rich. Copyright © 1984 by Adrienne Rich. Copyright © 1975, 1978 by W.W. Norton & Company, Inc. Copyright © 1981 by Adrienne Rich. Used with the permission of the author. "A Red Sweater" by Fae Myenne Ng first published in *The American Voice* and *The Pushcart Prize XII: Best of the Small Presses (1987-88)*; reprinted by permission of the author. "Secrets of an Unkosher Home" by Jean Roberta first published under the title "Sisters" in *Secrets of the Invisible World* by Jean Roberta, Lilith Publications, Montreal, Quebec, 1988; reprinted by permission of the publisher. "Design" by Dawn Raffel first published in *North American Review*; reprinted by permission of the author. "Waiting" by Budge Wilson first published in *University of Windsor Review* and *The Journey Prize Anthology*, 1989; reprinted by permission of the author. "Funny Women" by Shay Youngblood, first published in *The Big Mama Stories* by Shay Youngblood, Firebrand Books, Ithaca, New York, 1989; reprinted by permission of the publisher.

Contents

Introduction

THE LAST TIME I visited my parents, I found a photograph from the 1950's of my two older sisters and me, in which we look very sisterly. We are dressed in identical polka-dotted pajamas with nightcaps to match, sitting lined up according to size on the living room floor. We look pretty silly, but the picture made me feel nostalgic anyway.

I remember that my middle sister was with me the day I purchased my first grown-up book. I was eleven and over-whelmed by the choices the bookstore offered me, until my sister helped me pick *Jane Eyre*. That same year, my oldest sister took me to Washington, D.C., the most sophisticated traveling I'd done up until then. I am still an avid buyer of books, and a traveler who, like my sister, maps out most of the details before leaving home.

Of course, not all my memories of my sisters are sweet. They sometimes locked me out of their room or refused to play with me, and they still call me their "baby" sister even though I am thirty-five. But they have had a profound influence on me and on what I have made of my life, and that is what led me to this anthology.

A few years ago, someone suggested to me that sisters, perhaps more than mothers, are the prototypes for our relation-ships with other women as friends and lovers, because they are our first female peers. The more I thought about it, the more it made sense for me as a lesbian and a feminist and the more I became interested in what other women had to say about their experiences with their sisters.

What I found among published work was very little in the way of nonfiction and even less in terms of fiction. Most of the nonfiction was either literary criticism about works written a hundred years ago, explorations of sisters in classical mythology or popular fairy tales, or analyses of the relationships of famous sisters, like Virginia Woolf and Vanessa Bell. And while it was all very interesting, what I really wanted to read were contemporary stories that addressed some of the questions raised by the articles and essays I'd come across. That was the start of this collection. I wanted to encourage women writers to think about the complexity of the sister relationship and to turn their talents to that area, much in the same way they began tackling the mother/daughter relationship several years ago.

This is a book about sisters, for sisters, our first female friends and allies. They were more like us than our brothers or parents. Through them, we learned to have relationships with other women. Maybe we've mimicked those first relationships in adulthood. Or maybe we've improved on them with our circle of women friends and lovers, who are, we might say, our metaphoric sisters.

These fifteen stories form a palette of our experiences. Some resonate with the jealousies of growing up. "Yours were the top drawers with the pretty glass knobs," writes Julia Alvarez, "the left side of the closet that was closest to the mirror." Others proclaim a fierce devotion, born of being sisters. "I had lots and lots of other friends who were more interesting," Budge Wilson's narrator tells us, reminiscing about childhood; but when it came down to it, she always chose her sister's company first.

While we might look to our sisters for the symbolic roots of our relationships with women lovers, Shay Youngblood startles us with her portrait of two women who are *literally* both sisters and lovers.

In other stories, sisters face each other as adult survivors. "How many times did my sister and I have to hold them apart?" asks Fae Myenne Ng's character about her parents. The Jamaican sisters of Donna Weir's "Gal Pickney" struggle to balance their feelings about their mother and the culture she represents with their new life in the United States. Jean Roberta depicts sisters with a "dark secret" who try to find some common language other than violence.

The sweet and silly memories are here, too. Bárbara Selfridge paints an unforgettable scene of four middle-aged sisters romping on the beach like girls, adorning their bare breasts with seaweed leis. In my "Kay, Grown Up," a young girl invades her teenage sister's underwear drawer, unsure what she's looking for. And Wendy Ann Ryden's baseball fans remind us that many sisters become each other's lifelong companions and best friends and enjoy the kind of relationship idealized by the term "sisterhood."

I undertook this anthology for somewhat selfish reasons, to work out my own issues about having sisters and how they have influenced my other relationships. In the process, I discovered that I am not alone, that women harbor feelings about their sisters that are often contradictory, painful and dear all at the same time. Maybe I'm just sentimental, but I hope that these stories will make us all—no matter how long it's been or how great the distance—want to pick up the phone and call our sisters.

Paula Martinac
Brooklyn, New York
July 1989

yin and yang

Marianne Paul

CANADIANS ARE RUGGED. We can handle winter. It has been programmed into our genes from the time of Champlain. We collectively delight in the freak blizzards that periodically jump out and yell "Boo!" at Californians. The slickest media campaign can do no more to promote national unity than a sheet of ice sending American sun worshipers skidding into telephone poles and across our television screens because they don't have snow tires.

The humidity of summer: now that is what gives us trouble. The kind of heat that is stifling, like today, and what do I see, but a lady wrapped in a winter coat like a hot dog in a bun, leather boots on her feet as if the coat is not enough to keep her warm. And all this during an ungodly and unpatriotic heat wave, as if the rest of the country were out of synch with the calendar, and not her.

I turn my car away from Arista's attic loft, and hear my sister honking her disapproval since I am invited for dinner and bound to be late, and over-steamed vegetables are unpalatable even to her dedicated vegetarian taste. With relief, I realize the sound originates with the car behind me, where a man waves his fist angrily in my direction, a more soothing sight than Arista eating soggy vegetables and making me feel guilty because I am late and chose to be a commercial artist.

Three corners into the street, and I spot the lady again. I deduce that she is not forced by circumstance to carry her possessions wherever she goes. The hem of the coat fashionably

11

covers the knee, neither drowning the shins nor exposing the thighs like the brigade of Salvation Army castoffs that take drill practice up and down this very sidewalk each winter. The boots are leather, and from their nearly new condition, have not suffered a winter of stalking the streets in search of a warm grate.

The lady ducks into the park. I ditch my car in a no-standing zone and continue the chase by foot. I find her pretending to be perfectly sane, sitting on a bench and reading a magazine. I sit on the bench too, also pretending to be perfectly sane, studying the lady and noticing, with the pride of parenthood, that the magazine features my artwork.

"I did that," I tell the lady as a lead-in to the obvious question about her clothing.

"Wrote the article?" she asks, looking up from her reading, obviously impressed.

"No, designed the art for the computer advertisement."

"Oh," the lady says, and then studies my work. "I like the way you combine the creative and the pragmatic in the same presentation."

"Thank you."

The comment surprises me; I had not expected a lady who wears winter clothes in summer to be articulate.

"If you will allow me to comment further—"

"Please do." What could I say?

"—your art suggests the Chinese Tao, the creative force, if you will, the yin and yang in perfect balance, opposite, equal and necessary partners in this amusement ground we call existence."

"I hadn't thought of it in quite that way." I don't know whether to laugh or leave. Instead, like a fool, I sit and listen.

"There are many ways to view a work of art—"

"Of course—"

"—and art is reflected in many things, even in an advertisement for computers."

The lady stands, slipping the magazine under her arm in an action miming goodbye. "Now, if you will be so kind as to excuse me—"

"No, I mean yes, of course, but first, I want to ask a question."

The statement of my intent makes me sound like a disciple at the feet of a guru, and I feel absurd. The lady waits patiently while I stumble for words.

"Why are you wearing—those clothes?" I blurt out, as if I have asked something truly important, like how the universe began.

"Why do you ask?"

"It just struck me as odd—"

"Because it is different?"

"Well, yes."

"And you want me to give you a reason for my actions?"

"I was just curious—"

"Walk a mile in my moccasins."

There is amusement in the lady's eyes, and I assume it is because she has mixed her "images," so to speak, Chinese folklore and Native people cliche.

"Moccasins won't exactly produce the same effect as wearing your winter coat and boots," I laugh.

"Then be my guest. Take the coat and boots," the lady says, shedding her winter clothes like a caterpillar emerging from its cocoon.

It may seem strange that I knock at the door instead of simply turning the knob and entering the loft. According to popular myth, sisters exist on the same side of the closed door, sharing teddy bears and secrets in the privacy of a common bedroom. But this is not a commercial for detergent, where I burst on stage, praise the value of family, and intimately confide the perfect product for getting clothes whiter than white.

Arista answers my knock. She smiles that tiny smile that is not really a smile at all, but a frown in disguise.

"Glad you could make it," she says, meaning the vegetables are soggy, and I am late and chose to be a commercial artist.

"Sorry," I apologize. "I got caught up in this project, a layout for a fashion spread, and lost track of time."

"It's beyond me how you could lose track of time doing something as mundane as a layout for a fashion spread. Sounds like a clock-watcher to me."

I ignore the comment rather than try to explain the merit of my work. Explanations sound feeble in the presence of Arista, and I inevitably feel guilty as hell for being successful, living in a condominium apartment with a view of the lake, having a bank account that is never overdrawn, and giving Christmas presents that aren't homemade.

"Work isn't the only reason I'm late."

Arista doesn't ask any questions, although I have given her the perfect opening. After a pause, I continue talking for the sake of conversation.

"I saw the most bizarre sight—"

"A billboard with your latest advertisement on it?"

"No—thank you—a lady, can you believe it, dressed in a winter coat and boots. In this weather!"

"Likely a bag lady."

"No, she wasn't, and we had the strangest conversation, something straight from 'The Twilight Zone,' or at least, from a George Lucas movie. You know what I mean. I expected her to say 'May the Force be with you' when she left."

"Bag ladies are depressing, with their poverty and all, but what would you know about poverty? Let's eat."

Arista serves the perfect meal to suit the image of a starving-artist vegetarian: spaghetti smothered in meatless tomato sauce with a side order of broccoli. I stab a forkful of soggy broccoli, and promise myself a fast-food feast on the way home. Arista refuses to eat animals, which of course rules out hamburgers, although shrimp and sushi are part of her diet when she can afford them, which is not the same as eating cows and pigs and lambs and chickens, or so she tells me.

Arista pours the red wine. I think she has already had a few glasses herself, because the bottle is half empty. This bottle is not the same bottle that housed the wine in the store, but a corkless carafe with an image of a bunch of grapes stamped on it, the kind of bottle with the brim pushed out wider than the neck as if life itself is being squeezed up and away, the kind of bottle that should only exist in an ad for an Italian restaurant.

My sister tells me about her latest art exhibition, how difficult it is to choose just the right pieces to make a cohesive statement, how the paintings must unite to demonstrate a central theme, how some of the watercolors have a good chance of selling but not being a commercial artist, profit is secondary to her. She has more compelling reasons to paint than money, such as self-expression, communication of the human spirit, and the portrayal of the nature of the universe.

I drink another glass of wine.

Arista's apartment is typical of what you may imagine from a Fine Arts graduate. I don't say that in a negative way, nor do I mean to impose stereotypes, but being in advertising, I notice these things.

An easel is positioned near the skylight, brushes lie on a nearby table as if part of a window display, a palette waits ready to indulge the creative whim whenever it happens to strike, a coffee-table book sits with its pages straddled to the works of the Group of Seven, and a ceramic jug features long feathery stalks that resemble wheat.

"You really should buy yourself some decent clothes," Arista is telling me. "You look so uptight in those pleated skirts and silk blouses you wear to work, although I am sure they cost you a fortune."

I push the last noodle around my plate with the fork. I like the clothes I wear, never feel that they are wrong until I visit Arista.

"Something cotton would be nice, something loose, something that breathes," Arista continues while emptying the wine into her goblet and then leaving the table to refill the bottle.

I feel a wave of self-doubt edging upon me with the slow and stubborn determination of a tide.

"Come, let's retire to the living room," Arista says after dinner, her voice whining, like the sound of a bow against the string of a violin in the hands of a beginner.

The living room is not a room at all but a corner of a multi-purpose space that serves every capacity except cooking. We sit on big fringed "Made-in-India" pillows that are tossed with staged carelessness around a Persian-style rug.

Arista places the wine on a small table that resembles an orange crate. She is barefooted. I remove my shoes and shove them into my purse before she can comment, feeling somehow that Arista is right, even though she hasn't said aloud that I should really buy myself a pair of sandals.

Arista sits cross-legged on the rug. She looks thoughtfully into her goblet, tipping it in such a way that the smooth surface of the wine expands to fill the space. Then, she moves her hand in a circular motion, creating a storm at sea, which makes me feel seasick with anticipation.

"Everyone thought you would be the artist in the family," Arista begins.

"I *am* an artist," I say, although without much confidence, the claim sounding like a lie against the backdrop of orange crate furniture, the easel and the skylight and my long-haired sister.

"You were so *good*, showed so much *promise*, always winning those poster contests as a kid, being awarded that scholarship in high school to go to summer art school."

The humidity is stifling, even though a window is open. I feel the heat sitting on my face and chest with the weight of a fat lady, so I unbutton the top of my blouse. Perhaps it is the effect of the wine, but the air has thickened so that breathing is difficult, and I begin to panic.

"I can't understand why you chose to go to a university that specializes in commercial art, and why you took that minor in business—"

I look around the room at works in various stages of development, some hanging in frames on the wall, others matted ready for framing, others half filled with form, waiting definition from

Arista's brush. She is good and, in time, will be very good.

"I guess you sold out to the highest bidder," Arista says with triumph, as if the whole night, and perhaps our whole lives, has built towards this one statement. The wine that pulses through her body and flushes her cheeks gives her the courage and right to say, not simply imply, what she believes to be true.

The evening is still more day than night, it being midsummer, with the sun at the beginning of its return to the winter solstice. I drive back through the events of the last few hours, tracing the path from the moment I storm out of Arista's attic loft like a fool to the conversation with the lady on the bench.

I circle the block, feeling guilty because Arista's accusation may be true, and wishing I drove a cheap Chevette instead of a brand new Volvo, as if that could be sacrificed to my confusion and appease the angry gods of my self-doubt.

The air conditioner in my car is broken, and the heat is stifling without sign of relief. It is too hot to be roaming the streets unless you are a Bruce Springsteen-type in a '57 Chevy, arm hanging out the window, a pack of cigarettes stuffed under the sleeve of your tee shirt, the car radio blaring rock-and-roll with the fervor of belief. But that image is too intense, and I stop near the park hoping to escape the heat under the trees.

I know that what I do is insane even as I do it, but I go to the back of the car, slip the key into the lock, open the trunk, take off my shoes and put on the boots of the strange lady.

I know that what I am going to do next is even more insane, if insanity may be measured in degrees, but I reach into the trunk and pull out the coat. I push my arm through a sleeve and catch the corner of the coat around my back and pull it across my shoulders and push my arm through the other sleeve and do up the buttons.

No one has noticed me, and I consider dashing into the car and racing home and throwing the coat and boots into the incinerator, except there isn't an incinerator in my condominium, and the furnace is hibernating for the season. So I

17

walk around the block, trying not to meet the stares of yuppies who have braved the inner core for the pleasures of an evening stroll, trying not to advertise my unease with the mocking disapproval of lovers too young to be entwined in each other's arms in such defiant displays of passion.

I find escape within my discomfort. The boots are small, squeezing my toes and heels with the jeering promise of blisters. The fur lining makes my feet cry with tears of sweat. The coat is hot and heavy and irritates my patience, and I feel my heart beat faster and my body temperature rise, and I wonder if I will faint, or even die.

I think of the monks who wear sackcloth for penance and the nuns who whip themselves with rosary beads for atonement and wonder if this is the intent of the lady, if bearing the cross of these boots and coat in this deathly heat is a ritual of cleansing meant to wash away secret sin. I wonder if I am doing penance, and I find the truth shocking.

The sidewalk merges into the park and the trees, and I sit on the bench. The sky is darkening, and I am moved by the fullness of the moon against the emptiness of the sky. I wonder if the moon is aware that paired with the sky it is art. I think about my work and how I lose myself in the beauty of the act of each creation, how the whole day passes and feels like a few minutes, how I choose and shape each image with the care and attention of love.

I look about me and see that the city is full of creation, most of it mundane, if you view it simply as buildings and roads and billboards crowding each other, candy wrappers discarded on the ground, and weeds pushing up between the cracks in the sidewalk as you hurry by. But then I begin to see the lines and shapes in another way, and how they intersect and interact to make the whole, and I see the architect behind the lines and shapes as sure as God, and the creative force that moves the weed to reach for life between the cracks of the sidewalk. The weed is not aware of the distinction between itself and the flower, because from this viewpoint, there is no distinction, only art.

And I begin to cry a bit, because there is no deep dark sin, no need for penance or atonement, and I am not my sister, and I have my own reasons. And then I laugh, because I feel wretched and look absurd in this winter coat and boots on a night when the heat is stifling and sits on my face and chest with the weight of a fat lady. And somehow, in this one moment, tears and laughter are both appropriate.

A woman joins me. I look into her face and see the question begging to be asked. Before she can ask it, I take off the coat and boots and lay them on the bench beside her.

The breath of the wind cools my skin, and the heat is no longer stifling. I smile with the relief of abandoning my burden and at the invitation I have placed beside this woman. And then, I leave.

Kay, Grown Up

Paula Martinac

WHEN SHE WAS in high school, my sister Kay used to spend most Saturday afternoons lying on her bed on her stomach, propped up on her elbows, her Keds crossed casually in the air, writing books. Actually, they were short stories, but she made individual books out of them, folding sheets of typewriter paper in half and stapling them together at the crease. She wrote a story in longhand inside, stopping when the pages were filled, and made a collage on the cover from pictures cut out of *Life* and *National Geographic*. All of our magazines had holes in them, and my mother got furious with Kay for destroying them. "Why can't you just *look* at the pictures, like other people?" she'd say.

Now we'd call Kay's creations artist's books. Then they were just her silly stories. My mother actually called them that. "Kay writes silly stories with sad endings," she explained to me, when I was old enough to wonder what Kay did all those Saturday afternoons on her bed. "She writes about people she couldn't possibly know anything about, people in France and Hawaii."

"How do you know?" I wondered, innocently.

"I just do," my mother said, turning a little pink. "You can tell by the covers. Well, pretty soon Kay'll forget all about writing stories. She's so petty, the boys have always paid her so much attention. She'll get married young, just like I did."

Kay wouldn't let anyone read her stories. She kept them in a Gimbel's box under her bed. If I came into her room when she was working on one, she covered it with a pillow. I always wanted to read her books, but I knew I was too young and insignificant to ask.

"What do *you* want?" She was never that cross when she wasn't writing.

"Want to play Mousetrap?" I often had to beg my sisters to play with me. "Please?" Because they were teenagers, Kay nine years older than I and Bub seven, they just as often refused, swatting me verbally out of the way like an annoying fly.

"I'm *working*," Kay said, pushing her determined chin into the pillow. "Go find Bub."

Kay was the first person I knew who called writing work. But it was years before I remembered that she had.

I was eight years old when I wrote my first story. It hadn't occurred to me that writing was something I, like Kay, could do. But one week, instead of a book report, Sister Theresa had us write a short story and design the cover. None of us had made up something on paper before, though we'd told our share of tales. Sister Theresa didn't confine our young imaginations.

"What should we write about?" someone asked.

"Anything you like," she answered. "An animal, a friend of yours, a place, a game—anything you can think of. Then draw a picture on a cover sheet with your name and the title of the story. You can write it out or print it or ask someone in your family to type it for you."

My eyes widened at the word "type." I had been intrigued by the brand new Olympia typewriter that Kay had gotten for Christmas. My mother was very proud of the gift. "It's important for you to have a skill, in case you need to make a living someday," she said, as my sister unwrapped it. "Suppose your husband dies or loses his job and you have to support your family." Kay looked a little disappointed, maybe because it was the same size as a portable record player, or because she couldn't look far enough ahead to marriage and widowhood.

"Sister Theresa says we have to type it," I said when I reported my homework to my mother.

"Really?" Standing at the stove, she looked at me skeptically over her shoulder. "Well, maybe I can do it for you. I'm pretty rusty though."

"I bet I could do it," I said.

"No, Robbie, even Kay hasn't really learned yet, and she's taking a typing class." She shook her head and continued stirring a pan of gravy.

"I'd do it with one finger," I persisted, choosing one and holding it up. "I'd be real careful. I'd go slow."

My mother turned around, wiped her hands on a terrycloth dish towel, and looked at me cautiously. "Well," she said finally, "we'll see."

When it was Sunday afternoon and time to type the one and a half pages of my story, my mother lifted the typewriter onto the kitchen table and started warming up. "Now is the time for all good men," she said aloud, as she pecked, but on the page it came out, "Now is tje ti,e for a;; good ,en."

"Why don't you look at the keys?" I asked, trying to be helpful.

"You're not supposed to," she said, frowning. "I haven't typed in twenty years," she added, apologetically, peering over the keys to the mess she'd made on the paper. "Is this due tomorrow?"

I nodded and she sighed, pulling the paper out of the roller with a snap. I patted her shoulder.

"Can I try?" I asked. "I'll do it with one finger."

"That will take forever. No, go see what Kay's doing. Tell her I want her to help you."

Kay was lying on her bed, listening to the rock 'n' roll station on the radio and reading her English homework. Since she wasn't working, she got up eagerly to help.

"Sure," she said, slapping her book closed. "It'll give me some practice."

She didn't want to type in the kitchen. She carried the typewriter back to the bedroom, where she set it on the floor between her bed and Bub's. We sat resting our backs against her bed, her with her legs around the typewriter, me with mine splayed in imitation of her.

"'Gillie was a soft brown fawn,'" she typed slowly, with all her fingers and no mistakes. I sat mesmerized by the thumping of the keys against the paper, the way my words appeared in type as if by magic. When she reached the bottom of the page, she read it over for mistakes, made a few changes with correction tape, then smiling contentedly at her work, pulled the sheet out of the carriage and handed it to me.

"This is a nice story, Robbie," she said, the corners of her deep green eyes crinkling into a smile. "This is an A+ story for sure."

I leaned against her gently. She didn't seem to mind, even though her arm was slightly restricted. At the top of the next page, she got a phone call from her current boyfriend.

"Wait for me," she said, "I'll be back."

But it was too long to wait. I got up and went to the bathroom twice. I touched everything in her bedroom once. I peeked into her underwear drawer. When Kay finally came back, it felt like she had been gone for hours. I was sitting with my legs around the typewriter, picking out the letters with my index finger, which had begun to feel cold and stiff. Gillie the fawn had just gotten shot.

"I have to get ready to go out, Robbie," Kay said. "Johnny wants to go to Isaly's for a milkshake." She stared down at the sheet in the typewriter. She couldn't believe I'd gotten so far. "Well, you seem to be doing okay," and she brushed her hand lightly across the top of my head, pushing the stray hairs out of my eyes. "And only using one finger!"

I continued to thump at the keys while her bath water ran. She was humming something that sounded like "Johnny Angel." It wasn't long before Gillie the fawn had recovered from his wounds.

23

No one wondered about it when Kay stopped lying on her bed on Saturdays, writing books. It seemed like a natural progression. It happened after high school, when she started Katherine Morris Business School. She took the secretarial course and worked part time as a file clerk to help pay her tuition. It was understood somehow that she'd get married soon and that four years of college would be a waste. My parents had to have money for Bub, the brain, to go to college.

After she started business school, Kay and her best friend Sue Kusak used to spend every Friday night at Teenworld Dance Club. They dressed up in the tightest pants their mothers would allow, teased and sprayed their hair till a hurricane wouldn't muss it, plucked their fair eyebrows off then drew them back on again in dark brown, and hopped into Sue's light blue Valiant. It was at Teenworld that Kay met Frankie Montana, to whom she became engaged and whose heart she later broke.

Now on Saturday afternoons, Kay and Sue went to Southland Shopping Plaza and picked out new clothes at Penney's for the dates they'd made for that night. Sometimes, if my mother insisted, they took me with them, but I was just as often busy writing stories. In fact, by the time I was eleven, I'd written a book of stories and two novellas at the typewriter. The first novella sounded suspiciously like *Jane Eyre*, and the second had a little too much of *Oliver Twist* about it. Though she'd frowned on Kay's stories, my mother thought it was cute and clever that I'd taken to writing so young, that I spent my summer vacations hunched over a typewriter instead of outside in the fresh air. "She's a little brain, isn't she, just like Bub," she'd say to my father. Her attention spurred me on. Sometimes I typed so furiously it stopped sounding like a typewriter. Our next door neighbor actually thought the sound came from a sewing machine. There were days when my finger went numb, and that was the only thing that got me to quit.

I never progressed beyond one finger, but Kay became a competent typist, eventually working her way up to eighty wpm. Her skills got her a job as a secretary for United Airlines, where she became glamorous, too. She had so many clothes my mother moved some of them into my closet. Hanging in there together, her matching outfits made my plaid school jumper look even worse. She bought everything at the downtown stores now, not at Southland. In fact, she had credit cards at stores in other cities, like Filene's and Wanamaker's. Once she bought me a sweater at Lord & Taylor. With her free airline passes, she traveled every few weeks. I think the first place she went was Paris. It must have been, because I was still young enough to appreciate the Marie Antoinette doll she brought back for me. She wore eye shadow and jewelry that matched her dresses perfectly, and she got her hair done once a week at a beauty parlor by a man named Anton.

All this made her too worldly for Frankie Montana. She gave him back the diamond he'd bought at Southland, after she began to notice how little it shone.

"Kay," my mother said, "I know Frankie might not be very flashy, but you *are* twenty-one and not getting any younger."

"There's more to life than Frankie Montana," Kay sighed. But maybe she never quite figured out what. Or maybe she had trouble believing she was right and my mother was wrong. Or maybe she just got tired of having to find new girlfriends to travel with all the time, because the old ones were getting engaged and married one by one.

She got married herself at twenty-three, after getting her own apartment and finding out she was pregnant. Her husband Ted was a text book salesman she met on a trip to a dude ranch in Arizona. He brought her history and geography books to read, while she was waiting for the baby.

After Kay got married and Bub went away to graduate school, my mother redecorated the room they had shared. She made it into a den with a nautical theme. Many of the decorations were souvenirs Kay had brought back from trips to Hawaii, Tahiti, and the Caribbean.

Under Kay's bed she found the Gimbel's box full of stories.

25

There must have been a hundred of them. I leafed through the covers—*Nanette Jourdan, Aloha Girl, Ten Days in Tahiti*—but something kept me from flipping them open.

"Do you want them?" my mother asked, and I grimaced. It seemed a little like the time I had looked through Kay's underwear drawer.

"What should I do with them?"

"Better ask Kay," I said.

The next time Kay came to visit, looking uncomfortably pregnant, like she'd swallowed a watermelon whole, my mother asked what she should do with her old roller skates and the box of stories. Kay decided to take the skates, in case she had a girl, but she stood looking at the closed lid of the Gimbel's box, her arms folded over the baby in her stomach. My mother opened it for her, a bit impatiently, then went to check on the laundry.

Kay peered into the box, the covers blurring together into one big collage of the world. She lifted *Ten Days in Tahiti* from the pile and examined the cover closely.

"I hardly remember doing this," she said, incredulously. "I didn't know anything about any place then." She opened the cover and read a few lines to me from the first page. "'In Tahiti, when the sun sets, the sky is blue and lavender and crimson all at the same time, with streaks of deep orange for accent. It made Diane both happy and sad to look at it.'" She looked at me quizzically, as if she'd read something of someone else's for the first time and didn't understand it. "Now how did I know that?" she asked.

I shrugged my shoulders. I had never figured out how I knew what it was like to be wounded fawn, an English governess, a thieving orphan.

"Do you want them?" she asked, and now it seemed like there was only one choice. I nodded yes. I kept them in the same box, under my bed, and read them one by one, till I was sure I had been around the world and back.

A Red Sweater

Fae Myenne Ng

I CHOSE RED for my sister. Fierce, dark red. Made in Hong Kong. Hand Wash Only because it's got that skin of fuzz. She'll look happy. That's good. Everything's perfect, for a minute. That seems enough.

Red. For Good Luck. Of course. This fire-red sweater is swollen with good cheer. Wear it, I will tell her. You'll look lucky.

We're a family of three girls. By Chinese standards, that's not lucky. "Too bad," outsiders whisper, "... nothing but daughters. A failed family."

First, Middle, and End girl. Our order of birth marked us. That came to tell more than our given names.

My eldest sister, Lisa, lives at home. She quit San Francisco State, one semester short of a psychology degree. One day she said, "Forget about it, I'm tired." She's working full time at Pacific Bell now. Nine hundred a month with benefits. Mah and Deh think it's a great deal. They tell everybody, "Yes, our Number One makes good pay, but that's not even counting the discount. If we call Hong Kong, China even, there's forty percent off!" As if anyone in their part of China had a telephone.

Number Two, the in-between, jumped off the "M" floor three years ago. Not true! What happened? Why? Too sad! All we say about that is, "It was her choice."

We sent Mah to Hong Kong. When she left Hong Kong thirty years ago, she was the envy of all: "Lucky girl! You'll never

27

have to work." To marry a sojourner was to have a future. Thirty years in the land of gold and good fortune, and then she returned to tell the story: three daughters, one dead, one unmarried, another who-cares-where, the thirty years in sweatshops, and the prince of the Golden Mountain turned into a toad. I'm glad I didn't have to go with her. I felt her shame and regret. To return, seeking solace and comfort, instead of offering banquets and stories of the good life.

I'm the youngest. I started flying with American the year Mah returned to Hong Kong, so I got her a good discount. She thought I was good for something then. But when she returned, I was pregnant.

"Get an abortion," she said. "Drop the baby," she screamed.

"No."

"Then get married."

"No. I don't want to."

I was going to get an abortion all along. I just didn't like the way they talked about the whole thing. They made me feel like dirt, that I was a disgrace. Now I can see how I used it as an opportunity. Sometimes I wonder if there wasn't another way. Everything about those years was so steamy and angry. There didn't seem to be any answers.

"I have no eyes for you," Mah said.

"Don't call us," Deh said.

They wouldn't talk to me. They ranted idioms to each other for days. The apartment was filled with images and curses I couldn't perceive. I got the general idea: I was a rotten, no-good, dead thing. I would die in a gutter without rice in my belly. My spirit—if I had one—wouldn't be fed. I wouldn't see good days in this life or the next.

My parents always had a special way of saying things.

Now I'm based in Honolulu. When our middle sister jumped, she kind of closed the world. The family just sort of fell apart. I left. Now, I try to make up for it; the folks still won't see me, but I try to keep in touch with them through Lisa. Flying cuts up your life, hits hardest during the holidays. I'm always sensitive then. I feel like I'm missing something, that people are doing something really important while I'm up in the sky, flying through time zones.

So I like to see Lisa around the beginning of the year. January, New Year's, and February, New Year's again, double luckiness with our birthdays in between. With so much going on, there's always something to talk about.

"You pick the place this year," I tell her.

"Around here?"

"No," I say. "Around here" means the food is good and the living hard. You eat a steaming rice plate, and then you feel like rushing home to sew garments or assemble radio parts or something. We eat together only once a year, so I feel we should splurge. Besides, at the Chinatown places, you have nothing to talk about except the bare issues. In American restaurants, the atmosphere helps you along. I want nice light and a view and handsome waiters.

"Let's go somewhere with a view," I say.

We decide to go to Following Sea, a new place on the Pier 39 track. We're early, the restaurant isn't crowded. It's been clear all day, so I think the sunset will be nice. I ask for a window table. I turn to talk to my sister, but she's already talking to a waiter. He's got that dark island tone that she likes. He's looking her up and down. My sister does not blink at it. She holds his look and orders two Johnny Walkers. I pick up a fork, turn it around in my hand. I seldom use chopsticks now. At home, I eat my rice in a plate, with a fork. The only chopsticks I own, I wear in my hair. For a moment, I feel strange sitting here at this unfamiliar table. I don't know this tablecloth, this linen, these candles. Everything seems foreign. It feels like we should be different people. But each time I look up, she's the same. I know this person. She's my sister. We sat together with chopsticks, mismatched bowls, braids, and braces, across the formica tabletop.

"I like three pronged forks," I say, pressing my thumb against the sharp points.

29

My sister rolls her eyes. She lights a cigarette.

I ask for one.

I finally say, "So, what's new?"

"Not much." Her voice is sullen. She doesn't look at me. Once a year, I come in, asking questions. She's got the answers, but she hates them. For me, I think she's got the peace of heart, knowing that she's done her share for Mah and Deh. She thinks I have the peace, not caring. Her life is full of questions, too, but I have no answers.

I look around the restaurant. The sunset is not spectacular, and we don't comment on it. The waiters are lighting candles. Ours is bringing the drinks. He stops very close to my sister, seems to breathe her in. She raises her face toward him. "Ready?" he asks. My sister orders for us. The waiter struts off.

"Tight ass," I say.

"The best," she says.

My scotch tastes good. It reminds me of Deh. Johnny Walker or Seagrams 7, that's what they served at Chinese banquets. Nine courses and a bottle. No ice. We learned to drink it Chinese style, in teacups. Deh drank from his rice bowl, sipping it like hot soup. By the end of the meal, he took it like cool tea, in bold mouthfuls. We sat watching, our teacups in our laps, his three giggly girls.

Relaxed, I'm thinking there's a connection. Johnny Walker then and Johnny Walker now. I ask for another cigarette and this one I enjoy. Now my Johnny Walker pops with ice. I twirl the glass to make the ice tinkle.

We clink glasses. Three times for good luck. She giggles. I feel better.

"Nice sweater," I say.

"Michael Owyang," she says. She laughs. The light from the candle makes her eyes shimmer. She's got Mah's eyes. Eyes that make you want to talk. Lisa is reed-thin and tall. She's got a body that clothes look good on. My sister slips something on, and it wraps her like skin. Fabric has pulse on her.

"Happy birthday, soon," I say.

"Thanks, and to yours too, just as soon."

"Here's to Johnny Walker in shark's fin soup," I say.

"And squab dinners."

"'I Love Lucy,'" I say.

We laugh. It makes us feel like children again. We remember how to be sisters.

I raise my glass, "To 'I Love Lucy,' squab dinners, and brown bags."

"To bones," she says.

"Bones," I repeat. This is a funny story that gets sad, and knowing it, I keep laughing. I am surprised how much memory there is in one word. Pigeons. Only recently did I learn they're called squab. Our word for them was pigeon—on a plate or flying over Portsmouth Square. A good meal at forty cents a bird. In line by dawn, we waited at the butcher's listening for the slow churning motor of the trucks. We watched the live fish flushing out of the tanks into the garbage pails. We smelled the honey-crushed cha sui bows baking. When the white laundry truck turned into Wentworth, there was a puffing trail of feathers following it. A stench filled the alley. The crowd squeezed in around the truck. Old ladies reached into the crates, squeezing and tugging for the plumpest pigeons.

My sister and I picked the white ones, those with the most expressive eyes. Dove birds, we called them. We fed them left-over rice in water, and as long as they stayed plump, they were our pets, our baby dove birds. And then one day we'd come home from school and find them cooked. They were a special, nutritious treat. Mah let us fill our bowls high with little pigeon parts: legs, breasts, and wings, and take them out to the front room to watch "I Love Lucy." We took brown bags for the bones. We balanced our bowls on our laps and laughed at Lucy. We leaned forward, our chopsticks crossed in mid-air, and called out, "Mah! Mah! Come watch! Watch Lucy cry!"

But she always sat alone in the kitchen sucking out the sweetness of the lesser parts: necks, backs, and the head. "Bones are sweeter than you know," she always said. She came out to

31

check the bags. "Clean bones," she said, shaking the bags. "No waste," she said.

Our dinners come with a warning. "Plate's hot. Don't touch." My sister orders a carafe of house white. "Enjoy," he says, smiling at my sister. She doesn't look up.

I can't remember how to say scallops in Chinese. I ask my sister, she doesn't know either. The food isn't great. Or maybe we just don't have the taste buds in us to go crazy over it. Sometimes I get very hungry for Chinese flavors: black beans, garlic and ginger, shrimp paste and sesame oil. These are tastes we grew up with, still dream about. Crave. Run around town after. Duck liver sausage, bean curd, jook, salted fish, and fried dace with black beans. Western flavors don't stand out, the surroundings do. Three pronged forks. Pink tablecloths. Fresh flowers. Cute waiters. An odd difference.

"Maybe we should have gone to Sun Hung Heung. At least the vegetables are real," I say.

"Hung toh-yee-foo-won-tun!" she says.

"Yeah, yum!" I say.

I remember Deh teaching us how to pick bok choy, his favorite vegetable. "Stick your fingernail into the stem. Juicy and firm, good. Limp and tough, no good." The three of us followed Deh, punching our thumbnails into every stem of bok choy we saw.

"Deh still eating bok choy?"

"Breakfast, lunch and dinner." My sister throws her head back, and laughs. It is Deh's motion. She recites in a mimic tone. "Your Deh, all he needs is a good hot bowl of rice and a plate full of greens. A good monk."

There was always bok choy. Even though it was nonstop for Mah—rushing to the sweatshop in the morning, out to shop on break, and then home to cook by evening—she did this for him. A plate of bok choy, steaming with the taste of ginger and garlic. He said she made good rice. Timed full-fire until the first boil, medium until the grains formed a crust along the sides of the pot, and then low-flamed to let the rice steam. Firm, that's how Deh liked his rice.

The waiter brings the wine, asks if everything is all right.

"Everything," my sister says.

There's something else about this meeting. I can hear it in the edge of her voice. She doesn't say anything and I don't ask. Her lips make a contorting line; her face looks sour. She lets out a breath. It sounds like she's been holding it in too long.

"Another fight. The bank line," she says. "He waited four times in the bank line. Mah ran around outside shopping. He was doing her a favor. She was doing him a favor. Mah wouldn't stop yelling. 'Get out and go die! Useless Thing! Stinking Corpse!'"

I know he answered. His voice must have had that fortune teller's tone to it. You listened because you knew it was a warning.

He always threatened to disappear, jump off the Golden Gate. His thousand-year-old threat. I've heard it all before. "I will go. Even when dead, I won't be far enough away. Curse the good will that blinded me into taking you as wife!"

I give Lisa some of my scallops. "Eat," I tell her.

She keeps talking. "Of course, you know how Mah thinks, that nobody should complain because she's been the one working all these years."

I nod. I start eating, hoping she'll follow.

One bite and she's talking again. "You know what shopping with Mah is like, either you stand outside with the bags like a servant, or inside like a marker, holding a place in line. You know how she gets into being frugal—saving time because it's the one free thing in her life. Well, they're at the bank and she had him hold her place in line while she runs up and down Stockton doing her quick shopping maneuvers. So he's in line, and it's his turn, but she's not back. So he has to start all over at the back again. Then it's his turn but she's still not back. When she finally comes in, she's got bags in both hands, and he's going through the line for the fourth time. Of course she doesn't say sorry or anything."

I interrupt. "How do you know all this?" I tell myself not to come back next year. I tell myself to apply for another transfer, to the East Coast.

"She told me. Word for word." Lisa spears a scallop, puts it in her mouth. I know it's cold by now. "Word for word," she repeats. She cuts a piece of chicken. "Try," she says.

I think about how we're sisters. We eat slowly, chewing carefully like old people. A way to make things last, to fool the stomach.

Mah and Deh both worked too hard; it's as if their marriage was a marriage of toil—of toiling together. The idea is that the next generation can marry for love.

In the old country, matches were made, strangers were wedded, and that was fate. Those days, sojourners like Deh were considered princes. To become the wife to such a man was to be saved from the war-torn villages.

Saved to work. After dinner, with the rice still in between her teeth, Mah sat down at her Singer. When we pulled out the wall-bed, she was still there, sewing. The street noises stopped long before she did. The hot lamp made all the stitches blur together. And in the mornings, long before any of us awoke, she was already there, sewing again.

His work was hard, too. He ran a laundry on Polk Street. He sailed with the American President Lines. Things started to look up when he owned the take-out place in Vallejo, and then his partner ran off. So he went to Alaska and worked the canneries.

She was good to him, too. We remember. How else would we have known him all those years he worked in Guam, in the Fiji Islands, in Alaska? Mah always gave him majestic welcomes home. It was her excitement that made us remember him.

I look around. The restaurant is full. The waiters move quickly.

I know Deh. His words are ugly. I've heard him. I've listened. And I've always wished for the street noises, as if in the traffic of sound, I believe I can escape. I know the hard color of his eyes and the tightness of his jaw. I can almost hear his teeth grind. I know this. Years of it.

Their lives weren't easy. So is their discontent without reason?

What about the first one? You didn't even think to come to the hospital. The first one, I say! Son or daughter, dead or alive, you didn't even come!

What about living or dying? Which did you want for me that time you pushed me back to work before my back brace was off?

Money! Money! Money to eat with, to buy clothes with, to pass this life with!

Don't start that again! Everything I make at that dead place I hand. . .

How come. . .
What about. . .
So. . .

It was obvious. The stories themselves mean little. It was how hot and furious they could become.

Is there no end to it? What makes their ugliness so alive, so thick and impossible to let go of?

"I don't want to think about it anymore." The way she says it surprises me. This time I listen. I imagine what it would be like to take her place. It will be my turn one day.

"Ron," she says, wiggling her fingers above the candle. "A fun thing."

The opal flickers above the flame. I tell her that I want to get her something special for her birthday, ". . .next trip I get abroad." She looks up at me, smiles.

For a minute, my sister seems happy. But she won't be able to hold onto it. She grabs at things out of despair, out of fear. Gifts grow old for her. Emotions never ripen, they sour. Everything slips away from her. Nothing sustains her. Her beauty

35

has made her fragile.

We should have eaten in Chinatown. We could have gone for coffee in North Beach, then for jook at Sam Wo's.

"No work, it's been like that for months, just odd jobs," she says.

I'm thinking, it's not like I haven't done my share. I was a kid once, I did things because I felt I should. I helped fill out forms at the Chinatown employment agencies. I went with him to the Seaman's Union. I waited too, listening and hoping for those calls: "Busboy! Presser! Prep Man!" His bags were packed, he was always ready to go. "On standby," he said.

Every week. All the same. Quitting and looking to start all over again. In the end, it was like never having gone anywhere. It was like the bank line, waiting for nothing.

How many times did my sister and I have to hold them apart? The flat *ting!* sound as the blade slapped onto the linoleum floor, the wooden handle of the knife slamming into the corner. Was it she or I who screamed, repeating all of their ugliest words? Who shook them? Who made them stop?

The waiter comes to take the plates. He stands by my sister for a moment. I raise my glass to the waiter.

"You two Chinese?" he asks.

"No," I say, finishing off my wine. I roll my eyes. I wish I had another Johnny Walker. Suddenly I don't care.

"We're two sisters," I say. I laugh. I ask for the check, leave a good tip. I see him slip my sister a box of matches.

Outside, the air is cool and brisk. My sister links her arm into mine. We walk up Bay onto Chestnut. We pass Galileo High School and then turn down Van Ness to head toward the pier. The bay is black. The foghorns sound far away. We walk the whole length of the pier without talking.

The water is white where it slaps against the wooden stakes. For a long time Lisa's wanted out. She can stay at that point of endurance forever. Desire that becomes old feels too good, it's seductive. I know how hard it is to go.

The heart never travels. You have to be heartless. My sister holds that heart, too close and for too long. This is her weakness, and I like to think, used to be mine. Lisa endures too much.

We're lucky, not like the bondmaids growing up in service, or the newborn daughters whose mouths were stuffed with ashes. Courtesans with the three-inch feet, beardless, soft-shouldered eunuchs, and the frightened child-brides, they're all stories to us. We're the lucky generation. Our parents forced themselves to live through the humiliation in this country so that we could have it better. We know so little of the old country. We repeat names of Grandmothers and Uncles, but they will always be strangers to us. Family exists only because somebody has a story, and knowing the story connects us to a history. To us, the deformed man is oddly compelling, the forgotten man is a good story. A beautiful woman suffers.

I want her beauty to buy her out.

The sweater cost two weeks pay. Like the forty-cent birds that are now a delicacy, this is a special treat. The money doesn't mean anything. It is, if anything, time. Time is what I would like to give her.

A red sweater. One hundred percent angora. The skin of fuzz will be a fierce rouge on her naked breasts.

Red. Lucky. Wear it. Find that man. The new one. Wrap yourself around him. Feel the pulsing between you. Fuck him and think about it. One hundred percent. Hand Wash Only. Worn Once.

Secrets of an Unkosher Home

Jean Roberta

THERE IS A dark secret at the heart of my family, but it's not what you would expect. My father is a respected professor at the university, and you could search in vain for signs that he has ever abused his wife or two daughters in any physical way. Debbie and I, the grown children, have a long history of shocking, addictive, incestuous violence. She has threatened me with knives; I've thrown her on the floor and kicked her. We don't approve of such behavior, and we never plan it. It's something we never discuss at the dinner table.

I heard about Debbie's homecoming when I dropped in on our parents with my son Isaac, who was about a year old then. Our mother told me that the prodigal daughter was finally returning from her travels abroad, which included a year on a kibbutz in Israel. Deb had written to say that she would gladden our parents' hearts by living at home and going to the university where I hoped to get hired as an instructor in September. Oy vey.

Debbie would resent hearing me describe her as my younger sister, but I don't know how to explain our connection any other way. She would also resent hearing herself described as thinner, though she has always been a string bean. She looks enough like me to make the comparison apt, or perhaps I look like a darker and heavier version of her. She is a pale, thin streak of energy that bounces restlessly around a room, around the world. She could hold two or more jobs while saving for the things she wanted: travel, a stereo, a guitar, a motorcycle. She surrounds herself with friends, and although she asserts her opinions against all opposition, she has always defended her right to take up space, because she felt I'd been trying to crowd her out of the light since I was born seven years earlier. Ours was not the sisterhood of modern feminism. Ours was the tribal sisterhood of Leah and Rachel.

"You don't know what it's like," Debbie told our mother and me at the kitchen table. She was wearing a long, loose black cotton dress fastened with dozens of little buttons. Tied carelessly around her neck was some kind of Bedouin scarf with little coins on it. The outfit made her look even more svelte and dramatic than usual, and it brought out the golden highlights in her floating shoulder-length hair. She lit a cigarette. "Israeli men are sexist enough," she said, blowing smoke, "especially the sabras, but Arabs are worse. It's the Muslim culture. You just wouldn't survive in the Middle East, Miriam. No offense, but I know you."

She thought she was Deborah the prophet. And of course she couldn't imagine me surviving, because she thought women my age were either too weak to defend themselves or too reckless to stay out of dangerous situations or too stupid to think of the right move at the right moment. The heroines of her stories were young women with chutzpah who always landed on their feet.

Ike was toddling toward his aunt. "They're like little drunks," laughed our mother, "when they first learn to walk."

"Isaac, Isaac," sighed Deb dramatically, sweeping him into her arms. "My favorite nephew." She had written to tell me how excited she had been when she received the telegram in Dijon, France, informing her that she was an aunt. She had left for the kibbutz soon after that.

Ike squawked like a bird and struggled out of her arms. "Deb!" he said, looking smug. Talking was his latest accomplish-

39

ment. He patted her lap hard.

"Don't hit Aunty Debbie," I told him, grabbing his hand. Leave it to me, I thought. I couldn't help wondering what truce or conspiracy or rivalry or pseudo-parental relationship my sister would develop with my son. Did Deb blame me for beating her to motherhood? Did she want to get my little man into an alliance of Young Rebels against our parents and me, the Old Guard? What vicious child-taming practices would my sister accuse me of? At this point, I could only guess.

Deb flicked ashes off her dress. "Do you ever see his father?" she asked casually. She was wearing a condescending look that told me I had done something stupid, as usual, which she would never do. I felt my temperature beginning to rise.

"No," I said cautiously. I was sure I had told her in a letter that I had conceived by artificial insemination; letters are safer than conversations. But maybe I didn't tell her, or maybe she chose to forget. "The father isn't involved," I told her, measuring my words. "We agreed to that."

"Oh," she groaned, smirking. "You agreed. I won't even ask whether he sends money."

Our mother could smell blood, and looked worried. "We want to hear about the kibbutz, Deborah," she said urgently. "What kind of work did you do there?"

Deb stretched languidly. "I picked fruit for a while. That was hard, but I liked being out in the orchard. Then I worked in the kitchen. That was interesting, but I thought I would roast to death." She took a long drag on her cigarette. "The older couples were really conservative, you know, really orthodox and the men all had middle-aged paunches and the women were obsessed with their children, but most of the volunteers were young and progressive, left-wing. Most of them were university students from Europe and North America."

So that's what convinced you that it's trendy to get an education, I thought. I should have known she didn't pick that up from me.

"Remember Paul from New York?" She was referring to one

of the young men she had described in letters. I didn't feel it necessary to answer, since she was bound to tell her story anyway. "He's bisexual, but we got so involved that he even asked me to marry him. I know he was serious, but I couldn't see myself meeting his parents, getting married under a canopy and having babies and all that."

Of course, I thought, only idiots have babies. Deb flashed a snapshot, showing an earnest-looking youth with glasses and a new, tender-growth of dark brown beard against white skin. My son might grow up to look like that.

"We started using something," Deb was saying, "but by then it was too late."

A jolt of understanding passed through my center, from my clitoris to the crown of my head. Our mother looked alarmed.

"I got pregnant. It was an accident. At first I thought I was a late developer. I was growing breasts." She tried to laugh and didn't succeed. She couldn't look at us. "I finally got an abortion when I was almost three months along."

Our mother gasped loudly. "Deborah," she said, clutching her daughter's arm. "Was it done by a qualified doctor?"

Deb rolled the ash of her cigarette carefully against the rim of the ashtray. Her hands were shaking. "Oh, yes. Don't worry, Mom. He worked in a clinic with sterilized equipment and everything. But you know how I am with anesthetics. It didn't take the first time and I woke up while he was scraping—" She blew smoke. "I started screaming from the pain, so I had to have a general anesthetic. You wouldn't believe how much blood I lost."

"I'd believe it," I said before our mother could shower her with sympathy. "I bled for six weeks after having Isaac." I thought of something. "When did this happen?"

"I had the abortion six months ago," Deb said, not willing to let go of her story until she had received her share of sympathy and admiration. I could have guessed. After getting my news, she went straight to the kibbutz and found a boyfriend to play with.

You even dressed in black, I thought, to tell us your story. Is it because you're in mourning, or because you feel like a black sheep? I visualized some international headlines:

YOUNGER DAUGHTER OF PROFESSOR DIES IN BANGKOK FROM BACKSTREET ABORTION

CANADIAN ZIONIST DRUG-RUNNER GIVES BIRTH IN MEXICAN PRISON

"GIVING UP BABIES FOR ADOPTION IS A REVOLUTIONARY ACT," SAYS DEBBIE THE RED AFTER HAVING TWINS

Was I being fair? No. But she had never been fair to me either.

"Debbie," I asked her, "Do you know how developed a three-month-old fetus is? It has all its parts. Eyes, fingernails, internal organs, nervous system, skeleton, brain, hair, everything it needs. After that, it only needs to grow bigger. And the wall between the two sides of the heart needs to seal up just before birth. Did you see what they took out of you?"

"Miriam!" yelped our horrified mother, her eyes wide.

Deb stared at me in shock, then in hurt, then in rage. "What did you expect me to do, Miriam?" she spat. "Have the baby and raise it on the kibbutz? Or marry Paul and end up divorced? Or bring the baby home for our parents to raise, like you? Would you want me to be that irresponsible? I don't expect other people to pay for my mistakes, and I know I'm not ready for that kind of commitment. I'm not sure I'll ever have children. There are too many interesting things I want to do."

Isaac seemed to sense his aunt's mood. He ran from his pile of toys in the front room into the kitchen, clutching a fluffy toy dog in one arm and a plastic car in the other. "Deb!" he beamed at her.

My sister, on the brink of tears, scooped him into her arms as though the two of them were the only surviving members of our family. I could see the alliance forming, and I felt strangely

42

satisfied. "You're a good boy," she whispered. To the rest of the room, she said, "This child is so beautiful that I would never want to bring an unwanted baby into the world to be deprived. I think all children should be loved." She was gathering steam. "I'm not one of those women who believe in having children they can't afford to raise. I take responsibility for my own decisions."

"Deborah," I said, "I wasn't saying you should have had the baby. I think you did the most sensible thing, I really do. I just want you to realize what you did."

Deb's face clenched. "Do you really think I don't know what an abortion is?" Her voice was shrill.

Our mother wrung her hands, giving each of us a pleading look. "Girls," she said, "that's enough. Deborah, your sister didn't mean any harm. Miriam, Deb has gone through enough and it's over now so there's no point—"

Deb ignored her and yelled into my face, "Have you ever had your insides scraped with a sharp instrument? If I deserved to be punished, what about Paul? He told me his method was really safe, but he's not the one who got pregnant. Men don't give a damn. Why should they? And some women are stupid enough to go along with whatever men want them to do, just because it's easier that way and they think they'll be taken care of. Well, not me. I have my own life to live." She stabbed out her cigarette and angrily lit another. For a moment, I was afraid she would throw the lit match in my lap.

"Fine," I said, trying to keep my voice low. "Live your own life. Who's stopping you? But don't come here asking me for sympathy when you've never given me any."

"Sympathy!" she sneered. "Why do you need it? Because you're still afraid to strike out on your own and the only men you can find are turds who get you pregnant and run away? You're over thirty and you've never done anything. Are you still living with your friend what's-her-name?"

I wanted to grab her by the throat, but held onto the table instead. "Yes, I'm still living with Barbara because she's the woman I love, stupid! Why do you think we agreed to raise a child together? Why can't you ever see what's in front of your face?"

Deb glanced at our mother in shock and realized that our parents had known about me for a long time. Only Debbie, the baby, had been protected from the truth, as usual, while the rest of us had had discussions behind her back. This knowledge drove her wild. She opened her mouth.

"Do you ever think about anyone but yourself?" I interrupted. "Have you wondered how I feel? All your life you've had an audience." My voice was rising. "And you still expect me to give you a hug and try to make it better every time you fall down and hurt yourself, but all I get from you is a slap in the face—"

My sister was wreathed in agitated smoke. "I've never asked you for anything!" she shrieked. "You're the reason I had to get the hell our of here! You think you're such a hot shit! If I had never left home you'd still be telling me what to do and you can't even run your life!"

As though from a distance, I watched my own arm rise through the air. I slapped Deb with all my strength, and she jerked back. Her soft hair went flying.

"Mommy!" screamed my son. "Don't hit! Don't hit!" He had heard that message from Barbara and me often enough.

Deb lunged forward in a blind rage, but our mother threw herself between us. "Stop it! Stop it!" she begged, almost in tears. "What's the matter with you? Ever since you were children. When will we have peace in this house?" From the corner of my eye, I could see our father glowering in the doorway.

"Come on, Isaac," I said, reaching for him. "We have to go."

Our mother took this as a rejection of her peacemaking efforts. "At least stay for lunch!" she complained. "You don't have to leave yet. Your sister just got home and she has so much to tell." Insanity, I thought, thy name is Mother.

"No, Mama," I tried to say gently but firmly. "We really have to go home now."

I managed to keep a poker face until we got home to Barb, who read me like a book. Relief flooded me when I saw her tall form on the lawn as I pulled into the driveway. The sunlight brought out the colors of Barb's blue pants, gray sweater and sandy blonde hair. She looked cool and sensible, so different from the emotional young woman in black I had just left. "Not again?" was her greeting.

"Damn it!" I burst out, handing Isaac to Barb and beginning to cry. "Why every time?" I babbled. "That bitch! What does she want from me?" Barb tried to hold me and Isaac at the same time until I began to laugh.

"You don't have to go there," Barb murmured, "if it's that bad. Or go but don't stay long. Family life is no joke."

Barb carried our son into the house while I trailed behind, watching him in despair. He was giving her a sleepy smile. His childlike trust seemed simple—he allowed us to change his diaper, give him his bottle and put him down for his nap. But would he hate us in years to come? Would he come home from school with a dread of "lezzies" and "fags" and would I beat him like a wicked stepmother? Would his Aunt Deborah report me to the police, the Department of Social Services and the newspapers? I refused to imagine more headlines.

I was still tense with worry when our best male friends, Ted and Brian, came over with brandy to go with our after-dinner coffee. Isaac was already in bed, but Barb and I always hoped that the presence of gentle men in our house would somehow influence our son even when he was sleeping; we called Ted and Brian the Fairy Godfathers. God knows Isaac wasn't likely to learn love and patience from me.

We talked about my relationship with my sister, since it was clear to all that I couldn't keep my mind on anything else. Brian and Ted both echoed Barbara. "Can't you just stay away from your parents' house when you know she's there?" asked Ted.

"Or refuse to get involved?" asked Brian.

Very funny, I thought. Very simple. How little you understand.

"She's hard to ignore, isn't she?" Barbara asked.

"Yeah," I muttered.

Brian caught on. "It sounds as if you still care for her."

"She admires you," said Barb. "That's why she competes with you."

"When we were kids," I told my companions between gritted teeth, "she used to follow me around, bugging me. 'Miriam, tell me a story! What are you doing? I'm telling! Give me some!' But she was too proud to let me protect her from bullies at school, because she didn't want anyone to think she couldn't fight her own battles. And she paid me to make her a dress when she was sixteen, because she thought I was a good seamstress and she wanted to be woman who paid her own way. She thinks she's the Wandering Jew, an outcast from society. But now she wants to follow in my footsteps by living at home and taking art classes. She drives me berserk."

Ted chuckled. "Why not write her a letter?" he suggested. "You don't have to send it, but you might feel better if you write down everything you want to say to her."

That night, after the men had gone home and my mate had gone to bed, I sat up late, thinking. I had an imaginary conversation with Debbie. "So sister, do you have some idea what you want out of life?" I asked her.

"Of course," she answered. "I'm not confused like you. I'm going to take some courses, travel some more, maybe set up a small business or two. Open a restaurant, something like that. Then I'll settle down in a challenging profession and find someone who will never break my heart."

"How will you find and attract this paragon?"

"I have good judgment and good instincts, Miriam. I'm not like you."

"So you say. Will your lover be male or female? Jewish or otherwise? From what country? Forgive my curiosity. I'm eager to learn from the resident sage."

The Debbie in my imagination grew furious, despite being unreal. "That's just like you, Miriam!" she yelled. "What a stupid attitude! You've got such a fucking small, conservative mind! No wander you'll never get anywhere when all you can do is run other people down and ask bitchy questions!"

"Excuse me," I said. "I should have known you would be a great success at life in general and find a generic human being to love."

In spite of my exhaustion, I began writing:

Dear Deborah, my only sister in the world,

You probably don't remember your own childhood the way I do, but believe me, you were always a special person. Our parents probably favored me because I was the first-born, but that doesn't mean you were an irrelevant after-thought. Do you think I would have had a child of my own if I hadn't loved you when we were growing up? I wanted to protect you from all harm, even though that isn't possible.

We both call ourselves feminists (yes I know you don't believe I fit that label) but what does that mean if we each hate the only woman we can call "sister" in the most literal sense? I don't want to hurt you, but how else do you expect me to react when you constantly sneer, criticize and try to one-up me?

Debbie, I've known for a long time that neither of us could lead a conventional life and be the nice girl we were each raised to be. Our parents love both of us, but it seems we were born to break their hearts by stepping off the traditional path of feminine self-sacrifice. Not that our father believes our mom ever gave up anything for him; on the contrary. I think both our parents believe that a certain level of disappointment in marriage—and in life— is necessary to the maintenance of a kosher home, and I know they believe they are doing the right thing by suffer-ing in silence over their uncontrollable daughters. I think the silence is killing us all.

I can't believe that you've never guessed why all my

closest friends have been women. Why do you always accuse me of being the spineless dupe of worthless men? If you do it to prevent me from telling you the truth about my life, you've succeeded. If you do it to build up your own ego, you've obviously failed, since you can never put me down enough to feel safe yourself. You can't imagine how you hurt me by insisting that no one could use me without my consent. I notice you don't apply that rule to yourself or the women you respect.

I've known for years that I am a woman who loves women, and I can't pretend this had nothing to do with you. I might have turned out this way even if you didn't exist, but you do exist, along with the other female people who influenced me when I was growing up. I feel very lucky that I finally found a good woman who could love me back. If you feel threatened by my relationship with Barbara, I can't help you. We are who we are.

I'm glad you seem to love your nephew. Like you, he was born into a difficult situation, and he will need all the love he can get. But if you ever try to turn him against me, so help me Goddess, I will break your bones. *(I later crossed out this sentence.)*

In some cultures, in some religions, they use dolls for some very serious purposes. You should know about that. For every baby dead at birth, for every miscarriage and every other half-assed possibility that could not be brought to term, the mourner dresses a doll in the color she associates with grief, and buries it with due ceremony. The mourner lights incense or a candle or the weed of her choice and lets her regrets waft away on the smoke. She says some suitable words to each doll, like this:

My niece or nephew, hail and farewell. May you find a place in the world someday, and may the womb you came from recover completely.

Deb's image of me, may you shrink down to my actual size and stop being the monster shadow at her back.

My memories of my baby sister, may you vanish back into the past where you belong, and stop forming false images between me and the woman Deb has become.

If all these dolls were laid to rest, Deb, we might be able to see each other clearly. If they can't be laid to rest, I hope we both have the courage to bury our hopes of ever accepting each other.

We were lucky to be born into the generation between gas ovens and the (possible) nuclear holocaust to come. While we're alive, and while we both have the urge to create new life in spite of everything, let's not burn up with our own rage.

Love,

Miriam

Ted was wrong. Writing this letter wasn't enough to relieve my feelings. I had a knot in my stomach for three days afterwards, and nothing Barbara could say to me made it go away. I realized that my relief would come, if ever, when I had mailed the letter to the party for whom it was intended. On Barb's advice, I added this postscript:

If you are still on speaking terms with me, Barbara and I would like to invite you over for dinner. We'll wait to hear from you to decide on the time.

I mailed the letter to Deb at our parents' house and waited. After two weeks had gone by with no word, I decided she wasn't going to answer. Then when I last expected it, she phoned.

"Miriam," she muttered, "can you meet me for coffee in the Arts Building cafeteria tomorrow? I'm free at two-thirty." She probably chose this location because it made up in neutrality for what it lacked in privacy. I accepted her terms.

My sister was not hard to spot. The Bedouin scarf now covered her head, and her jangling, flashing earrings hung almost to her shoulders. She was sitting at a table that appeared to be a gathering place for the New Wave crowd on campus. She agreed to come with me to a more secluded corner.

Deb wouldn't admit to having read and digested my letter, but what else was this about? I waited for her opening shot. "Miriam," she began, staring at a packet of breath mints on the table, "how can you tell if you're a gay person?" She shook a mint into her hand and avoided my eyes.

"The same way you can tell whether it's time to have a child," I said. "You get a feeling. In a lot of cases, you fall in love with someone. Usually you have to go through a lot of hopeless crushes before something mutual happens. I should know. But even before that, you know you're different. If you try going out with some guy, it feels wrong."

"Um," she acknowledged. "It's dangerous to be that way. Other people can cause trouble."

"Yes."

"Is it worth it?" she asked me.

"Yes," I said simply.

"Some people can go either way," she reminded herself aloud. "Are there some women who can't get along with men but they're not really lesbians?"

"Neither gay nor straight?" I laughed. "I suppose anything's possible. We all have to find out for ourselves what works. But first we have to figure out how we really feel, and that's amazingly hard. I went through a period of thinking I was neither gay nor straight."

Deb looked surprised. "You did?"

"Oh yeah. School was a way out. I was going to be an academic and social activist, and that way I wouldn't have to be sexual. I wouldn't have to feel, or think about who I really loved. It hurt too much."

"Yeah," she admitted. Her eyes were clouded.

"One thing that helps," I said quietly, "is remembering that life is short."

Deb gave me a sarcastic look. "Jews and women have an advantage when it comes to that," she said. "We get reminded." We were both silent for a minute, remembering the sight of our own blood.

I suddenly noticed her jittery hands. "Are you trying to stop smoking?" I asked.

"Yes. I want to live as long as possible," she smirked. "Our parents say I can entertain when they go out, so—"

"But they never go out."

Deb looked impatient. "They say they'll go, if only to visit their friends. I'd like to invite you and Barbara over, with Isaac." She seemed to have forgotten our invitation to her. I remembered that my sister is a proud, touchy woman who wants to be a hostess, a giver, an expert, a queen. She would probably cook us something elaborate.

"That would be nice," I smiled. "You have our number." We parted with promises to get together, promises as fragile and dependent on our passing moods as all other commitments, even between people who know each other well. I went home to tell Barbara about the success of Round One.

Once A Friend

Terri de la Peña

S HE SLID IN QUIETLY, padding across the living room carpet. When Mama and I glanced up at her sudden approach, Toni offered a perfunctory smile.

"You sure came back fast." I helped Mama spread assorted pattern pieces on the dining room table.

"I have to study." Toni fiddled with the tousled fringe of her macramé bag. "What're you making?"

"Sylvia's blazer." Mama expertly pinned the tissue-paper pattern to the burgundy velvet.

"Isn't it neat?" I grinned and caressed the plush nap.

"Classy." Toni remained standing, arms crossed. "Mama, do you know a Consuelo Luna?"

"*Cómo no*? Consuelo's in the Altar Society, and just had a baby. *Por qué me preguntas?*"

"Laura and I went to visit her in the hospital tonight."

"*Consuelo y Laura's mama son muy amigas.*" Mama tossed Toni a mischievous glance. "How did you handle your part of the conversation, eh? Lots of pauses between words? Or did you let Laura do all the talking?"

Showing some annoyance, my sister shrugged. "Laura knows her. I didn't say much."

"Toni, you should be ashamed of yourself. You don't even try to speak Spanish. *Que sin vergüenza!* Now Consuelo's going to think I've raised a girl with no manners." Flustered, Mama nearly jabbed herself with a pin. She picked up the scissors and began to cut out the blazer's sleeves.

"They weren't even talking to me, Mama. Anyhow, I get by with Spanish when I have to. As long as I understand it, who really cares?"

"Mama, concentrate on what you're doing," I interjected frantically. "You almost cut those sleeves in half." I gave my sister a rough nudge. "Why don't you go study, Toni? I can tell when you're in a bad mood. Can't you see we're trying to work?"

Glaring, my older sister didn't move. "I'm trying to talk to Mama, if you don't mind—"

"Girls," Mama reprimanded, rapping her knuckles on the table. "*Basta! Pues, que tienes,* Toni?"

"Nothing." Looking sulky, she picked up the pattern folder and inspected its printed diagrams. She seemed to be killing time. "The Lunas are a really huge family," Toni remarked after a moment.

"*Consuelo's esposo tiene como cuatro o cinco hermanos.*" Mama picked up the scissors again, ignoring our sibling tension. "All the Luna boys are gardeners."

"All of them?"

Filled with impatience, I couldn't understand my sister's preoccupation with the Lunas, whoever they were. I resented her intrusion into our sewing session and wanted her to leave.

"*Si,*" Mama continued. "*Y no hablan inglés.* They're as bad as you, Toni. Those boys don't even try to speak English." Mama's round cheeks dimpled with her teasing tone.

Eyes downcast, Toni did not respond to Mama's prodding. She headed into her bedroom and closed the door.

"She's the moodiest person I've ever seen." I carefully fastened a side panel of the pattern to the velvet.

"Sylvia, I say the same thing about you sometimes. But at least you go out with your friends. Toni just hangs around—except when she goes someplace with Laura."

"She's too wrapped up in school."

"She can't help it, *hija.* Toni has to keep up her grades. College isn't like high school." About to snip the side panel, Mama stopped. "*Mira,* Sylvia. You accuse me of not concentrating.

53

Look who's talking. You pinned this backwards. The nap has to fall the same way, remember?"

With an embarrassed giggle, I hurried to remove the pins.

"You look like you've lost your best friend." Hours later, I paused in the threshold of Toni's book-lined bedroom. She was sitting dejectedly at her desk, her sociology textbook open.

"I almost have."

"Toni, what's the matter?"

Rubbing her eyes, she grabbed a silver barrette from the edge of the cluttered desk and secured it in the thick hair at the nape of her neck. With her hair pulled back, she appeared more forlorn, her dark eyes filled with tears.

"When Laura phoned after dinner, she asked me to go with her to the hospital to take a gift to her mother's friend Mrs. Luna. I told her I really needed to study tonight, but she practically begged me to go with her."

I plopped down on Toni's quilted bedspread.

Toni gathered her thoughts. "There was a whole gang of people in Mrs. Luna's room. I felt kind of shy, but I figured Laura'd introduce me to them. As soon as we got there, she bounced up to Mrs. Luna and started a half-English, half-Spanish conversation. Sylvia, she forgot I even existed. I stood in the doorway like a complete idiot. I don't think anyone noticed me."

"That doesn't sound like Laura," I said.

Toni rested her chin on her hand. "Tell me about it. Especially since she'd begged me to go with her. Laura had a great rapport with Mrs. Luna, when she'd given me the impression she hardly knew her. I felt really out of it, so I stood in the corridor for a while, 'far from the madding crowd.'

"A few minutes later, I heard Laura's voice and thought she was ready to leave. Was I ever wrong. She walked out with a real *Mexicano* type—black wavy hair, mustache, not bad looking, to be honest—but the kind of dude who's just crossed the border. Sylvia, they were holding hands."

"What?" Intrigued, I waited for more details.

"All of a sudden, they're in this mad clinch in the corridor, just a few feet from me. They acted like they didn't even know I was there. I felt like a voyeur. I turned the nearest corner and wound up in the nursery, staring through the glass at a bunch of crying babies.

"I was still there when Laura showed up, real nonchalant. Right away, I started shooting dozens of questions. She claimed all those relatives had made her nervous, and by the time she remembered me, I was gone. She apologized, but I still think she was rude. Then she told me the dude's name is Fabian Luna."

"One of the gardeners?"

"Can you believe it? Ms. Laura Esparza, a junior at Cal State, is stuck on a Mexican gardener who can't even speak English. Sylvia, she's going to marry him."

I stared at Toni. "Is she crazy?"

"Crazy in love," she muttered. "When I said she could've at least confided in me, she got upset. We're supposed to be best friends, but she hadn't told me anything 'cause she claims I wouldn't understand. Well, she's right, Sylvia. I don't. Do you?"

"No way."

"She's even quitting school and getting a job to help pay for their wedding in January. Sylvia, I'm dazed. This has been going on for months, and she never even told me." Sniffling, Toni reached for a kleenex and blew hard.

I stared at her, trying to come up with an explanation. "Maybe there's been family pressure. Mama said the Lunas are good friends with Laura's family. Laura's twenty years old. Maybe they think she's practically an old maid."

"I think that definitely has something to do with it, but Laura denies it. She claims she loves this Fabian dude."

"What's he like?"

Toni switched off her gooseneck lamp and slammed her sociology textbook. "She lured me there to see them in action, but didn't have the courtesy to introduce me to him. She was so inconsiderate—to me, anyway. Not to anyone else. Why did she beg me to go with her if she spent the whole time ignoring me?"

"No wonder you were grumpy when you got home. Why didn't you tell Mama about it?"

Wrapped in her fleecy bathrobe, Toni rose and leaned against her desk. She opened and closed her long-fingered brown hands while she talked.

"Mama's always kidding me about being snotty to *Mexicanos*. I didn't need to hear that tonight. Sylvia, I have nothing in common with *Mexicanos*. I was born here, and English—not Spanish—is my native language."

"But Mama was born in Sonora," I reminded her.

"When she came here, she learned English and became a citizen. You heard what she said about the Lunas. They don't even try. So what the hell are they doing here? This Fabian character probably wants to marry a citizen to stay here permanently. And Laura happens to be the one who caught his eye."

"Did you tell her that?"

"Didn't have the nerve. What do you think?" Crossing her thin arms, she frowned.

"You have a point." I traced the intricate swirls on her multi-colored quilt.

"If I said that to Laura, she'd think I'm jealous. Nothing could be further from the truth. I wouldn't trade places with her for a million dollars. She'll wind up with six kids and zero future."

"Well, she must love this dude. In all fairness—"

"Would you marry a *Mexicano* who expected you to live the traditional way?" Her level gaze met mine.

"I don't think so."

Moving from her desk, Toni sat beside me. "You know you wouldn't, Sylvia. Look at Mama and Dad. His family was here for generations. And when Dad married a Mexican, they criticized him. But Mama's exceptional. She doesn't feel tied to the old ways. She's—"

"Assimilated, acculturated," I cut in. "Sort of, anyway. She still speaks Spanish a lot. She even thinks in Spanish."

"But her English is damn good, accent or not. And who's the real boss around here? It isn't Dad, even though he likes to think so. Mama runs the show. I hate to say it, but Laura doesn't have that strong a personality. This Fabian already has her under his thumb. After all, she's quitting school."

"Maybe that's what she wants, Toni."

"She's too damn infatuated to think straight. How can they have a coherent discussion? Laura's Spanish isn't much better than mine."

"Maybe they use the language of love," I joked.

"Necking in a hospital corridor—isn't that the pits?"

I giggled and gave her a playful shove. But she didn't share my laughter. I leaned closer. "This really bothers you, doesn't it?"

Sighing, she nodded. "I thought I knew Laura. Now I don't think I ever did." She cast me a sidelong glance. "Remember those crazy dialogues Laura and I used to write for Spanish class?"

"Something about two *Mexicanas*?"

"Hortensia and Josefina. We wrote skits about them to practice our Spanish. We'd laugh so hard we'd get stomach-aches. I never thought Laura'd actually turn into Hortensia. I can't believe it." She surveyed me. "I have to talk her out of it."

That night, I lay awake and pondered my sister's dilemma. Soon I might have to face similar situations. At seventeen, I already had friends who planned to marry right after high school. Yet, unlike my sister, I had numerous other classmates who were college-bound like myself. Toni and Laura had been inseparable since their high school freshman year. Studious and shy, Toni had not cultivated many other friendships. No wonder she was shaken by the abrupt, even stealthy, announcement of Laura's engagement. With characteristic stubbornness, Toni was determined to change Laura's mind. I had my doubts about her being able to do that. Behind her detached demeanor, Toni was sensitive, vulnerable. Out of protectiveness, sibling loyalty, and outright curiosity, I had reluctantly agreed to accompany Toni to lunch with Laura.

"What about teaching, Laura? That's what you've always dreamed of." Toni continued her persuasive tactics while we sat in a booth at Fuji Gardens.

Shaking her long brown hair, Laura set down her fork. With her delicate features, she was much more attractive than my scowling sister. "Toni, I really want a family—kids, the works."

"I don't believe you." Toni pointed her chopsticks for emphasis. "I've known you since you were fourteen years old, lady. All you've ever talked about is teaching. How long've you known this dude, anyway? Sounds like he's been messing with your mind."

I leaned back and wished I'd gone shopping instead.

"You don't have to be insulting," Laura snapped. "My mind's made up, and nothing—"

"Look, I want to know why there's such a rush to get married? Is he going to be deported?"

"Toni, lay off," I whispered.

Laura touched my hand. "Let her talk, Sylvia. She has to get this out of her system." She turned to my sister again. "Toni, I admit I should've told you sooner. But I didn't want to hear your put downs about marriage. Remember when we went to Julie Ortega's wedding? You were so sarcastic that day."

"Because Julie married a bum."

"I suppose you think Fabian's a bum, too."

"That isn't the point, and you know it, Laura. What I really have trouble dealing with is your decision to live a traditional Mexican lifestyle. How can you? What does Fabian know about our way of life? Would you even bring him to this restaurant, for instance? You've had over two years of college. How can you marry a gardener from Jalisco? Doesn't that seem totally incongruous?"

"Not at all."

Toni sighed, exasperated. With the flailing chopsticks, she

almost knocked over her tea cup. "Laura, I've tried putting myself in your place, and it simply doesn't work. I can't picture myself coming home from the library after a busy day of cataloguing books, and finding an uneducated husband watching *novelas* on KMEX.

"I mean, being bi-cultural is enough of a hang-up. We're already marginal people, teetering between two worlds. We've talked about this before, Laura, and we've both admitted not being totally at ease with with either Anglos or Chicanos. I know for a fact I wouldn't return to the past. I want to advance, not regress. You've had opportunities most Chicanas dream about, but you're rejecting them to be a baby machine for a—"

"Wetback," Laura stoically supplied.

"I wasn't going to say that."

"You were thinking it." Laura faced her. "I'm sorry you don't understand this, Toni. Listen, I've changed. Maybe you won't, but some of us do. Fabian's an honest, decent man, and he respects me. I've dated more than you have. He's not money-mad or career-oriented—maybe he isn't even too smart, but he cares about his family in Mexico and sends them money—"

Toni's eyes widened. "Laura, are you serious? Suppose he's so family-oriented that he has a wife there, too? It's been known to happen. What do you really know about him?"

"Plenty." Sipping her tea, Laura looked steadily over the china rim at my sister. "Toni, we're not getting anywhere. You'll never like him, will you?" Her measured words were tinged with sadness, but not regret.

"How the hell do I know? You haven't even introduced me to the dude. Lady, you acted incredibly weird that night. How can you expect me to be open-minded now? I have feelings, too."

"I've already apologized. What do you think of this, Sylvia?" Laura asked suddenly.

I nearly choked on my rice. Both of them scrutinized me. Toni's eyes narrowed, perhaps wary of sisterly subterfuge.

"Laura's, it's your life," I said nervously. "Just don't be mad at Toni for what she's said."

"You don't have to talk for me," my sister muttered.

"I want to explain something to her."

Shrugging, Toni sighed, playing with her chopsticks. Her teriyaki steak lay neglected on her plate.

I turned to Laura. "Toni's dedicated to finishing her education. That's why she can't relate to your quitting school to marry Fabian. She'd never consider anything like that because she wants to go on to graduate school and become a librarian. She expects other people to share her drive, especially you, since you're her best friend."

"Sylvia's exactly right." Toni beamed at me, then grew serious again. "If there's no hope of reaching a goal, I suppose the only thing to do is quit. But when opportunity's wide open, it's insane to give up."

"So now I'm insane." Laura dipped her tempura into its sauce.

"Laura, can't you see the inconsistency of your behavior?"

"Why do I have to follow you, Toni? Have you ever thought of that? If you want to be a librarian, hiding in the stacks, that's your business. You're more at home with books, anyway. But I'm not. I want to marry Fabian and that's what I'm going to do. Quit putting your standards on me."

"If marriage means losing my individuality, I'll never have anything to do with it." My sister's voice shook. "And if your marriage means losing our friendship—"

Tensely, they stared at each other across the table.

I had heard enough. My head ached. I slithered from the booth and tossed my share of the bill onto the tablecloth.

"I'll meet you at the library," I called over my shoulder.

"Sylvia." Past midnight, Toni caught me as I tiptoed to my room. I had been out with friends and glad to escape her problems for the evening.

"Why aren't you asleep?" I was irked by her big-sister vigilance.

"I've been reading. Talk with me a while." She was framed in her amber-lit threshold. Through her pale nightie, I could see her bony figure. Sighing, I reluctantly followed her into the bedroom, knowing I was too spaced out to be her confidante.

"You smell like pot."

"Shhh. It's no big deal." Yawning, I collapsed on her rumpled bed. On the furrowed pillow, I noticed a paperback novel, *The Member of the Wedding*, by Carson McCullers.

Grabbing the book, Toni swiftly paged through it. She sat beside me. "I want you to listen to this. And tell me who it reminds you of."

"Okay." Closing my eyes, I relaxed against her warm bed, ready to float into sleep.

"'She belonged to no club and was a member of nothing in the world. Frankie had become an unjoined person who hung around in doorways, and she was afraid.'"

I wished I didn't have to open my eyes.

"Sylvia, don't fall asleep." She nudged my shoulder. "That's me, isn't it?"

"It's a character in a book, not you."

"Do you think I might be jealous of Laura?"

"You're hallucinating. I'm the one who's stoned."

She ignored me. "I mean, maybe I'm jealous of her decision to live with a man. Maybe I'm jealous of the sexual aspect."

Baffled, I blinked at her. She seemed uninterested in men and hardly ever dated. Even though I was three years younger, I probably had more experience. In that shapeless nightie, with her long hair in a thick braid, she looked almost Victorian.

"Toni, you probe too much. You're concerned about Laura's future, that's all. As her friend, you have a right to be."

Lying beside me, she kept the worn book in her hands. "Sylvia, be honest. Am I an asexual bookworm, hiding in the stacks, like Laura said?"

I chose my words carefully and addressed them to the eyelet edging of her collar rather than to her earnest face. "You're an introvert, and you're shy. That doesn't mean you're hiding. I

61

bet if you met a guy with the same interests, you'd get out of yourself."

Touched by her confusion, I leaned closer. "What'd Mama talk with you about? Did she tell you to date more?" I had seen her and Mama sequestered in Toni's bedroom when I had left earlier.

Toni nodded. "But she knows school takes so much of my time. She didn't pressure me."

"You told her about Laura. And Mama thinks you might be jealous."

She sighed. "She didn't come right out and say that, but I read between the lines. The truth is—and please don't tell Mama this—I'm not jealous of Laura, but of Fabian." She spoke rapidly, getting it out. "Well, it's logical, isn't it? He's stealing my best friend away. He's going to be between us from now on—if she wants to continue the friendship. She won't be able to run off and have lunch with me, or go shopping on impulse like we've always done. He's going to come first. And that isn't fair."

"That's the way life is."

"For women, Sylvia. Laura's life'll completely revolve around him. Of course, if he's a good lover, I suppose that'll compensate some for the loss of her personal life. Otherwise, it's a lousy trade-off."

I had to smile. You're really cynical."

"Read some feminist books when you get a chance. They'll change your outlook."

I lay back, folding my arms behind my sleepy head. "What else did Mama say?"

"To butt out."

"Are you going to?"

"I've already said my piece, Sylvia, and it didn't work. Listen, there's another passage in this book that's really appropriate." Slowly, she read it to me. "'The conversation about the wedding had somehow been wrong. The questions she had asked that afternoon had all been the wrong questions... She could not name the feeling in her, and she stood there until dark shadows made her think of ghosts.' Ghosts of a friendship," Toni whispered. She put the book beside her. "I guess I'll have to listen to Mama."

She rested next to me for several moments. From the corner of my eye, I saw her frowning at the dim ceiling until a flickering smile crossed her face.

"What?" I asked with drowsy interest.

"Check this: Laura Luna. Doesn't that sound absurd?"

I giggled. "Like an exotic drink. Bartender, I'll have a Laura Luna, please."

Rocking with unrestrained—relieved— laughter, we clumsily bumped into each other on her narrow bed, giggling like children. At last, regaining my composure, I tottered to my feet.

"Think you can sleep, Toni?"

"I hope so. If not, I'll read some more."

Surprising myself as much as her, I leaned over and kissed her cool forehead.

"Sylvia, you absolutely reek of marijuana," she grumbled. "Shhh."

In the two months between that disastrous luncheon and the wedding, my sister rarely saw or heard from Laura. Although we attended a couple of bridal showers in her friend's honor, both times Toni suggested leaving early, discouraged by Laura's preference for her prospective in-laws.

According to Toni, the unsophisticated Luna women cared more about the quantity of Laura's bridal gifts than about the mediocre quality of her future. I was inclined to defend the well-meaning women—after all, I enjoyed the risque trivialities of wedding showers—but I couldn't deny the truth of Toni's perception. Unlike her, I wasn't depressed by it; she moped for days.

By the morning of the wedding, Toni seemed to be in better spirits. Standing outside the parish church after the Spanish ceremony, she looked fashionable in a mauve crepe dress, her black hair gathered into a sleek topknot. When she and Laura shared an *abrazo* on the church steps, I noted some stiffness in their attitudes; neither looked directly at the other. At the wedding reception that afternoon, their remoteness was even more pronounced.

Within the crowded Knights of Columbus hall, resonant with brassy *mariachi*, Toni and I sat together and sipped champagne. Our parents, whirling on the dance floor, had been lenient with alcohol privileges that day. Since my sister had already drunk three plastic goblets full, she appraised the festivities with a bleary gaze.

"Laura only lets older women cut in," Toni remarked. "A little while ago, Maria-Elena Ramirez tried to dance with Fabian, and Laura practically wrenched him away—with a firm smile, of course. She sure wants to hold on to that guy."

"She loves him."

"Laura Esparza no longer exists."

"Toni, when're you going to get over this? It's boring."

"It's very hard to accept. I was positive we'd graduate together. That's impossible now. We don't have much in common anymore. Maybe we never did."

I studied the bubbles captured in the pale champagne and said nothing.

"Laura said I was 'hiding in the stacks,' remember? Well, she's ready to hide in the kitchen—or the bedroom. Think of it, Sylvia. In time, you're supposed to have a husband supporting you, and kids depending on you. You could become so identified with that, that you really wouldn't be yourself any more. To some women, I guess that's security—it's non-threatening and safe. To me, it's stagnation."

"And to Laura?" I finally looked up.

Toni shrugged. "She's convinced she's chosen the right path. I just wish she'd given herself more of a chance. Why'd she have to rush into this?"

I leaned my chin on my hand. "Maybe she's pregnant."

"She said she isn't. That was one of my first questions."

"You didn't leave any stone unturned, did you?"

With a trace of a smile, she shook her dark head. "Sylvia, you don't have to sit here with me. Mama and Dad're having a great time—just look at them. You love to dance, too. Go on."

"Meanwhile, you'll get quietly bombed."

"There's always a first time. And I have a good reason."

One of the Luna brothers, who had been flirting with me all afternoon, finally succeeded in persuading me to dance. His rapid-fire Spanish left me tongue-tied. I smiled a lot to make up for my lack of vocabulary. Escaping, I returned to the table and found my breathless parents chuckling over their fancy footwork on the dance floor. They told me Toni had gone to the restroom.

She wasn't in any of the narrow stalls nor anywhere else in the hall. Outside, I found her propped against the stucco structure, her head tilted back, her once sleek coiffure slightly disarrayed.

"Are you all right?"

"I had to get out of there. Too loud, too much smoke. I think the booze got to me. I'm really dizzy."

"The ocean air'll do you good."

"Sylvia, go back in. I'm okay."

"Did you leave because Laura's going to throw her bouquet?"

At that, she looked away. "Mama would've pushed me to catch it. In the first place, I don't want to. In the second, I'd probably fall flat on my face. I could barely walk out here."

"Don't move, Toni. I'll be right back."

Several minutes later, I sheepishly returned to my sister, holding the bouquet of white carnations and baby's breath.

"Are you kidding?" Toni laughed giddily.

"Everybody fumbled for it, and all of a sudden, it was in my hands."

"A likely story."

"Look, I don't want this thing either." Friskily, I tossed the delicate flowers into the air and caught them.

Toni kicked off her high heels and bent to retrieve them. Her movements were deliberate. "Sylvia, I'm going for a walk."

"I'll go with you." I swung the bouquet as we strolled past the gaudy row of paper-flower-covered cars. Without her shoes, Toni walked steadier, taking countless deep breaths. Beside her, I held the unwanted bouquet, its white satin ribbons trailing.

"What happened at the end of *The Member of the Wedding*? You never told me."

"Frankie gets a phone call from a new friend."

"An upbeat ending."

"McCullers ends it on a fairly positive note." Toni glanced at the bouquet. "I thought you were getting rid of that."

"I am, but I hate to throw it away. It's pretty."

"Leave it there." Halting, she pointed toward a bus bench on the corner. The only person sitting there was an elderly woman, surrounded by hefty shopping bags. Oblivious to the rumbling traffic, she dozed in the late afternoon sun.

I liked Toni's suggestion, but hesitated to approach the woman. "What if she wakes up?"

"I'll do it."

Handing me her shoes, my sister took Laura's bouquet and briefly caressed its flowers. She reached the bus bench and gently lay the blossoms beside the gray-haired woman's hand, the smooth white ribbons a poignant contrast to her wrinkled skin.

Toni had tears in her eyes when she walked back to me.

"McCullers would've like that," she said.

Design

Dawn Raffel

I T WAS MY MOTHER who told me about the attack on Ann. The call had come late the night before, after I'd eaten my usual stack of graham crackers and gone to bed. In the morning, my mother edged into the story so cautiously that I later suspected she'd rehearsed. "I'm afraid I have some difficult news," she began, "about your sister." What I felt at first was more impatient than upset: "difficult" was old news with Ann, and as far as my mother was concerned, I knew from experience how long it could take to get to the point of the story. "Your sister was walking home from the bus stop last night," my mother said. "She was going her own way, truly minding her own business. . ."

"Actually, she saw him first while she was still on the bus," my father said. He was not interrupting my mother, who wouldn't stand for interruptions, so much as talking to himself. His voice was agitated.

"Saw *who*?"

"*Him*." My mother glared at my father, then sighed. "All she could tell the police was that he looked lopsided and wore a ratty blue jacket. I can't say that's very helpful."

"Police? What happened?" I asked, feeling fearful for the first time.

"He followed her off at her stop and started trailing her down the street. She stopped in a drugstore, that one down the block from her apartment. She bought some Dentyne. By then she figured she'd lost him, he'd given up and it was safe to go back outside. It was only nine o'clock." Her voice took on a pleading tone, and I thought I saw her eyes fill behind her tortoise-shell glasses. "It's not as if it was one or two in the morning. It was only nine. She swears it was only nine."

"But what *happened*? Is she okay?"

"Nothing critical happened, thank God," my father said. "Not rape or anything."

The low-down, I eventually learned, was that Ann had had her face shoved into the pavement, her glasses shattered and her knees scraped raw before her screams sent the attacker fleeing with her purse. "She will heal," my father said. "I hope."

My parents had been very concerned with what was critical and what would come to heal ever since my sister had started seeing her first psychiatrist six years earlier. Ann was now on psychiatrist number four. This one, my mother said, had described her as "iffy." Recently he had started calling my mother long distance almost every week. I didn't know much about psychiatry, but it smelled like a ratty kind of betrayal to me. Ann was twenty-two years old and lived a hundred miles away from us in Chicago—and besides, she was an artist. She not only deserved an inner life that was none of our business, I thought; she required it. At any rate, she *had* tried to please our parents. She had earned the college degree they wanted her to have. She had landed a job they regarded as decent and that she regarded as drudgery. According to Ann, the position of administrative assistant at the Browncow Farm Equipment Company was no kind of life for a woman with her qualifications, and I had to agree. When I imagined my sister at work, I saw her sitting at a desk constructing barns out of typing paper. Nearby, girls with names like Jolene, new arrivals to the Windy City, would sit polishing their fingernails in jewel tones.

"We're going to visit Ann," my mother announced one night about two weeks after the attack. Her voice was dangerously cheerful.

"When?" I asked. I was sitting at the kitchen table, rereading *The Great Gatsby* for an assignment. I'd most recently heard that Ann's knees were healing nicely, and that she had chosen an attractive new pair of glasses. The fact that she'd successfully discouraged us from making a family pilgrimage to her apartment seemed natural. Our visits usually consisted of my mother bringing a CARE package of canned tunəfish and volunteering my father to rehang the curtains. Inevitably, we would end up having dinner at the Surf 'N' Turf Inne, where a great time was had by no one.

"Now," my mother said.

My father was already pulling on his ancient car coat, and I could see that "we" didn't include me.

"It's a little bit of an emergency, honey." My mother slipped into her imitation lamb's wool jacket. "I know you'll be fine. We'll be back in the morning, and if you have any problems, you can dial Aunt Lucy."

I tucked a place mark into my book and closed it. "Would someone care to tell me what's going on?" I said. Then, thinking I might have more success if I chose the right words, I asked, "Is something critical happening?"

"I don't know." My father pulled out his keys. "She's depressed." He paused for a moment. "But don't worry."

Then my mother gave me a peck on the cheek and the two of them were gone. My mother's floral scent hung in the air. I sat staring at my reflection in the darkened kitchen window for a while, and I thought about calling my friend Lori, but didn't. Finally, I turned on Johnny Carson and made a bowl of red popcorn, using Ann's recipe with paprika.

Ann and I used to make red popcorn almost every Saturday night when she was babysitting me and we were waiting for Dr. Cadaverillo to come on at one. I was supposed to be in bed by ten, and Ann always acted as if it were an enormous favor to let me stay up, but I was pretty sure the truth was that she didn't want to have to watch alone. The show's dramatic vignettes were too campy to give us the creeps, but the emcee himself, with his sallow, bony face and rotted-out teeth, was the stuff of nightmares. Ann and I would sit mesmerized in front of the TV until we heard my parents' blue Cutlass pull into the driveway. Then the spell would be broken, and I'd have to hustle into bed at top speed and pretend to be asleep. I used to lie motionless while my mother checked me, the taste of red popcorn lingering in my mouth.

Besides the secret of Dr. Cadaverillo, Ann and I were bound by endless special projects. Ann had been the star of the James Madison Junior High School art department, and she never ran out of projects that required an obedient assistant at home. She didn't really have friends her own age, but she knew she could always pry me away from whatever book I was reading and put me to work. Together, we made houses out of cardboard and tin foil—she designed and I cut along the lines she drew, sticking Scotch-tape balls where she pointed. One winter we built an entire Alpine valley, with details so perfect it seemed you could move in, if only you weren't too big. I tried to save these treasures for the day Ann became famous, but somehow they were almost all eventually lost or destroyed in our damp basement.

On Valentine's Day each year, Ann and I always made dozens of elaborate, picture-perfect cookie hearts. Ann never received cards, and she said that the whole idea of a card exchange was pedestrian. I got into the habit of leaving the cards my classmates gave me in my desk at school, as a sort of courtesy, and I'd always hurry home to bake. We'd work for hours, and then, just as we'd be finishing the frosting stage, my mother would be sure to appear. "Who is going to eat all of these?" she would ask, lifting one or two from the piled-high platter and sucking in her stomach. "They're very pretty, but that's because you can't see what they do to your teeth." Then she'd giggle nervously. "They *are* tasty," she'd admit, lifting another, "and I know I can count on you girls to clean up."

It went without saying that I was the cleanup committee. Ann was a spiller, leaving a trail of ingredients on the floor. By the time anything came out of the oven, it was impossible to walk without sticking or crunching. I was good at mopping. Unlike my sister, I was neat and careful. I didn't have any real gifts of my own, unless you counted the precocious vocabulary that came from checking out books intended for the older grades. Such a meager claim to specialness, I reasoned, meant I couldn't afford to be moody.

"Dr. Shore thinks the attack was just the last straw," my mother said. "He even hinted she might have done something to prompt it. He always said she was 'iffy.'" She was explaining to me, as I sat at the table eating breakfast, about Ann's being checked into the psychiatric ward of a hospital in Chicago the night before. The kitchen smelled of rye toast. I thought of Ann's descriptions of bald Dr. Shore the shrink and took a swallow of juice.

"Dr. Shore called us last night and warned us that your sister was suicidal," she said, and I bit my toast. "You know, there are times when people talk about suicide because they're looking for attention, and times when they don't talk about it because they mean business. Your sister meant business."

"Can I see her?" I asked. I was worried, but I also figured Ann knew what she was doing. I could only imagine she was acting on an elaborate logic that eluded the family. They'd recently shown "Splendor in the Grass" at my school's movie night, and now I summoned up a picture of my sister looking like Natalie Wood in a crisp white hospital tunic. Surely she had something up her sleeve.

"I think it would be better if you didn't visit for a while," my mother was saying. "And I'd rather you kept this quiet. This is our little secret."

"Does Aunt Lucy know?"

"No."

"Well, what should I say if someone asks about her?"

"You will tell them that she's doing fine, that she's enjoying her job and finding it rewarding."

71

I didn't answer.

"Look, this is for her own good," my mother said and put a hand on my shoulder. I noticed she hadn't put on her makeup yet and her skin looked gray. "Try to understand."

"May I be excused?"

My mother nodded. I hadn't asked to be excused from a table since I was six, but at that moment the formality held a comfort I couldn't explain.

The next day after school, I went over to Lori's house where we cleaned out the refrigerator and made lists of boys we liked. We played our old game, Weird Geometry, in which we pondered various romantic configurations. My heart wasn't in it. I didn't care any more about the rumored triangle between our English teacher Miss Kellerman and the high school band leader and his wife—I had more important puzzles in mind. When I left for dinner, I thought Lori seemed relieved, and I know I was. I didn't trust myself in company; I kept swinging back and forth between a grownup's impatience with teenage trivia and a little girl's fear of being caught wearing lip gloss and a bra. I doubted that I would ever grow into the confidence that Ann had been born with, and knew I'd never have the power of someone who, for example, could ice a cake and then forbid me, at the age of eight, to lick the frosting that remained in the bowl. I remembered watching respectfully while Ann, who was then fifteen, selected a china figurine—a rosy-cheeked girl dressed in brown—and frosted it over. She had me believing this made perfect sense. She told me the doll's name was Miss Sugar Coat, and she got me to clean up afterward. Ann held the same nearly absolute power over my parents. "The secret," she'd said to me once, "is to get them worried enough."

In the weeks that followed Ann's admission to the hospital I avoided my friends, read less, and often failed to hear my teachers in class. I kept trying to reconstruct the scene of the attack in my mind, searching for some clue that would explain everything, or at least enough. But every time I tried to conjure up the face of my sister's attacker, I saw only Dr. Cadaverillo, the ratty blue jacket hanging on his emaciated frame.

Meantime, my mother placed calls to the hospital twice a day and began cooking elaborate recipes with names like Spicy Veal Tournedos and Chicken Fiesta Surprise. No one ate much. My father worked late, and on weekends he and my mother drove to Chicago. When they were both home, they cut wide swaths between each other. They exchanged sneaky sidelong glances, but never really met each other's eyes.

Up until then, I had taken for granted that my parents were a tight team. Ann used to refer to them as the Flying Wallendas. But where I'd always thought she was referring to the teamwork required to pull off their busy schedules—the club meetings and the parties and the evenings at the symphony—I suddenly wasn't sure. I remembered her saying something sarcastic about my mother's death-defying balancing act and my father's blind lifts—which I realized now was probably a reference to his fondness for medicine-colored liqueurs. That fondness grew as Ann's high school grades plummeted and the projects stopped cold and her black hair grew wild. He collected more and more bottles of syrupy blue and green and amber liquid, and he would sip three or four tiny glasses in the evening after dinner, licking his lips, savoring. I never saw him become clumsy or loud, but occasionally he talked to the furniture when he imagined no one saw. "I don't know," he would mutter to the upholstered living room chairs. Then he'd turn to the overfilled bookcase and say, "I don't know why she stays in her room and plays sad music. Why won't she talk to us? What's happened to my girl?"

"We can't allow this to become serious," my mother said often. She arranged for my sister to be seen by an adolescent psychiatrist who Ann said was a total idiot. Each week, Ann sat in his office and stared at the walls and refused to speak. She counted the little blue dots in the wallpaper and when we picked her up, she'd say "3016" or "3032"—unless she wasn't

73

speaking to us either.

Ann's periodic high school silences only lasted a day or two at a time, and I was always the first one she spoke to. My parents would bribe and cajole and offer her the planet on a stick if only she would utter a few syllables, but it was me she trusted. Now I was the only one in the family who couldn't see her. Every week, I asked to go along on the weekend visit, and each time my parents said no. They said they had to bow to Ann's wishes, and Ann wasn't ready.

"Ann sends her love," my mother would say to me every Sunday night when they returned. By the third week, I was seeing only the blown-up details of my mother's face as she spoke—the cracks around her lips where her lipstick had spread, the large pores in her nose. I felt betrayed and taken for a fool.

"Did you tell Ann I sent my love too?"

"Well, of course I did."

"But I didn't. I never sent any message. I'll bet Ann never did either." My mother was surprised into silence, and I added, "We're certainly a crafty family, aren't we?"

Then I saw real pain in my mother's eyes and felt guilty.

"This isn't like you," she said.

"I'm sorry."

"I know this is hard on you."

I nodded, mainly because it was the easiest way to stop her from talking. The image of Dr. Cadaverillo arose in my mind again, but he had lost his hold on me; it seemed clear now that both he and the real-life owner of the ratty blue jacket were little more, after all, than red herrings.

Just then my father, as if misreading my mind, said, "You know what kills me? What kills me is they never found the guy that did this to us. The cops have given up."

A week later, while my parents were making the drive home from Chicago, I got a phone call from Ann. I hadn't spoken to her in a month.

"This is your sister," she said dully. "It's rotten here."

"Ann." My cheeks felt hot, as if the call were from a boy I had a crush on.

"I'm trapped and I hate it here."

"I miss you. Can't you come home?"

"Even the food is terrible," she said, then giggled. "They actually feed us lima beans. And Jell-O with those slimy pears." There was a pause.

"Ann. . .?"

I heard her start to cry, and before I could compose myself to speak I heard a click and the dial tone. I looked up the number of the hospital, dialed, and asked to speak to my sister. I was sweating, despite my mother's insistence that girls "dampen," at worst.

"I'm sorry," the voice on the other end said. "The psychiatric unit does not accept incoming calls at this hour. Would you care to leave a message?"

I hung up. I thought of calling Aunt Lucy, whom my mother had finally confided in, but didn't. I called Dial-A-Horoscope and then the weather bureau and hung up again.

When Ann graduated from high school, my mother claimed it was "by the skin of her chin." She'd said so to Ann's face.

"I am not one of the three little pigs," my sister answered. She seemed proud of her record for truancy. That July she had gotten a job behind the shoe rental desk at Echo Bowl. After six months, she'd agreed to go to the local college, which had an art program, and she'd gotten her own apartment and made herself scarce. We often didn't see her for months. Sometimes I would take a bus and walk by her apartment, thinking I'd run into her, but I never did.

Toward the end of her senior year, my sister called and said that one of her huge, dreamy paintings had been chosen for the college art show. We all dressed up and went to the student union for the opening. The painting, done in blue and green oils, was a cluster of phantom houses atop a vague mountain, and it cast an immediate sense of longing over me that I couldn't understand. While my parents and Ann circulated, I stayed put, identifying myself to onlookers as the artist's little sister. A sweet-looking gray-haired woman said to me, "Your sister has an unusual sense of perspective." There was something false in her voice, and yet in that moment, I was able to put my finger on my sadness. However I might try to follow, there were places—secret villages of the mind—where Ann would travel without me. I searched the room for my family and saw them talking to strangers. I walked over to the refreshment table and got some pink punch in a styrofoam cup and some little party cookies on a napkin. I ruined my appetite for dinner.

Later, when we were all eating dinner in a restaurant, my mother said to Ann, "I feel as if we're all graduating. I think the hot soup is over."

"Cooled," Ann said. She turned to me; I was cutting a piece of veal into tiny bits. "Mom has always had a way with words."

Two months later, she had moved to Chicago.

Now my mother said, "It was only a matter of time; Dr. Shore said so."

"Maybe," my father said.

I kept my vow of secrecy about Ann's present whereabouts, but stories of things she had said and done years ago kept leaking out of me during the rare times I still spent with my friends. One day, Lori and I were eating leftover cold pizza out of her refrigerator and she accused me of being more obsessed with my flaky sister than Sally Coughman was with her nauseating boyfriend Scooter. I peeled a mushroom off my slice and threw it at her in a limp gesture. "Very funny," I said.

"Disgusting." Lori wiped her sleeve. "At least Scooter isn't nutsy."

"You don't know a thing about it." My voice had come out surprisingly hard and mean. "You know, you can be a real bitch."

"Jesus." Lori set her pizza down.

"Let's just drop it."

"Whatever you say. You're the *guest*." I was too ashamed to answer and she started eating again, pretending she didn't care.

Later that night, after a dozen false starts, I asked my parents whether Ann had been so different as a kid that other people would have been alarmed. My mother waited a long time before she answered. "You know," she finally said, "I think you thought your sister had a lot more in mind than she did. Not everything she does is by choice."

"Not everything anybody does is by choice," my father said, and it occurred to me to wonder how much he regretted. I was suddenly aware that my parents had never talked about Ann's future as an artist, and now I was embarrassed to mention it.

"I guess I always thought she was special," I said.

My mother looked at my father.

"Don't worry about it," my father said.

Two weeks later, Dr. Shore decided that Ann was ready for a halfway house. My parents let me come along on the final weekend drive to the hospital. We didn't leave for Chicago until late Sunday morning and my parent still didn't know whether Ann would let me see her, but I think they'd become worried about all the time I spent alone in the house.

We drove almost the whole way in silence.

"How does she look?" I finally asked.

"She's gained a lot of weight," my mother said. I hadn't been expecting that answer. In fact, I'd thought Ann might be dramatically wasted.

"You know," my mother said, "she's been ashamed for you to see her. She's put on close to forty pounds. She doesn't want you to see her like this."

"She's been doing pottery and ceramics in the art therapy room," my father said. "Isn't that nice?"

When we got to the hospital, I waited in the lobby while my parents went upstairs. I looked at some stuffed penguins in the gift shop. A few patients in green paper robes walked the hallways. There were a lot of tamped-out cigarette butts on the floor.

My parents finally came back down and my father said, "She's just not up to seeing you today."

"But I want to see *her*," I said.

"She wanted you to have this." My mother handed me a ceramic plate. "She made it in art therapy." The plate had been formed in a mold and Ann had enameled green and purple over the pattern of grape leaves that formed its border. In the center, she'd written in blue enamel, "For My Sister." I turned the plate over, avoiding my mother's eyes. A nurse or aide, someone with an awkward hand, had scratched Ann's name into the underside while the clay was still soft.

I couldn't think of anything to say. In the back seat of the car, I kept turning the plate over and over in my hands. It was very pretty, but it was also the sort of thing anybody could have made in arts and crafts, even summer camp.

That night, I stayed up and ran a late-night retrospective in my head. The lifework of my sister: false houses and frosted figurines; secrets that she kept locked with her in her room for days, that she'd buried in silence and under the forty pounds of fat they said she'd gained. I kept thinking about all those cigarette butts on the hospital floor, then saw them lit, glowing with the seeds of cancer. I tried to force myself to cry because I thought I should; then the tears fell and my nose ran and I really couldn't stop. My mother must have heard me. She knocked on my door and came and sat on my bed like a visitor. Finally she said, "I hope you will believe someday that I tried."

The next week, I saw my sister at the halfway house. Her face was puffy and her hair was a black cloud and she was wearing an orange terrycloth robe and slippers. She had cutout paper snowflakes on her window, which overlooked an alleyway.

"Jill," she said, and the sound of my name was startling. She looked fat and scared, and suddenly I felt such a surge of love and grief that I was rooted where I stood. We faced each other with our hands at our sides. The moment passed and I embraced my sister as if, for all her size, she might disappear on the spot.

"Thank you for the plate."

"Do you like it?"

"Yes." Our voices were quiet, almost whispers.

"I picked that pattern myself," she said. "It was my choice."

"Yes." I turned then, so she couldn't see the look in my eyes. "I was hoping it was."

Waiting

Budge Wilson

"**Y**OU MUST REALIZE, of course, that Juliette is a very complex child." My mother was talking on the telephone. Shouting, to be more exact. She always spoke on the phone as though the wires had been disconnected, as though she were trying to be heard across the street through an open window. "She's so many *sided*," she continued. "Being cute, of course, is not enough, although heaven knows she could charm the legs off a table. But you have to have something more than personality."

I was not embarrassed by any of this. Lying on the living room floor on my stomach, I was pretending to read *The Bobbsey Twins at the Seashore*. But after a while I closed the book. Letting her words drop around me, I lay there like a plant enjoying the benefit of a drenching and beneficial rain. My sister sat nearby in the huge wingbacked chair, legs tucked up under her, reading the funnies.

"I hope you don't regard this as *boasting*, but she really is so very *very* talented. Bright as a button in school—three prizes, can you believe it, at the last school closing—and an outstanding athlete, even at eight years old."

Resting my head on my folded arms, I smiled quietly. I could see myself eight years from then, receiving my gold medal, while our country's flag rose in front of the Olympic flame. The applause thundered as the flag reached its peak, standing straight out from the pole, firm and strong. As the band broke into a moving rendition of "Oh, Canada," I wept softly. Wet and waterlogged from the last race, my tears melded with the chlorine and coursed attractively down my face. People were murmuring, "So young, so small, and so attractive."

"And such a *leader*!" My mother's voice hammered on. "Even at her age, she seems forever to be president of this and director of that. I feel very blessed indeed to be the mother of such a child." My sister stirred in her chair, and coughed slightly, carefully turning a page.

It was true. I was class president of Grade 4, and manager of the Lower Slocum Elementary School Drama Club. I had already starred in two productions, one of them a musical. In an ornate crepe paper costume composed of giant overlapping yellow petals, I had played Lead Buttercup to a full house. Even Miss Prescott's aggressive piano playing had failed to drown me out, had not prevented me from stealing the show from the Flower Queen. My mother kept the clipping from *The Shelburne Coast Guard* up on the kitchen notice board. It included a blurred newspaper picture of me, with extended arms and open mouth. Below it, the caption read, "Juliette Westhaver was the surprise star of the production, with three solos and a most sprightly little dance, performed skillfully and with gusto. Broadway, look out!"

Mama was still talking. "Mm? Oh. Henrietta. Yes. Well, she's fine, I guess, just fine. Such a serious responsible little girl, and so fond of her sister." I looked up at Henrietta, who was surveying me over the top of her comics. There was no expression on her face at all.

But then, Henrietta was not often given to expression of any kind. She was my twin, but apart from the accident, or coincidence, of our birth, we had almost nothing in common. It was incredible to me that we had been born to the same parents in almost the same moment, and that we had been reared in the same house.

But Henrietta was my friend, and I, hers. We were, in fact, best friends, as is so often the case with twins. And as with most close friends, there was one dominant member, one submissive. There was no doubt in this case as to who played the leading role.

Henrietta even looked submissive. She was thin and pale. She had enormous sky-blue eyes surrounded by a long fringe of totally colorless eyelashes. Her hair was a dim beige color without gradations of light or dark, and it hung straight and lifeless from two barrettes. Her fingers were long and bony, and she kept them folded in her lap, motionless, like a tired old lady. She had a straight little nose, and a mouth that seldom smiled, that was serious and still and oddly serene. She often looked as though she were waiting for something.

Untidy and flamboyant, my personality and my person flamed hotly beside her cool apathy. My temper flared, my joy exploded. With fiery red cheeks and a broad snub nose, I grinned and hooted my way through childhood, dragging and pushing Henrietta along as I raced from one adventure to the next. I had a mop of wild black curls that no comb could tame. I was small, compact, sturdy, well-coordinated and extremely healthy. Henrietta had a lot of colds.

When I start talking about Henrietta and me, I always feel like I'm right back there, a kid again. Sometimes, you know, I got fed up with her. If you have a lot of energy, for instance, it's no fun to go skiing with someone who's got lead in her boots. And for heaven's sake, she kept falling all the time. Scared to death to try the hills, and likely as not, going down them on the seat of her pants. "Fraidy cat! Fraidy cat!" I'd yell at her from the bottom of the hill, where I had landed right side up, and she would start down the first part of the slope with straight and trembling knees, landing in a snowbank before the hill even got started. There were lots of fields and woods around our town, and good high hills if you were looking for thrills. You could see the sea from the top of some of them. The wild wind up there made me feel like I was an explorer, a brave Indian squaw, the queen of The Maritime Provinces. Sometimes I would let out a yell just for the joy of it all—and there, panting and gasping and tripping up the hill would be old Henrietta, complaining, forever complaining, about how tired she was, how cold.

I guess I really loved Henrietta anyway, slow-poke though she was. I had lots and lots of other friends who were more interesting. But it's a funny thing—she was nearly always my first choice for someone to play with.

There was a small woodlot to the east of the village, on land owned by my father. We called it The Grove. It had little natural paths in it, and there were open spaces under the trees like rooms, or houses, or castles, or whatever you wanted them to be that day. The grove of trees was on the edge of a cliff over-hanging some big rocks, and at high tide the sea down there was never still, even when it was flat oil calm. So it could be a spooky kind of place to play in, too. I loved to go there when it was foggy and play Spy. It was 1940 and wartime, and by then we were ten, going on eleven. From The Grove we could sometimes see destroyers, and once even a big aircraft carrier. In the fog, it wasn't hard to believe that the Germans were coming, and that we were going to be blown to bits any minute.

We never told Mama or Papa about going to the cliff when the mist was thick. Henrietta hardly ever wanted to go on those foggy days. She was afraid of falling off the cliff onto the rocks, sure she would drown in the churned-up water, nervous about the ghostly shapes in the thick gray-white air. But she always went. I used to blackmail her. "If you don't go, I'll tell Mama about the time you pretended to be sick and stayed home from school because you didn't have your homework done and were scared of Miss Garrison." Or I would just plain order her around. "I'm *going*, Henrietta, so get a move on and *hurry*!" She'd come padding out of the house in her stupid yellow raincoat, so that she wouldn't get a cold in the wet wind, and off we'd go—me fast and complaining about her slowness, and her slow and complaining about my speed. But she'd be there and we'd be together and we'd have fun. I'd be the Spy, and she'd be the poor agonized prisoner of war, tied up to a tree by a bunch of Germans. Sometimes I'd leave her tethered good and long, so she'd look *really* scared instead of pretend scared, while I prowled around and killed Germans and searched for hidden weapons. Or we'd play ghost, and I'd be the ghost— floating along on the edge of the cliff, and shrieking in my special death-shriek that I saved for ghost games. It started out low like a groan, then rose up to a wail, ending in a scream so thin and high that it almost scared *me*. Sometimes, if she was especially wet and tired, Henrietta would start to cry, and that *really* made me mad. Even now, I can't stand crybabies. But you had to have a victim, and this was something she was extra good at. No point in handing out my death-shriek to a person who wasn't afraid of ghosts. No fun to have the Germans tying up someone who was big and strong and brave, partcularly when the Germans weren't actually there and you had to think them up and pretend the whole thing. One time when we went there with a bunch of kids instead of just us two, I forgot all about her being tied to the tree, and got halfway home before I raced back the whole half mile to untie her. She never said a word. It was snowing, and there were big fat snowflakes on those long white lashes of hers, and her eyes looked like they were going to pop right out of her head. I said I was sorry, and next week I even bought her a couple of comic books out of my allowance money, when she was home sick with bronchitis. Mama said she should have had the sense to wear a scarf and a warm hat, being as she was so prone to colds, and that's certainly true. She never told on me, and I don't know why. She sat up against the pillows and colored in her coloring book or read her funnies, or more often she just lay there on the bed, her hands lying limp on the quilt, with that patient, quiet waiting look of hers.

When the spring came, a gang of us would go out to The Grove on weekends to practice for our summer play. Year after year we did this, and it had nothing to do with those school plays in which I made such a hit. We'd all talk about what stories we liked, and then we'd pick one of them and make a play out of it. I would usually select the play because I was always the one who directed it, so it was only fair that I'd get to do the choosing. If there was a king or a queen, I'd usually be the queen. If you're the director, you can't be something like a page or a minor fairy, because then you don't seem important enough to be giving out instructions and bossing people around, and the kids maybe won't pay attention. Besides, as my mother pointed out, I was smart and could learn my lines fast, and you couldn't expect some slow dummy to memorize all that stuff. Henrietta's voice was so soft and quiet that no one could ever hear her unless they were almost sitting on her *lap*; so of course it would have been stupid to give her a part. She couldn't even be the King's horse or the Queen's milk-white mule, because she was so darn scrawny. You can't have the lead animal looking as though it should be picked up by the SPCA and put in quarantine.

But she was really useful to the production, and it must have been very satisfying for her. She had to find all the costume parts, and she rigged up the stage in the biggest clearing among the trees, making it look like a ballroom or a throne room or whatever else we needed. She did a truly good job, and if it weren't for the fact that I can't stand conceited people, I probably would have told her so. I liked Henrietta the way she was. I didn't want her strutting around looking proud of herself and putting on airs. One time one of the kids said, "Hey, Henrietta, that's a really great royal bedroom you made," and right away she started standing and moving around in a way that showed she thought she was a pretty smart stage manager. I can't stand that kind of thing, and I knew the others wouldn't like it either. So I said, "Oh sure! And the king must have just lost his kingdom in the wars. Who ever heard of a king sleeping on a pile of branches or having an old torn dishtowel at the window? Some king!" And everyone laughed. I always think that laughter is very important. It makes everyone happy right away, and is a good way to ease tensions.

We had a lot of fun practicing for those plays. No one went away for the summer. No one needed to. The sea was right there beside the village, with a big sandy beach only a quarter mile away. Some of the fishermen let us use their smaller flats for jigging, and we could always swim or dig clams or collect mussels. Besides, the War was on, and people weren't spending money on cottages or trips. It seemed to me that everyone just stuck around home, saved paper and counted their ration stamps, and listened to the news on the radio. There was a Navy base nearby, and sometimes sailors came to dinner. They'd tell us about life on the base, and all the dangers they were expecting and hoping to experience when they started sailing to Europe. I envied them like anything, and couldn't for the life of me see why you had to be eighteen before you joined the Navy, or why they wouldn't let girls run the ships or use the guns. Henrietta said she didn't want to be a sailor anyway, because she'd be too scared, which of course is only what you'd expect. Apart from that, there wasn't much excitement. So the play practices were our main entertainment, and in August we put on the play in front of all our mothers and fathers, uncles and aunts, and the sisters and brothers too young to take part.

The play we put on in 1942 was about a rich nobleman called Alphonse, who falls in love with an exquisitely beautiful but humble country girl called Genevieve. I played the part of Genevieve, and it was the nicest part I had ever played. In the last scene, Genevieve and the nobleman become engaged, and she gets to dress up in a very gorgeous gown for a big court ball. I had a real dress for this scene, instead of the usual pieced together scraps of material dug out of old trunks from our attics. My mother let me use one of her long dance dresses from when she was young. It was full of sequins, and even some sort of fluffy feather stuff, and it was pale sapphire blue and very romantic looking. I had trouble getting into it, because I was almost thirteen and sort of big through the middle. But my mother put in a new zipper instead of the buttons, and I was able to wear it after all. I had to move a little carefully and not take very deep breaths, but I was as tall as Mama, and I felt like a real woman, a true beauty. The neck was kind of low, but I was pretty flat, so I didn't need to worry about being indecent in front of Harold Boutilier, who played the part of Alphonse. Mama put a whole lot of make-up on me, covering up the pimples I was starting to get, and I thought I looked like a movie star, a genuine leading lady.

The zipper wasn't put into the dress in time for the dress rehearsal, but Harold wore a big bow at his neck and his mother's velvet shorty-coat, with a galvanized chain round his waist that looked like real silver. He had on his sister's black stockings and a pair of high rubber boots, and he looked very handsome. Up until that year he had just seemed like an okay boy to me, as boys go, but that summer I spent a lot of time watching him and teasing him and thinking about him when I went to bed at night. I guess I had a big crush on him. And I was pretty sure that when he saw me in that blue dress, he'd have a crush on me right away too.

On the day of the play, our families started arriving at The Grove theater a full hour before we got started. It didn't rain, and there wasn't even one of those noisy Nova Scotian winds that shake the trees and keep you from hearing the lines. My mother was hustling around backstage helping with clothes and make-up. Mostly she was fussing with my face and my first costume and telling me how pretty I looked. We had rigged up eight bedspreads, some torn and holey, some beautiful, depending on the fear or the pride of the mothers who lent them, and behind this strung-out curtain, we prepared ourselves for the two o'clock production. Henrietta was moving quietly about on the stage, straightening furniture, moving props, standing back to look at the effect. Later on, just before the curtain went up, or rather was drawn aside, she went off and sat down against a tree, where she'd have a good view of the performance, but still be out of sight. If any of us needed anything, she could get it without the audience seeing what she was doing.

In the first part of the play, the Nobleman ignores the beautiful peasant girl, who comes on dressed in rags but heavily made up, and therefore beautiful. He is of course looking for a wife, but no one even thinks of her as a possible candidate. She does a lot of sighing and weeping in the first scene, and Alphonse rides around on his horse (George Cruikshank) looking handsome and tragic. Harold did this very well.

I could hardly wait for the last scene in which I could get out of those rags and emerge as the radiant court butterfly. Yet I put all I had into the first scene, because in the due course of time, Alphonse turns down all the eligible and less beautiful women of the land, and retires to a corner of the stage to brood, while George Cruikshank stands nearby, munching grass. To a roll of drums (our wooden spoon on Mrs. Eisner's pickling kettle) Genevieve arrives on the scene, and as he turns to look at her dazzling beauty, he recognizes her for what she is—not just a poor commoner, but a young woman of great charm and loveliness, worthy of his hand. At this point in the play, she places her hand on her breast and does a deep and graceful curtsy. He stands up, bends to help her rise, and in a tender and significant gesture, kisses her outstretched hand.

And that's exactly how we did it, right there on the foxberry patch, which looked like a rich green carpet with a red pattern, if you happened to have the kind of imagination to see it that way. I thought I would faint with the beauty of it all. Then the string of bedspreads was drawn across the scene, curtain hoops squeaking, and the applauding audience awaited the final scene.

I didn't waste any time getting into my other costume. Dressed in my blue gown, I peeked through the hole in Mrs. Publicover's bedspread to assess the audience. I had not had time to do this up until now, but Mama had dressed me first, and she had six other girls to get ready for the ball scene. The crowd outside was large. There must have been forty-five or fifty people of various sizes and ages, sitting on the cushions placed on top of the pine needles. The little kids were crawling and squirming around like they always do, and mothers were passing out pacifiers and bags of chips and jellybeans and

suckers to keep them quiet during intermission. One little boy—
Janet Meredith's brother—was crying his head off, and I sure
as fire hoped he'd stop all that racket before the curtain went
up. While I watched all of this, I looked over to the left, and
saw three sailors coming through the woods. I knew them.
They'd been to our house for supper a couple of times, but I
never dreamt we'd be lucky enough to have the Navy at our
play. My big scene was going to be witnessed by more than
just a bunch of parents and kids. There was even a little group
of Grade 12 boys in the back row.

We were almost ready to begin. Backstage, most of the make-
up was done, and Mrs. Elliot was standing by the tree, making
up Henrietta just for the heck of it. Henrietta had set up the
stage and handed out the costumes, and she was putting in
time like some of the rest of us. She just had on that old blue
sweatshirt of hers and her dungarees, and it seemed to me that
all that make-up was going to look pretty silly on someone
who didn't have a costume on, but I didn't really care. If Henrietta wanted to make a fool of herself, it wasn't going to bother
me.

In the last scene, all the courtiers and aristocrats are milling
around in the ballroom, waiting for the nobleman to arrive with
his betrothed. The orchestra is playing Strauss waltzes (on Mrs.
Corkum's portable wind-up gramophone) and you can see that
everyone is itchy-footed and dying to dance, but they have to
wait around until Alphonse arrives with Genevieve. It is a moment full of suspense, and I had to do a lot of smart and fierce
directing to get that bunch of kids to look like they were happy
and excited and impatient all at the same time. But they did a
really good job that afternoon. You could see that they thought
they actually *were* Lords and Ladies, and that they had come
to a real live ball. At this point in the scene, suddenly there is
a sound of trumpets (little Horace Miller's Halloween horn) and
Alphonse comes in, very slow and stately, with Genevieve on
his arm. She is shy, and enters with downcast eyes; but he
turns around, bows to her, and she raises her head with new

pride and confidence, lifting her arms to join him in the dance.

We did all this beautifully, if I do say myself, and as I started to raise my arms, I thought I would burst with the joy and splendor of that moment. And as it turned out, burst is just about exactly what I did. The waltz record was turned off during this intense scene, and there was total silence on the stage and in the audience. As my arms reached shoulder level, a sudden sound of ripping taffeta reached clear to the back of the audience. (Joannie Sherman was sitting in the last row, and she told me about it later). I knew in one awful, stupifying moment that my dress had ripped up the back, the full length of that long zipper. I can remember standing there on the stage with my arms half raised, unable to think or feel anything beyond a paralyzed horror. After that night, whenever I heard that accident victims were in a state of shock, I never had to ask the meaning of that term. I knew. Joannie told me later that the whole stage full of people looked like they had been turned to stone, and that it really had been a scream to see.

Suddenly, as quiet and quick as a cat, Henrietta glided onstage. She was draped in one of the classier bedspreads from the curtain, and no one could have known that she wasn't supposed to be there. I don't know how anyone as slow-moving as Henrietta could have done so much fast thinking. But she did. She was carrying the very best bedspread—a lovely blue woven one that exactly matched my dress. She stopped in front of me, and lifting the spread with what I have to admit was a lot of ceremony and grace, she placed it gravely over my shoulders. Fastening it carefully with one of the large safety pins that she always kept fastened to her sweatshirt during performances, she then moved backwards two paces, and bowed first to me and then to Harold, before moving slowly and with great dignity toward the exit.

Emerging from my shock with the kind of presence of mind for which I was noted, I raised my arms to their proper height, and prepared to start the dance with Alphonse. But Harold, eyes full of amazement, was staring at Henrietta as she floated off the stage. From the back of the audience, I could hear two long low whistles, followed by a deep male voice, exclaiming, "Hubba! *Hubba!*" to which I turned and bowed in graceful acknowledgment of what I felt to be a vulgar but nonetheless sincere tribute. The low voice, not familiar to me, spoke again. "Not *you*, pie-face!" he called, and then I saw three or four of the big boys from Grade 12 leave the audience and run into the woods.

Somehow or other I got through that scene. Harold pulled his enchanted eyes back onstage, and the gramophone started the first few bars of "The Blue Danube," as we began to dance. Mercifully, the scene was short, and before long we were taking our curtain calls.

"Stage Manager! Stage Manager!" shouted one of the sailors, and after a brief pause, old Henrietta came shyly forward, bedspread gone, dressed once more in her familiar blue sweat-shirt and dungarees. The applause from the audience went on and on, and as we all bowed and curtsied, I stole a look at Henrietta.

Slender, I thought, throat tight. Slender, not skinny anymore. All in an instant I saw everything, right in the midst of all that clapping and bowing. It was like one of those long complicated dreams that start and finish within the space of five minutes, just before waking in the morning. Henrietta was standing serenely, quietly. As the clapping continued, while the actors and actresses feverishly bobbed up and down to acknowledge the applause, she just once, ever so slightly, inclined her head, gazing at the audience out of her astonishing eyes—enormous, arresting, fringed now in long dark lashes. Mrs. Elliot's make-up job had made us all see what must have been there all the time—a strikingly beautiful face. But there was something else there now that was new. As I continued to bow and smile, the word came to me to describe that strange new thing. Power. Henrietta had power. And what's more, she had it without having to *do* a single thing. All she needs to do, I thought, is *be*.

The terrible injustice of it stabbed me. There I was, the lead role, the Director, the brains and vigor of our twinship, and suddenly, after all my years in first place, it was she who had the power. Afterwards I looked at them—the boys, the sailors, *Harold*—as they gazed at her. She was only sauntering around the stage picking up props. But they were watching, watching, and I knew, with stunning accuracy, that there would always be watchers now, wherever she might be, whatever she wore, regardless of what she might be doing. And I also knew in that moment, with the same sureness, that I would never have that kind of power, not ever.

The next day, Mama stationed herself at the telephone, receiving the tributes that came pouring in. A few moments per call were given over to a brief recognition of my acting talents and to an uneasy amusement over the split dress. The rest of the time was spent in shouted discussion of Henrietta's startling and surprising beauty. I lay face downward on my bed and let the words hail down.

"Yes indeed. *Yes*. I quite agree. Simply beautiful. And a real bolt from the blue. She quite astonished all of us. Although of course I recognized this quality in her all along. I've often sat and contemplated her lovely eyes, her milky skin, her delicate hands, and thought, 'Your time will come, my dear! Your time will come!'"

"Delicate hands!" I whispered fiercely into the mattress. "Bony! Bony!"

I suppose, in a way, that nothing changed too drastically for me after that play. I continued to lead groups, direct shows, spark activities with my ideas, my zeal. In school, I did well in all my subjects, and was good at sports too. Henrietta's grades were mediocre, and she never even tried out for teams or anything, while I was on the swim team, the baseball team, the basketball team. She still moved slowly, languidly, as though her energy were in short supply, but there was a subtle difference in her that was hard to put your finger on. It wasn't as though she went around covered with all that highly flattering grease paint that Mrs. Elliot had supplied. In fact, she didn't really start wearing make-up until she was fifteen or sixteen. Apparently she didn't need to. That one dramatic walk-on part with the blanket and the safety pin had done it all, although I'm sure I harbored a hope that we might return to the old Henrietta as soon as she washed her face. Even the sailors started coming to the house more often. They couldn't take her out, of course, or *do* anything with her. But they seemed to enjoy just looking at her, contemplating her. They would sit there on our big brown plush chesterfield under the stern picture of Great-great-grandmother Logan in the big gold frame, smoking cigarette after cigarette, and watching Henrietta as she moved about with her infuriatingly slow, lazy grace, her grave confidence. Her serenity soothed and excited them, all at the same time. Boys from Grades 9 and 10 hung around our backyard, our veranda, the nearest street corner. They weren't mean to me. They simply didn't know I was there, not really.

I didn't spend much time with Henrietta anymore, or boss her, or make her go to The Grove in the fog, or try to scare her. I just wasn't all that crazy about having her around the entire time, with those eyes looking out at me from under those long lashes, quiet, mysterious, full of power. And of course you had to trip over boys if you so much as wanted to ask her what time it was.

Every once in a while I'd try to figure out what the thing was that made her so different now; and then, one day, all of a sudden, I understood. We were down at the beach, and she was just sitting on a rock or something, arms slack and resting on her knees, in a position I had often seen over the years. And in that moment I knew. Everything else was the same: the drab white skin, the bony, yes, bony hands, the limp hair. But she had lost her waiting look. Henrietta didn't look as though she were waiting for anything at all anymore.

Gal Pickney

Donna Weir

1.

THE ROOM SMELLED strongly of Johnson's Baby Powder mingled with the lingering odor of stale piss from Junior's carefully concealed bedwetting of the night before. He had covered the pissed-on sheets with clean, dry ones, but the stench had risen at noon, to join forces with the clammy, hot blasts of air emitting from the long defunct air-conditioner. Together they inhabited the room with a presence that was as commanding as it was unbearable.

Shirley was standing in front of the mirror in canary yellow panties and a bra that used to be white but was now a yellowish brown from numerous encounters in the washing machine with all varieties of multicolored clothing. She was fully coated in Johnson's Baby Powder and could have been mistaken for an Egyptian Mummy, but for the wide grin with which she greeted Maxine as she entered the room.

"You missed a spot, Sis," Maxine said, poking Shirley in the belly button, the only spot that was still brown, and only because it was too deep to have caught any of the indiscriminate shower of powder.

"Thanks," Shirley grinned impishly as she dunked the bottle of powder into her belly button, covering the red carpet in white dust.

"Did our color-struck mother finally convince you that you would be more beautiful if you painted your body white, Shirl, or was this your idea?" asked Maxine, as she carefully maneuvered her way around Junior's bed to plop down onto the disarray of bedclothes, books and dirty underwear that lay bunched up in the middle of Shirley's bed.

Shirley smirked at her sister in the mirror. She had heard that kind of dig before and refused to fall for it this time. She knew that Maxine was probably looking for an excuse to resume that discussion they had started on Martin Luther King Day. And since she neither fully understood nor particularly cared about the whole Black/White thing that Maxine was so hung up on lately, and moreover was in no mood for one of her sister's long-winded "college girl" lectures, she ignored the bait. As far as she was concerned, if White people were still making Black people ride at the back of the bus, Mommy would not have brought her to America, no she wouldn't, and that was that.

From the bed, Maxine watched Shirley walk over to the closet. Her body was smooth and tight and brown as custard-apple. She moved with an unconscious grace that had been handed down from Granma Matilda, had skipped both her mother and Maxine, to abound all the more bountifully in Shirley's slender limbs. Her slightly bowed legs, which might have detracted from the physical allure of some less blessed creature, seemed to enhance Shirley's shapely figure. Her hips (which should have been boyishly flat like her mother's and Maxine's) rounded and flared. If she looked like this at fifteen, Maxine wondered, imagine how she'd look later when the pimples and blackheads cleared up to reveal the healthy skin underneath. She reminded Maxine of their cousin Doris, who had the same figure and used to drive the men into a lecherous craze whenever she wore pants. Having been Doris' constant companion when the two were girls together in Jamaica, Maxine had gotten used to the wild catcalls and dirty talk that came from the men on the street corner. Talk that was meant to flatter but instead offended Doris, and eventually drove her into ankle-length skirts and baggy pants.

Maxine watched her sister with envy and pride. She had always been on the chubby side herself. Even when her legs

95

had grown long and graceful, the rest of her had remained round as if reluctant to part with its baby fat. She blamed her mother for her long legs, wide waistline and flat hips and was always envious of girls with the hourglass figure. It was both a shock and a relief when she came to the States and found there were actually people in the world who dreamed of having slim thighs and long legs. However, she was not too comforted for long, for later she discovered that this was merely the dream of TV White girls. Her real-life companions and relatives were a constant reminder that a tiny waistline, big hips, and a bottom that moved when you walked were still and always would be the womanly figure for Blackfolks. Her sister Shirley fit the description to a T.

Maxine was secretly pleased that Shirley was growing to resemble her in looks if not in build, though the smart-assed brat would rather die than admit it. And nobody's fool had ever called Maxine ugly. Even her color-struck aunts and cousins had had to stop at "dark" when they took it upon themselves to describe her. "She dark fe true but her skin smooth and she have pretty looks" was the phrase (with not too many variations) that had reassured her that her blackness did not necessarily make her ugly. It was as if they were relieved and somewhat surprised that someone so plum-black could possess such luminous wide-set eyes, a cute upturned nose that flared and quivered like a high-strung pony's when she was upset or afraid, and high cheekbones that were a constant source of debate between Maxine and her mother. Her mother hated high cheek-bones and insisted that Maxine had inherited them from her father, "who everybody knew came from a no-good breed and was a wotless ole nigger." At this, Maxine would break out into what her mother described as "marketwoman" laughter, while pointing out her mother's own very prominent cheek-bones. She chuckled softly now at the memory of her mother's face, star-apple purple at the suggestion that she too had a jawbone "sharp enough to cut a man's throat."

Shirley's voice broke into her sister's daydreaming. "What'cha laughing at, you don't like it?" She was dressed in a pair of black sweat pants and a long oversized white shirt. The shirt was falling off Shirley's thin shoulders, despairingly.

"Well, that depends on where you're planning to wear it to," Maxine replied.

"What's wrong with it?" Shirley asked, rolling her eyes up into her head like a cement mixer in full motion.

"Nothing, if you're going to a costume party you'll make a fine Raggedy Ann," said Maxine. She walked over to the closet and took out a red midi-blouse and a straight denim skirt that she had given Shirley last Christmas. "Here, wear these if you wanna look like somebody," she sassed.

Shirley glanced at the skirt and back at Maxine and wriggled her nose. She had worn that skirt to LaTanya's sweet-sixteen party and it had hugged her butt so tight that 'Tanya's cousin T.J. had kept sliding his hand down to her waist as they danced. She had tried not to say anything 'cause he was so fine and she wanted to invite him to the movies the next day, but he had not gotten the message even after she had pushed his hand away three times. She finally had to smack his face and call him a jerk right there on the dance floor and he had walked away from her saying, "You not that cute anyway" and went to dance with freckle-face Deidra who thought she was so cute because she had light eyes and naturally curly hair. Later Tanya told her that ever since that night T.J. and Deidra had been going together.

Besides she had twenty million other reasons for hating stupid tight-fitting skirts. Everyone was always gawking at her and mistaking her for a slut. It started two years ago. One day, shortly after turning thirteen, she discovered that she had a slut's body. The men who owned the twenty-four-hour grocery store across the street had known her since she was a shy little girl, who had just stepped off the plane into the sucking, burning, turn-your-fingers-blue cold, and had immediately taken refuge beside the heater in their shop refusing to budge an inch in the direction of the schoolyard, whose inhabitants were as cold and as cruel as the iceberg that they inhabited for almost half the year. Always making fun of her, saying she talked funny. Hiding her gloves so they could watch her fingers turn bluish-purple as she stood alone on the playground crying for the familiar faces of Karen and Janice and wondering where the sun had disappeared to.

These nice Jamaican men were her mother's friends. They had driven her to school more than once when she was too scared to brave the cold. Suddenly one day, they were saying good morning to her chest. She looked at them and saw that they had not changed. Only she had. She knew that it was her fault and she was ashamed. Ashamed of herself for becoming a slut overnight and causing them to look at her that way. So she found an ally in winter, made her peace with the cold. She buried her body under layers of shirts and sweaters, jackets and coats. And when summer rolled lazily around she tried to repeat the camouflage. But the summer's heat and her sister's pleading had worn down her resistance. She had began to dress almost normally again, except for the standard tee shirt worn under summer clothing to conceal telltale bra marks.

Maxine's sassiness evaporated into the tense silence. She too was remembering. The day Shirley had burst into the living room, flung her bookbag at the TV, and run into her room screaming loud and urgent enough to wake Granma Matilda from her grave. Common sense had told Maxine that she would get nowhere by probing, so she had gotten into the bed with Shirley instead and had lain there quietly, watching her sister's back arch like a scared cat's. Finally, Shirley had blurted out, "They're looking at me nasty again. Those men across the street." Maxine had lain there stunned into an even deeper silence. She had wanted to tell her sister that they looked at her nasty too, but she was too busy absorbing the shock that those men considered her baby sister old enough to be seen in that way. Why, Shirl was young enough to be their granddaughter.

Now, watching the way Shirley glanced suspiciously at the

skirt, Maxine prayed fervently that her sister had gotten over that pain-filled period of self-hate. She hoped that Shirley's baggy look was a reflection of the new fashion statement and not another cruel onslaught of growing pains.

"I dare you to try it on," Maxine challenged. "I bet you look like flat-butt Annie in it anyway."

"Who you calling flat-butt Annie?" Shirley returned, clearly offended. "I bet I look better in it than you." Shirley tugged the skirt over her hips and fastened the zipper deftly, slipped her arms through the blouse, then her head, and stood there in front of the mirror, mesmerized by her own image. She looked good, she looked better than good, and she knew it. She began to twirl and grin, the dimple twinkling mischievously in her chin. She twirled, faster and faster, and her head began to grow, and grow dizzy. She stood up on tiptoe and pirouetted like a ballerina and fell rather ungracefully onto the bed.

Then she remembered that there would be boys at the party. Yes, hopefully there would be boys. Cute boys and boys who thought they were cute. Boys with razor-sharp tongues, who serenaded your butt in on-the-spot rap-attacks. Boys with cool clothes, and hot hands. Boys like T.J. who were not content to look without touching. She quickly unzipped the skirt and stepped neatly out of it.

Maxine stared at her sister in confusion. She was trying to ride with the waves of emotion crashing in rapid succession across Shirley's face. It was an exercise in frustration. Maxine sighed.

"You never did say where you're going," she prodded.

"Oh, Kimberly is having a party," Shirley replied off-handedly.

"Oh? Does Mama know anything about this?" Maxine inquired sharply.

The cement mixer in Shirley's head malfunctioned. Went into fast-forward. Rolled all the way back until only the whites were showing. "I was going to tell her after I got dressed," she lied.

"So, you're getting dressed for a party that you possibly, no, quite probably, won't be allowed to set foot in, right? I know you always saying how you were not cut-out for college, but I didn't know you was this dumb."

Shirley had slipped on a hot pink jumpsuit that was almost her size, and was carefully applying Vaseline Petroleum Jelly in very liberal portions to her lips. She glanced sheepishly at her sister in the mirror, the dimple in her chin winking, though she was not smiling. "Will you tell her for me?" she asked cautiously.

Maxine hesitated for a while. "I don't know, it's already eight o'clock, and you have a bad attitude. And a nine o'clock curfew, remember!"

"Yeah, yeah, yeah, I know," Shirley snapped. "How could I forget, I'm the only girl in America who has to be home at nine o'clock. But she listens to you. She'll say yes if you ask her. Please, Max. Please!" Shirley pleaded, fixing Maxine with a look that made it impossible for her to say no.

2.

JEAN STOPPED SPEAKING to the Lord right after her mother died. Now, she referred all things, good or bad, to a more receptive source—her mother Matilda. While Jesus never gave her any sign that he was sympathetic to her problems, Mumma always came to her in dreams and told her things. Like the time when Junior was a baby and had the fever. She had heard Mumma's voice interrupting her dreams calling, "Jean, Jean, wake up and see to de baby." But she had wanted so much to finish that nice dream, she had refused to listen. Mumma had reached out her hand and slapped her so soundly that her eyes flew open instantly. The baby was lying by the edge of the bed, choking on his tongue. His face was blue, his body was soaking wet and his eyes were bulging, big and dead looking.

For days she had walked around thanking Mumma for saving her son's life and showing everyone the fingerprints from her dead mother's slap, but no one believed a word of it. Jean didn't try very hard to convince them; she just let it go at that. As long as Mumma was looking out for her, it didn't matter what anyone else thought or believed. She just kept right on talking to Mumma. She had an ant's nest full of parables to fill Mumma's ears tonight. She gathered all the ironing into a basket, put up the board and began talking to her mother as she ironed the children's clothes.

"You know Mumma, ah jus get another letter from dat dam whorish dawg, ah sey ah married to. Say him not coming back to New York 'cause him ha fe wuk too hard in de cold and him woman and pickney need him down dere more dan we. Imagine dat, eh? Ah slaving away cleaning dat white woman behind, trying to save every penny ah earn fe buy a house so snow won' freeze and sun won' bun him pickney dem, and before him stay here and help me him run gawn back to dat dutty gal and her lickle sore foot pickney. Ah know ah shudda never did sen fe him in de firs' place. But de lawyer did tell me sey if de pickney dem come widout dem fadda, de government woulda put all a we pon welfare. And you never raise me fe go pon poor list, at all, at all. It too low down and dutty, and dem treat you worse dan a dawg wen you go fe pick up de check. Ah didn' lef me daddy dead lef house and lan to live in dis man country on pauper roll. Afta me no cripple. Long as me hearty and strong me gwine wuk hard fe better me life, wid or widout dat dutty bum. But ef ah ever ketch him ass back a New York ah gwine dash hot oil inna him face. Dat dutty tarra tarra clath. But is how him coulda do it, eh Mumma? Afta me dun tek him out de gutta and tun him inna gentleman. Every day me worry se de pickney dem gwine tek afta him dutty ways and tun out wotless like him. Dey say chip no fall far from de block and is true. Dat Shirl acting more like him every day. See letter jus come say she still a miss class and nah do her homework. Ah tell you Mumma, ef ah did know sey a so raisin' dem hard, ah woulda never have de firs' one. Why you never tell me. . ."

Jean stopped mumbling and looked up as a shadow fell across her ironing board. She smiled as she realized who was blocking her light. "Oh, is you? How you manage fe drag youself from you dear Auntie fe come look fe you ole good fe nuttin madda?"

Maxine chuckled softly in her belly as she walked over and kissed her mother. "Hi, sexy girl," she teased. "Still talking to youself?"

"Pshaw, ah tired a telling you we not de same size. Who you tink you calling girl, eh? You tink cause you taller dan me dat mek you a woman? You betta have some respec', you hear. Ah'm still you madda."

Maxine laughed heartily and remarked, "Ah notice you making up big scandal over girl, you ain't complainin' 'bout sexy." She was preparing to plop down on her mother's perfectly smooth bed but Jean cleared her throat, eloquently. Maxine straightened, said "Oops, ah almost forgot that was sacred grounds," walked over to the armchair and sprawled there instead, her long legs kicking the closet door.

Jean turned her attention back to the pants she was ironing. She touched her index finger to her tongue, and then to the face of the iron. The slow hiss told her it was now hot enough to press cotton but not hot enough to burn it. She picked up the iron and went to work on the seam in Malcolm's pants. "What you looking at so?" she asked, as she felt Maxine's eyes burning a hole in her back.

"Nuttin, ah jus' wondering whose throat 'Big-Brother' planning to cut with dat knife edge you pressing into his pants, dat's all."

Jean laughed and sucked her teeth. "But is what you know about ironing, though. Wid dem double seam ah see walking around in you jeans! Ah pray to God de man you marry know a iron from a pen, cause you don' know de difference. Gal, you tink dis is ironing? You should see de way you Granny use to iron pants. When she finish wid it de pants stan' up straight like a living man in deh." She took her hands off the board, and placed them on her hips, arms akimbo. "As a matter of fact, ah hear story dat long time 'fore she even had me, your Granny 'Tilda press a pants and lef it fe stan' up while she run to de kitchen to turn a breadfruit she was roasting on de coal-pot. When she come back, all she see is de pants-foot bruking de corner. So she tek off afta de pants. But the pants waist look 'round and see her coming and tell de pants foot fe pick up speed and away it went down the rocky road. It give you Granny such a race and she still never catch up to de run-a-way pants. Dat's why ah stop starching pants de minute ah come to dis man country. Ah don't able chase no pants thru dem ya wicked streets, ah might lose more dan me wind."

Maxine chuckled. As she watched the mischievous looking dimple winking in her Mama's chin she thought, "Right now, she looked just like Shirl." And remembered her mission. "Mommy?" she ventured.

Jean stopped moving the iron across the board and turned too quickly, startling the guile on Maxine's face. The last time Maxine had called her Mommy was on the phone, and she hadn't been able to see her child's face. She had answered the phone without waking up and the call became an extension of a bizarre nightmare she'd been having. But the hysterical voice at the other end of the line was no dream. It was real, real terrified, and it was calling her Mommy!

Maxine got hysterical every time Reagan appeared on TV but she only called her Mommy when she was in pain, or trouble. To block out the vision of her child lying hurt, bleeding or in jail somewhere, she had yelled into the receiver, "Max, gal, calm youself and tell me wat's de matter wid you!"

Then the whole story had come pouring down like a riverbed after a hurricane. How the white kids, and the teachers, and the cold, and the hicks, and all the rest of the uncivilized world in upstate New York were ganging up on her daughter, and how she was going to kill herself or come home—whichever was easier. And Jean, who had never understood why Maxine, after so many years of living without a mother in Jamaica, had insisted in running off upstate to college, after spending only one year with her, had had no problem telling her daughter to "stop all dat foolishness and come home, right now."

And Maxine had done just that. But Jean had never gotten over the shock that six months after coming home Maxine had left again. This time to go live with her Auntie. She was hurt to the core but refused to admit that it had anything to do with her. She was a damn good mother. The fact that she had sent for all six of them, three years after setting foot in dis man's country, attested to that. Wasn't her fault that the children had gotten so rotten living on their own back home, that they considered themselves too big for some discipline.

But Jean had no time to dwell on why Maxine had chosen her aunt over her. She had to find out what it was that was making her daughter resort to her baby name for her. "Wat's wrong now? Wat kinda trouble you in?" she asked, glancing suspiciously at Maxine's stomach.

Maxine snorted in disgust, sucked her teeth, and said, "Ah'm not in no trouble, Mama. You always on the lookout for that kinda trouble. Ah wonder what you gwine do when you fine what you lookin for one a these fine days."

Jean stared at her daughter for a second, then burst out, "But you ever se me dying trials. You wondering wat ah gwine do... You betta worry 'bout wha you gwine do ef trouble find you before you ready fe it. Me done have all my troubles and you and you sistah is de biggest ones. Pshaw, but wat dis pickney gal disturbing me peace fa when ah trying to box-out dese couple pieces a clothes. Wat she run in here crying Mommy like a baby fa when she got nuttin betta to tell me dan how she wondering wat ah gwine do. Since you so quick to pull you tongue on me, it shouldn' be nuttin too great you crying Mommy 'bout. So wat 'appen? You and dat bway fall out again?"

"Oh, Mama, there you go again, assuming the worst," Maxine replied in a more conciliatory tone. "Is nuttin like dat. Ah jus was gwine ask ef you know 'bout Kimberly party since Shirl got her heart set on going but too scared to ask your permission."

Jean chuckled softly and asked, "Is dat all? Is dat why you come in here crying Mommy? So dat ah can let you sistah go run de streets wid her Yankee friend and combolo. Who she tink you is, God almighty? But Lord, ah raise some smart gal pickneys, eh? One in de room fixing up to go to a party she didn't tell me nuttin 'bout and de other one in here crying Mommy like she mash her finger in de door. Ah musta been lying on de wrong side when ah get dese two." She shook her head from side to side and picked up the iron.

"Mama, it really wouldn't look right ef you didn't send Shirl to Kimberly's sweet sixteen," Maxine persisted. "After all, Kimberly's Mom did send her to Shirl's. It gwine look real funny, like you have something against her or something. Look, don' worry yourself about Shirl and boys. She can take care of herself. She not as dumb as you tink. And anyway, you remember dat story you use to tell me about dat girl whose father always lock her up in the house cause he was afraid some man might trouble her? And how him use to follow her everywhere, even to de toilet. But de girl was meeting a lover every night in de toilet while her father wait outside de door. When de ole man tek a stock him daughter pregnant, and him walk 'round saying dat is fat she fat cause him never let no man get near her. Well is de same ting you trying to do to Shirl. You can' hide her from de world because somehow or other de world gwine fine her."

Jean turned around and stared at Maxine long and hard. "You tink all ah worrying 'bout is her belly, don't you?" she asked. "Ah worrying 'bout her belly, her back, her head and all de res of her. You know dat jus de other day dey fine a little boy dead behind de projects. Overdose from crack. You hear me! You tink dis is a nice place we livin' in?" Her voice cracked and grew hoarse as she said, "And is me alone and God care 'bout wha 'appen to me pickney dem. So ef ah don' worry, den is who gwine do it? Dem good-fe-nuttin daddy him run gawn back to Jamaica cause him too damn lazy to stay here and help we wuk so we can have a betta life. Is me alone, you hear me. And it rough. It rough, you hear. You jus wait until you have you family and you will understand what me talking 'bout. You jus wait! Aaaaah sah!!!"

Jean rested her hands on the ironing board and placed her chin between her cupped palms. Her back was turned to Maxine. She was quiet for a long time. When she spoke again, she sounded tearful and beaten. "Awright, you win. Ah don' want Kimberly Madda carry bad feelings fe me. Because ef anything 'appen to anyone a de kids, when ah gone a work ah know she would help out till ah get home. Tell de gal fe get dress and gwan, but don' set foot out ya widout her bredda Junior, and don' set foot in ya after eleven, or her batty gwine have fe answer fe it tomorrow morning."

3.

MAXINE SPRINKLED THE Comet liberally over the sponge, and bent down to scrub the tub. She checked the clock on the bathroom wall. Eight o'clock. Where was Norman? She hoped he hadn't gotten lost changing trains. How could someone live in Brooklyn and not be able to find his way to Queens by subway? Didn't it ever occur to him that he might have to take public transportation sometime? But she had to admit, she too missed the old blue jalopy. It had afforded them the luxury of getting up and taking off at a moment's notice. Far away from the scrutiny of nosy relatives who never recognized when you grew up. Those days were gone. She sighed wistfully. At least for now, anyway. Maybe if she saved enough this summer, she would be able to afford something better than that lemon by graduation next year.

Graduation. She said the word over slowly in her mind. How good it sounded. To be the first one of Mama's children to graduate from college. And she owed it all to Auntie Val despite her nosiness. She could not have made it through City College without her support. After Maxine left upstate, she never thought she would get the chance to finish college. Mama wanted her to get a full-time job to help with the rent, since her husband had taken off to Jamaica to be with his sweetheart. Malcolm was holding down a good job at the mechanic shop and helping her out real good, and she felt that Maxine should try to do the same. After all, she had struggled and worked and saved for three years to bring them to this country, only to have that bum desert her and his four children. Malcolm and Maxine were not his and Maxine was glad of that. She hated him. He was everything her Mama said he was and more. She had begun to feel like a real scum when Mama started accusing her of being just as ungrateful as he was. She was prepared to forget about college and get a job to help her mother pay the bills, but six months of listening to Mama blame everyone for what her husband had done was all Maxine could stand. It was Maxine's fault for never treating him with any respect. It was Malcolm's fault for always intervening whenever Mama and her husband had a fight. It was Aunt Valerie's fault for calling him a bum to his face when he quit his construction job. As far as Maxine was concerned, it was Jean's fault for being stupid enough to bring him here in the first place. Night and day, day and night she carried on about it and wouldn't let anyone in the house get any rest. Maxine also caught hell for dating. The men she was seeing were going to treat her the same way. Maxine tried to tell her mother she wasn't planning to marry any one of them or get pregnant, but Jean was on a rampage. She started beating up on the children. All except Malcolm. Maxine got the worst of her wrath for some inexplicable reason. She couldn't seem to do anything right.

When Maxine left to live with Aunt Valerie, Shirley became the beating stick. And she gave as good as she got, for Shirley was no angel. She didn't like school and she was always getting suspended for playing hooky, or fighting. Even Maxine had to admit that sometimes Shirley gave Mama more than enough reasons to beat her.

Maxine finished scrubbing the bathtub and reached into the cabinet for the Pinesol. Here we go again, she thought, bending over the toilet bowl. Funny how folks never complained about food when it goes through the mouth, but when it comes out at the other end—whew! Lord have mercy! she chuckled.

The sound of footsteps descending the stairs two at a time broke into her reverie. Surely that couldn't be Norman! Seconds later, Shirley bounced in, with Norman in tow. Maxine straightened up, arms akimbo. "Now, where did the two of you find each other?" she smiled. "No, don't tell me. Norman got lost and went straight to Mama's house and she asked you to walk him over here, right?"

"Not even close," Norman replied in a mock huff. "I found my way here quite all right, and rang the kitchen bell several times but no one answered. I was just going around to try the front door when I met your sister coming through the gate. She let me in."

Maxine glanced suspiciously at Shirley. "You mean to tell me that you came here of your own free will?" she asked, turning abruptly on Shirley.

"Yes," Shirley replied sheepishly.

"Hmmm, you must be growing out of that me-myself-and-I phase," Maxine replied with a pleased smile. Then her head jerked up as if remembering something. "You wouldn't happen to be dropping by to pick up that new jumpsuit I bought you, would you?" she asked suddenly.

Shirley shook her head in an emphatic no.

"Good," Maxine replied. "Because if your memory serves you right, you will also recall that I promised I would send it to your cousin Nadine in Jamaica if you played hooky one more time this semester. Uh, uh, don't even try to deny it. Someone saw you hanging out by my old high school with Kimberly and LaTanya. I hope when you start high school next fall you will go there every day, since you seem to like it so much already. And I don't mean hanging out by the gates, either."

Shirley walked away from Maxine's eyes. She didn't mind

the anger too much. It was the hurt and disappointment that she couldn't bear to face. Why was Maxine so much like Mom sometimes? Why didn't she just chill out and be like her friends' sisters? She walked over to the bedroom and turned on the little black and white TV. "227" was on. It was her favorite show. She loved Sandra. She could hear Norman and Maxine talking in the bathroom. She hoped they weren't discussing her, but just in case she turned up the volume. She didn't want to hear any of it.

Maxine left Norman and went into the bedroom to talk to Shirley. "Did you eat yet?" she asked.

"No," Shirley replied, "I left before Mama finished making dinner."

"Okay, then I'll fix something for you and Norman." As she got to the door, she turned to ask Shirley if she would care to join her in the kitchen, but her sister's eyes were glued to the TV set. She shook her head bemusedly and continued up the stairs.

Minutes later she could hear Shirley and Norman laughing. Their laughter floated up the stairway into the kitchen, mingling with the tantalizing smell of curry chicken warming over. She returned downstairs with two steaming platefuls of curry chicken over white rice and settled down to watch "Amen" and "The Golden Girls." During a commercial break, Norman got up, offering to wash the dishes.

"Okay by me," Maxine said, smiling, "but let me come upstairs with you. I wouldn't want Auntie Valerie to catch you alone in her kitchen with your hands in the suds." It was a standing joke in the family that Auntie Valerie was liberated in every way but one: she didn't allow men to set foot into her kitchen. She said all they ever did was make a goddamn mess for her to clean up.

Glancing at the kitchen clock Maxine noted that it was already after ten o'clock. She picked up the kitchen phone and dialed her mother's number. The voice at the other end sounded tired and exasperated. "Hi Mama," she called cheerily.

"Hi, sweetie-pie," the voice replied, perking up instantly. "I didn't know it was you, da'ling. Where you callin from?"

"Ah'm home. Ah just calling to tell you Shirl is here wid me. Ah notice it get late and ah figure you might be worried about where she is."

"So dat's where she is? De minute me step in dis house, she step out. And she didn't even say where she was going. Well, is full time she get home now. Dis place is full a druggies, and murderers, and God know wat else and dat chile would never listen to me and try to get off the streets before dark. Me talk to her 'til ah sick and tired. Me did tink you was stubborn but dis one beat all cock fight. At least you was 'fraid a beating. Dis one, she don' 'fraid a nuttin at all. Ah don' know wat else to do to get de chile to behave herself. She don' act like no Jamaican gal pickney at all, at all.

"Sometime ah sorry ah didn't leave her down dere 'til she grow big. Dis man New York is no place to raise no decent gal pickney. If you mek a mistake and put you hand on dem too hard dem claim that is abuse you abusing the chile. Pshaw, dey don' know de firs' ting 'bout discipline. The Bible say you not to spare the rod and spoil the chile, and de Lord knows ah tryin' me best. You was me firs' gal pickney and ah proud to see how good you turn out. But ef ah didn't discipline you, you wouldn't be in no college now trying to do all de tings ah could never hope fe do! No sir, ah sure you wudda throw weh you future pon man and pickney jus' like me. Ah glad ah did have de sense fe push you in de right direction and dat's wat ah trying fe do wid you little sister, but Lord ah run out a patience. Ah don' know wat else fe do."

Maxine listened to her mother go on and on about Shirl and wondered who she used to complain to about her when she was growing up. She remembered how angry she used to get when she caught Mama on the phone talking about her. She never knew who was the person at the other end but she hated them both for making her feel nasty, like a slut. Now she was that person at the other end listening to her mother complain about Shirley's misbehaving. She felt like a hypocrite. Shirley had witnessed many fights between her and Mama when she lived at home. It was to Shirley that she had gone when she decided to go away to college. Shirley had cried and begged her not to leave, and it had hurt her real bad to leave her sister behind, but she had done what she had to.

Returning home from that first horrible year in college, she had thought things would be better. But Mama had not changed. She still continued to treat her eldest daughter like a child. Maxine had left home to go live with Auntie Valerie after that last horrible fight, and this time Shirl had not cried. She had looked at her sister when she told her she was leaving for good this time and said, okay. Just like that. Okay. No tears. No nothing! It had cut Maxine to the quick that Shirley had given her permission to leave. She felt that Shirley had blamed her for making her life so chaotic. Screams in the night and cursing and name-calling and beating and tears, so many tears, her mother and sister hating each other out of too much love, too much protection, and Maxine wanted it to stop.

As she listened to her mother talk about Shirl, Maxine prayed that Shirl would hurry up and grow up. Eighteen, Lord Jesus, just let her turn eighteen and leave that house. She knew that Shirl didn't want to go to college and she didn't want to think about what her alternatives might be if she left home with no direction, but something had to give. Her mother would stifle the poor child protecting her to death. As she got off the phone with her mother, she promised her that she would talk to Shirl and immediately regretted it.

Leaving Norman to the pots and pan, Maxine returned to the basement. Shirley's eyes were still transfixed by the TV set in temporary flight from her troubled, confused thoughts. She wanted Norman to hurry up and go, so she could tell Maxine what had happened last night. Obviously, Mama didn't know yet, but she would find out as soon as Malcolm got home from work. Good thing he was working late tonight or Mama would have been killing her with beating right about now. She won-

111

dered if she should run away before Mama found out. She really couldn't take the cursing and the beating she knew awaited her. Maybe Maxine would let her spend the rest of the week with her until Mama's temper cooled down. She should have never sent Junior home. Malcolm would not have been suspicious enough to wait up for her if she hadn't done that. That sneaky, bad-tempered old red goat. Imagine sneaking up on someone in the dark and turning on the light. She had been so scared, she thought her heart was going to jump right out of her chest and land on his feet. And Carlos had been just as terrified. Well, more surprised than scared, really. Trying to act so cool saying, "Look man, I was just kissing her good night, nothing more, understand. . ." while backing away to the door. She could hear him tearing down the streets the moment his feet landed outside of her apartment. And she had stood there alone, her head hanging down to her knees, trying not to look into those accusing grayish-green eyes. Then she felt her head being yanked up and she prayed for her neck to snap by the time his eyes met hers.

"Me always did suspect you was a little slut," he whispered in a dangerously low and gravelly tone. He looked as if he was about to snap her neck for real, but changed his mind and released her, saying, "Ah ha fe go work before Mama wake up in de morning, but you just wait till ah get home tomorrow nite. Ah gwine mek Mama put you under heavy manners. You tink you is a woman? Well, we gwine show you who is de woman in dis house, you jus wait." Then he had walked away, slamming the door in Shirley's face.

She had wanted to die of shame, but when morning came her two eyes were still wide open, staring at the ceiling. It was only after she heard Malcolm slamming the door as he left for work that she allowed herself to fall in a troubled, nightmarish sleep.

Shirl was so deeply engrossed in her thoughts that she didn't notice that her sister had entered the room again. She jumped when Maxine spoke. "Does Mama know you're here, Shirl?"

Shirley looked up, startled. "Ahhmm, I don't know. I guess so."

"You guess so?" Maxine rebounded heatedly. "Aren't you tired of getting cussed out, slapped around? Don't you know you are supposed to call her when you're out after your curfew? You know she worries about you. How can you be so inconsiderate?"

Shirley rose and mumbled something about not knowing how late it was. She reached out to pick up the phone from the nightstand. "Don't bother. I already called her," said Maxine, "but next time you're out this late just give her a call and let her know where you are. It's only good manners and might even save your butt some sore spots, besides."

Shirley nodded and looked away quickly. She couldn't stand to see the softness in her sister's pleading eyes. A softness that belied the coarseness of her words. It made her feel guilty. Like Mama did. Like she had done something not only shameful but painful as well. She wondered why they made such a big deal out of everything. Her friends' folks never carried on like that about anything.

Norman returned complaining about how hot it was in the kitchen. Remembering she had not cleaned the bathroom mirror, Maxine got up and disappeared with Glass Plus and paper towels in hand. Shirley followed after her and stood hesitating in the doorway.

"Can I spend the night?" The question came out so breathlessly, tentatively, Maxine was not sure she had heard right.

"What was that" she asked, staring hard into the mirror.

"I want to stay with you tonight, can I?" her sister repeated, more firmly this time.

"Why?" Maxine asked. She was genuinely puzzled by the unusual request. Shirley had never before volunteered to spend any time with her. The few weekends they had spent together at the dormitories had always been her idea.

She had been forced to bridge the gap of a seven year age

difference with movies, window shopping, and an occasional visit to the skating rink at Rockefeller Plaza, whenever she could afford to rent skates. And Shirley always seemed to enjoy the attention that her big sister lavished on her on these rare occasions. She knew that she was singled out from among the other siblings, but although Maxine had caught her bragging more than once that she was her favorite, the girl had never once called her up to say hello or anything. She seemed to prefer the company of her friends, and Maxine understood that but was hurt nevertheless. Sister or no sister, it was too demeaning to yearn for an affection that was not reciprocated. And now, without any warning, Shirley was offering to spend time with her. Maxine wondered if something was wrong. Maybe Shirley wanted to talk to her without Norman around. She turned to face Shirley who was waiting expectantly at the door. "Look, if you want to talk to me we can go upstairs. No one else is up there."

Shirley hesitated for a while. Then, "Nah, it's okay, I don' wanna talk or anything. I jus' wanna spend the night. Can I, please?"

Standing there looking into her sister's eyes that were softer than she had seen them in years, softer than that morning years ago when Shirley had awakened to find her Mama gone far away on the plane and had sought out her sister to ask "Why?", Maxine almost gave in. Then she remembered Norman. She couldn't just send him back to Brooklyn after promising that he could spend the night. "Look, I'm not going to be here tonight," she lied. "Norman is taking me out and I probably won't be back until dawn."

"Oh, that's okay," Shirley replied. "I'll stay here and sleep until you get back."

Maxine was temporarily stumped by Shirley's unusual persistence. Then it occurred to her that Shirley was probably threatened by Norman's presence in her life. Hadn't she read it somewhere that baby sisters got that way when they felt they were no longer the focal point for their sister's affections? Yes, that's right. She had read it in a psychology book last semester. Oh, so that's what it was. Shirley didn't want Norman to spend the night, she thought. She was afraid if Norman got too close he would steal her big sister away from her. She decided that the situation called for directness and honesty.

"Look Shirl, you're a big girl now. You can't expect me to hurry home from my date just for you. How you think I'm gonna have a good time knowing you waiting here for me. How about next Saturday, eh? That will give me time and I won't make no plans, okay?". She drew Shirley to her in a tight squeeze. "Don't worry, nobody can take your place, not even Norman."

Shirley started to protest, but Maxine was no longer listening. "Oh, come on now. You can't always have things your way," she snapped. "Go put on your jacket. Norman and I will walk you home now."

4.

SHIRLEY LAY HUDDLED up on the bed in the thick darkness that was soothing after the storm that had just passed. She could taste the salty tang of blood on the roof of her mouth. Junior's pee hung heavy, stifling in the closed room. She tried to hold her breath so she wouldn't smell it, but she was sobbing too much to keep her mouth closed. She was squirming from side to side in the bed, partly to block out the vision of the last half hour, partly to discover an unsore spot on her body to rest on.

Just cut your wrist like you'd seen them girls do on that suicide movie on TV, and let your life bleed out onto the kitchen floor or in Her room. Let Her come home and find you dead on her bed. Covered up nice under her clean sweet-smelling-of-Downy sheets. Let Her raise the covers to find you there. Dead. Your blood all leaked out turning her nice sheets nasty smelling of blood, the way the kitchen smelled when she washed fresh

115

goat meat. Your face all black and blue the way she made it tonight. Your hands all cold and clammy. Your lips blue-purple-stiff. Let her think you only playing, not for real, the way she always think when she don' want to believe something. Let her start yelling for you to "stop dis foolishness, you hear me gal, a wat kinda fool you a play, answer me, me talking to you!" Then let her see you really not talking back. Not "back answering you own Madda." That you jus stone cold dead as anything that ever was dead. Then she would put her hand on her head and bawl or band her belly and holler, the way people use to do in Jamaica when somebody die. Then you could jus lie there in that dead place where people go when they die, and laugh at her. Maybe see Granma who died before you was one, and Granpa who died before you was born, and Daddy's father who died just a month ago in Jamaica, who you never even knew, cause as everybody know, "you daddy side a people dem is no good anyhow, don' want my children mixing up wid dem."

And when you was dead and gone you wouldn't have to listen to Her telling everyone what a wotless cruff you daddy was and how you was jus like him. You wouldn't have to worry 'bout the school calling Her up and saying how many weeks you had missed and making your crazy mother go even more crazy than she was. And you certainly wouldn't have to worry 'bout ole Red Ibo Malcolm snitching on you cause he was too much of a Mama's boy to get a girlfriend. You wouldn't have to worry about nothing. Not your dumb sister, who liked her boyfriend better than you, or your teachers, who thought you were Black and dumb, or your father, who liked his family in Jamaica better than you, or your mother, who never liked you anyhow, or stupid, pissy Junior, who was always following you about! When you was dead, you wouldn't have to worry 'bout nothing, nothing at all. Especially not your crazy mother, who you knew all along was crazy. She had proved it tonight when she was hitting you. It was as if she had gone someplace and forgot what she was doing. Holding you pinned to the fridge and pommeling you with her fists, her eyes all crazy and wild looking. And when she had grabbed your head and started hitting it against the freezer door, you knew that this crazy woman was going to kill you.

It was an uncanny feeling of certain death that had given Shirley that strength to pull away and try to escape, but Jean was grabbing after her again, and she knew that sooner or later she would have cornered her. Then she had glimpsed the knife lying on the counter and had grabbed it to ward off this woman who was not her mother but some stark-raving-mad woman, hungry for her blood. And it had worked. The woman's eyes had widened and focused on her for the first time, as she stood there with the knife gleaming in her hands, pleading for her life, "Don't come no closer. Don't hurt me anymore. Leave me alone. Stay away from me or I'm gonna kill you." Backing away from the kitchen, the knife held in front of her like a shield to ward off the life-threatening blows.

Her mother had stood there, paralyzed, the wildness slowly retreating from her eyes, shaking her head in disbelief, like she was trying to block out what she had just witnessed, shake it out of her memory.

Shirley's head was beginning to throb. Beat, beat, beat, like an African drum. Fusing and blending with the throb in her left arm until she couldn't distinguish between them. A familiar voice was trying to break through the fog that was clouding her head, making it feel full of cotton candy. Someone was calling "Shirl" and she wanted to answer, to tell the voice to go away, that it was too late. But the pain was filling her head, slipping and sliding through her ears, grasping at her throat and squeezing, cutting off her breathing, she was slipping down, down, down, and away.

Then she was climbing Hilltop to Uncle Son's guava trees. She was thinking what a funny name, Uncle Son. Whose Uncle? Whose Son? But she didn't care too much about that. He had the juiciest guavas on Hilltop, and she didn't care what her mother had said, Uncle or no Uncle, she was gonna get some of his guavas. Besides, her mother wasn't even here anymore. She had gone far away on a plane.

She was using her hands to part the branches that were getting tangled in her hair, using her bare feet to part the bushes. The thick overgrowth of thorns and shrubs and tangled weeds was doing a fierce tango with her feet. And then she was in the clearing. The earth was hot in places, cool in the shades. Teasing, tantalizing, flirting with her bare feet.

Now she was at the top of the guava tree, high up looking down into Kingston and she imagined that it was New York City. She could see the bright lights and fast cars, beautiful people, and streets shiny with gold. And she could see her mother, walking on the shiny street. She was shinier than the shiny street. See the mother. The mother is nice. The mother is pretty. The mother has long hair and light brown skin and the mother is smiling. The mother is holding out her arms. Wait mother, wait for me. I am coming mother. But the mother is disappearing down the shiny hole. Engulfed in the bright, bright lights. Glittering once, glittering twice, glittering—gone. And she started to shake the guava tree and the ripe fruits came tumbling down upon her head, bouncing off her shoulders, ripe and sweet and sticky, and plump pink flesh filling her mouth, rolling over her tongue, the seeds crunch, crunch, crunching on her teeth. She chewed up the skin, sweet, sour tangy taste at the back of her tongue. And it was heaven and earth and New York City. And not half as bad as mother warned her it would be.

5.

THE HOUSE WAS still as a tomb when Maxine entered. Where was everybody, she thought. Surely they couldn't still be sleeping. It was already eleven o'clock. She headed straight for her sister's bedroom. Sure enough everybody was still in bed. Must have had a late night, Maxine thought. The shades were drawn and she could barely make out the sleeping forms. Maxine snapped on the overhead light and her mouth flew open at what she saw lying before her. Eyes blinking rapidly, she slowly approached the bed. She was trying to blink away the apparition before her eyes. She wanted to replace the mass of bluish-purple flesh she saw lying on Shirl's bed, with the real Shirl. The Shirl with the supple, biscuit-brown skin and body bursting with youthful energy. But instead of Shirl, there was this broken, bruised thing lying on her sister's bed. It rolled over and she saw the face. It was swollen and purple and crusted over with welts and traces of blood.

Maxine stood and stared. Her brain refused to register that it was Shirl lying there looking more dead than alive. Slowly she walked over to the bed and sat down. Still in a trance, she picked up her sister's head and placed it in her lap. She began rocking Shirley back and forth, back and forth. Gradually the numbness eased out of Maxine's body and as her brain began to function, the tears began to come fast and hot down her cheeks. Gently, she laid down her sister's battered body and went over to the closet. She didn't think about what she was doing. If she stopped to think, she would change her mind. She grabbed a suitcase and started to pack Shirl's clothes. Realizing that Shirley had too many clothes, Maxine decided to take just what could fit into one suitcase. When she finished, she went in to the kitchen to call a cab and ran smack into Jean. They stood staring into each other's faces without saying a word. Jean was the first to look away.

"Ah sorry Max," she started. "How she look? Ah didn't mean fe beat her up so bad, but when Malcolm tell me dat him ketch her in de hallway wid some bway, me whole life flash cross me eye. Me see meself in her face, poverty and pregnant and wid not even a half-a-foot man standing by me side. Wen me try fe talk to her 'bout it, she get stubborn like a ole mule and ah swear is her daddy face me see spring up before me. Someting jus snap inna me and me start fe beat her. De force a de hatred me feel fe her daddy, me tek it out pon poor Shirl. Me never

119

member sey a she stan up before me, and wen me done beat her and see how she cut up and stay, me put me han pon me head and bawl. At daylight dis morning me run out go buy a plane ticket. See it ya. Me sending her back to Jamaica fe go live wid her daddy madda. When she reach eighteen, me a go file fe her again. Me don't want her fe stay here, cause she grieve me heart too much and me 'fraid to go catch trouble fe her. Me sending her back. See de ticket ya. Maxine... Max, say something, talk to me," Jean pleaded in a broken voice.

Maxine did not answer her mother. She had nothing to say. She knew she would never allow Jean to send her sister back to Jamaica. As fast as kids grew up in America, they grew up even faster in Jamaica. If Jean was afraid of Shirley getting pregnant here, she would be a grandmother sooner than she wanted to if she sent her back home. What did that man's mother know about her sister, anyway? She would never allow Shirl to live with a stranger. If her own mother could treat her like that, imagine what a grandmother who didn't know her would do. Jean could trade in her damn Air Jamaica ticket for a pass to Bellevue. From now on until Shirley was old enough and mature enough to live on her own, she would take care of her. After all, this was her sister. If it meant she had to get a full-time job and go to college part-time, fine! She only had a few months to go, anyway. And Shirley would be grown before she knew it. Thank God Aunt Valerie was the way she was. She was always saying Shirley could come and stay whenever she was ready. And she didn't give a damn what Jean said!

Maxine pushed past Jean and went to dial the cab number. Fifteen minutes later the cab arrived, and Maxine struggled down the stairs with the heavy suitcase. When she went back to wake Shirley, she found that Jean had already done so. Jean stood there holding her youngest daughter like she was drowning and needed something of her own to hang on to. Still dazed by sleep and the dull ache in her body, Shirley stood there calmly, letting her mother hug her.

"Grab your Teddy," Maxine said, her voice cracking just a little bit. "The cab is waiting."

Death of a Dillon Girl

Bárbara Selfridge

COUSIN CAROLYN DIED suddenly. The friends who found her dead in her apartment also found ballet tickets in her purse and lunch dates in her engagement calendar: these and many other signs, my mother tells me, that Cousin Carolyn hadn't known that death was coming, that she couldn't have been in much pain.

"Doesn't that sound nice?" Mommy asks across the dining room table. It doesn't really, but I don't bother to say so.

This is 1973 and Cousin Carolyn—my mother's cousin, not mine—had been sixty-eight. I am then twenty-two, long-haired, and convicted the year before of battery-on-an-officer (taking the rap for a striking U.C. secretary, also long-haired). I'm secretly proud of my twice-monthly visits to the probation officer.

My mother is then forty-eight, short, bespectacled, and prim-looking in her severe bun and lack of make-up. After working all through my childhood, she's reverted to unpaid slavery: remarriage and driving my little half-siblings to nursery schools and first grade. Occasionally she suggests that I can quit calling her Mommy, but I ignore all that letting-go garbage.

"Doesn't that sound nice?" Mommy says, cheerful and inexplicably charmed by her cousin's sudden death. It's typical of the way she transmits all bad news.

"The lawyer doesn't want us to touch any of Carolyn's watercolors," she continues, her high voice following me into the kitchen as I make myself another cup of tea. "He says they have to be appraised as part of the estate. Don't you think that's a simply fantastic compliment?"

Apparently my mother's *outré* remarks began at age three and were always known in the Dillon family as *Nonie's Bombshells*. Nonie is my mother's name, short for Lenore.

An only child who never married, Cousin Carolyn leaves everything to the four Dillon girls: Dillie, Anne, Phyllis, and Nonie. It comes to about five thousand dollars each. Outside of the old child-support checks from my father, the money is my mother's first direct income in six years—since quitting IBM to marry my stepfather. She says it makes her feel rich.

Also, there is loot. My mother returns from Cousin Carolyn's funeral with Navajo wall-hangings, watercolor paintings of my grandparents' converted chicken coop home on Vashon Island, and a silver serving spoon that came over on the Mayflower with my blue-blooded ancestor.

(Once in second grade, I did a show-and-tell about my great-great-great-great-great-great-great-great-great-great-great-great-great—thirteen greats in all—grandfather and equally great grandmother, but since turning socialist, I refrain from these disclosures of my Pilgrim stock.)

Mommy brings the kids old art deco watches and an opal ring she wants to save until Gwen turns thirteen. Gwen's birth six Octobers earlier—my mother over forty, divorced, and refusing to identify the father—was considered shocking behavior in an IBM employee. Extremely shocking for 1966. The Dillon girls rallied for it however, and even conservative Cousin Carolyn, the spinster, wrote that Gwen's baby picture hung by the door, "and every time I go out, I want to reach out and chuck her under that adorable little chin!"

(Gwen is the only inheritor of my mother's cleft chin.)

I inherit Cousin Carolyn's easel—for my own watercolors—a 1920's portable typewriter, and my pick from Mommy's paper-towel-wrapped wad of Cousin Carolyn's jewelry. I choose a clunky silver ring made from two French coins, one dated 1918, the other 1919.

"I thought you might like that!" my mother says, pleased with herself, and immediately I take offense. My life demonstrates a clear political opposition to jewelry, skirts, and all things feminine, but my mother is deliberately blind to that fact.

"I'm pretty sure both the ring and the typewriter came originally from your Great Aunt Josephine," Mommy continues, undaunted. "Aunt Jo was married to Daddy's older brother Edmond, but when we knew her she was a widow, running a very successful hotel coffee shop in Seattle. She served as inspiration to all of us, partly I suspect because she never remarried. After Uncle Edmond was killed in World War I, Aunt Jo went over and drove ambulances behind the French lines. We used to have pictures of her, all dressed up in her black hat and black uniform and looking radiantly happy. It makes sense that this ring comes from that time."

My mother is right. I do like the ring.

The inspiration for *my* life is my Aunt Dillie—short for Margaret Dillon—a former Communist Party member and children's book author, and the only one of the Dillon girls to inherit, as I did, a premature streak of white hair sprouting slightly left of the center part. During the family trauma of my arrest, Aunt Dillie commiserated with me: "They always think we're doing it to hurt *them*, don't they? Really, it's just something that we believe in, that we do for ourselves."

Aunt Dillie called Cousin Carolyn "Trixie," short for "Executrix" of my grandparents' will. She was also the closest in age to Cousin Carolyn and maybe because of that, my mother says, the most upset by the news of Cousin Carolyn's death.

"Dillie was so upset," Mommy reports cheerfully, "that she called up your Aunt Anne for consolation. Dillie said, 'Isn't it just like Carolyn not to tell anyone she was ill?' And Anne, who really wanted to cheer poor Dillie up, answered, 'I understand perfectly. I too have cancer and just came home from a month of radiation treatment in the hospital.' It was the first news any of us had of Anne's cancer and, on the whole, terribly effective at taking Dillie's mind off of Carolyn's death."

Aunt Anne's cancer is news to me too, but of course this is exactly how my mother would break it to me.

Mommy also reports that there'd been three funeral services for Cousin Carolyn, ironic for a lifelong loner. My Aunt Phyllis, the most dutiful of my mother's sisters and the only one with naturally curly hair, had actually been in Seattle the last week of Carolyn's life. She'd considered paying Cousin Carolyn a duty call, decided not to bother, and then felt so guilty she attended all three funerals.

My mother and Aunt Dillie joined her for the third service, and then the three of them traveled *en masse* to visit their fourth—Anne Dillon Bulling—in Eugene. Everybody laughed a lot, my mother tells me, and they said lots of "I love you's," and over the next few months they all found their way back to take turns, day and night, nursing Aunt Anne.

Six weeks later, I stuff my dirty clothes into my mother's washing machine and ask her, "Well, so what's the story?" She has a flight to Eugene in the morning, and I'm home from Berkeley, pressed into extended sibling-sitting.

Actually, despite my disgust over my mother's taste in second husbands, I love to come home. The kids always treat me as perfect, a relief after my ever-wary comrade sisters. "You never know exactly what Ellen Chatfield means when she talks," they complain. In fact, I'm scared of the heavy-duty politicos in the women's union, and never mention my battery-on-an-officer incident at all.

"Is Aunt Anne going to die?" I ask my mother.

"I think so." She answers in her highest, clearest voice—the one reserved for telling the absolute truth to direct questions from her children. Then she resumes her normal voice—still high, but not quite as crystalline. "Anne says she has utter faith in her doctor, whom she nick-named her 'once-a-day-lover.' Her plan is to hang on until the researchers arrive at a cure."

"Aunt Anne must have known she had cancer when she sent you that last birthday card," I say. "That's why it was so full of all that sappy January-birthday-cake business."

"'White cake with lots of white buttercream frosting,'" Mommy recites, and I realize, of course, she's just reread all of Aunt Anne's letters. That must have hurt.

"Anne apologized when we were there," my mother continues. "She admitted that all her letters lately have been a little saccharine."

Two summers earlier, Mommy and the kids and my stepfather drove up the Oregon coast—a trip Anne joined—and now all the photos from that trip are up on the bulletin board. In them, Aunt Anne wears white jeans and a navy windbreaker, her dark hair in a single braid down her back. She stands ankle-deep in a flat gray ocean, pants rolled up to her knees, with the baby Mikey on one hip and Bobby—two years old and still bald—on the other. The boys look relaxed and well-loved; Anne is radiant.

I also love the picture of Gwen—blonde hair, red socks, and a yellow plastic umbrella—posing with all the charm of a self-dressed four-year-old.

A letter to Aunt Anne keeps writing itself in my head. In it I remind her of the day ten years ago when we all tried to help Aunt Dillie and Uncle Dan civilize a piece of property they'd bought on Vashon Island. While Uncle Dan and my boy-cousins—Phyllis's kids— worked on shoring up the path down from the road, the four Dillon girls and I cleared beach. Reaching under the gentle back-and-forth of the Puget Sound, we found barnacle-covered rocks, and heaved them out of the way in order to create a strip of beach that wouldn't cut our feet.

I was twelve, wearing a red two-piece, and Aunt Dillie said she loved my long-legged colt look. My aunts and mother worked in the nude—naked except for the sneakers all of us wore to protect our feet. Aunt Dillie, with a bathing cap over her short bobby-pinned curls and breasts already beginning to lie flat like my grandmother's, looked particularly silly.

The four Dillon girls all *acted* silly. Aunt Anne hung ropes of seaweed, like leis, from each breast. In a minute, the others were imitating her, Mommy and Aunt Phyllis competing to see which pair of breasts could hold the most strands. I was a little awed, mostly terrified that some *Playboy* photographer would drive by in a speedboat and catch them.

My mother won with eleven strands. "Look at Nonie!" Aunt Dillie called, and in her voice I could hear that my middle-aged mother was still Dillie's fourteen-years-younger baby sister.

Aunt Anne, meanwhile, draped seaweed over her shoulder, catching a translucent green leaf on one nipple. "I like the casual look," she said. "A mermaid rising half-exposed from the waves."

That night everybody—even the boys—went skinny dipping at the beach near my grandfather's house. A police car pulled up just as we were climbing out of the Sound, and its spotlight caught Aunt Phyllis in her bra and bathing cap, bending over to step into her panties.

The sight paralyzed me and I refused to get out of the water. So did my cousins, but Aunt Anne told us not to mind the cop. "I'm sure he was much more embarrassed than Phyll was," she said.

Aunt Dillie added, "It's a silly law anyway."

("It's a silly law anyway." I believe that a lot now.)

In my head I tell Aunt Anne how that day on Puget Sound taught me what it was to be a Dillon girl, but unfortunately, the letter never gets written. It's too hard to write letters—or paint watercolors or read political theory—while taking care of the kids.

"You're not the boss of me!" Gwen taunts, defying the neighbor kids. "You're not the boss of me!" Bobby and Michael taunt, defying Gwen. "You're not the boss of me!" they all yell, all the time, and in my anti-capitalist heart, I try to take courage.

Mommy comes home ten days later. Farting was especially painful to Anne, she reports. And even though Aunt Anne's husband—Uncle Dick—had established a strict policy against pet cures, Mommy secretly fought the gas pains with Yoga techniques. "Your job is to breathe," she told Anne. "You just relax and concentrate on breathing in and out, in and out, and if that little gas bubble wants to wiggle its way outside, then you just let it."

My mother is speaking from the orange rocker, a thumb-sucking Michael squeezed in beside her. "It felt so illicit," she gloats, "but then I heard Phyll telling Anne—'Just concentrate on breathing in and out'—and I thought, Aha! A victory for my pet cure!"

Aunt Phyllis, five years older than my mother and two years younger than Anne, was dubbed *Head Dietitian and Bottle-Washer* and given the job of inventing nutritious milk shakes for Anne. "You know," Mommy says, "I always resented Phyllis. She had those Shirley Temple curls and got along with all the relatives and just altogether lacked any sense of the importance of being a tomboy. But now, in Eugene, she was the only one who could make anything that Anne would eat, and I thought she was just great."

"What about Aunt Dillie? What did she do?"

"Oh, Dillie got the really fun job!" My mother smiles at me. "She got to go up to Alberta to visit your cousin Davy." Cousin Davy is Anne's only offspring, a Vietnam War draft-dodger and would-be filmmaker. "Apparently, it's very hard for Americans to find work anywhere in Canada," Mommy says.

I can tell from her voice that my mother wants to adopt Cousin Davy; she's always wished I had an older brother. I'm eating cottage cheese and tomatoes on the couch, and don't bother to respond.

Uncle Dick, Anne's husband, had the job of reading aloud to her, the traditional nightly pastime of their thirty-year marriage. "I've always hated Dick Bulling," my mother says, "for the pre-laid-out suits and the exactly-three-and-a-half minute eggs and for just generally treating Anne like his own personal drudge, but this business of them reading aloud to each other was really nice. It was as if everything good about their marriage had been distilled down into that one act. I kept wishing you could have been there to see it."

I know exactly what that wish means. "You're too much," I say. "You want me to marry, and you claim my problem is never having the chance to observe a good marriage, but then the only good one you can find is admittedly rotten except for half an hour a day. It's just *not* very convincing!"

Mommy laughs, conceding the point, and then returns to her story about Dick Bulling. "Poor Dick. He's so bad at nursing, but he takes choosing the right books and reading to Anne very seriously, and it *is*. Then he only reads ten minutes before Anne falls asleep. She's in so much pain she hardly sleeps at all, so really, it was wonderful the way Dick's voice allowed her to relax, but there was poor Dick, feeling just terrible. It was hard for us to comfort him."

It also emerges, in my mother's stories, that a sizable chunk of the Dillon girls' bedside chatter centered on my lesbianism. As a point of fact, I'm not a lesbian—I have lovers of neither sex—but I *am* in an organization that deems *Coming Out to Your Family* a high-level political act, and not being one to shirk political duty, I'd *come out* to my mother.

"What I don't like," she'd responded at the time, really stricken, "is that you've ruled out half the population as your potential lovers."

"What about you! You've ruled out the other half by being heterosexual!"

"That's not true." My mother's voice was low, sincerely concerned. "I've always considered homosexuality the obvious solution to the problem of how to have sex after all the men die off. And certainly having a lesbian affair is on my list of things I want to do before I die."

I'm sure by this point, though, that my mother enjoys telling her sisters about *My Daughter, the Lesbian*. My supposed sexuality has become, like Gwen's bastard birth, *Another of Nonie's Bombshells*.

Aunt Dillie is supportive, naturally, telling Mommy to tell me that Great Aunt Josephine might have been a lesbian—"Just in case Ellen would like having a family precedent." Great Aunt Jo's possible lover was Miss Rutz—shortened by the Dillon girls to Aunt Rutzy—a woman who followed Aunt Jo home from France and then kept the books for her coffee shop.

"I think people actually called Aunt Rutzy 'head over heels' about Aunt Jo," Mommy says, unpacking in the bedroom. "Isn't it funny that I never suspected them of being lovers until now?"

"Didn't any of you ever read *The Well of Loneliness*?" I ask. "It's all about lesbians who drove ambulances during World War I!"

My mother moves to the bathroom to unpack her toiletries. "Oh," she says, "I think it was pretty standard reading for my generation. The point was that if you treat your daughter like a son, she'll grow up to be a lesbian."

"You're out of your head!" I say, following her. "You think everything is behavior! The whole book was about how it was in her genes from the very beginning!"

Mommy speaks to me in the bathroom mirror. "Anne said she thought it had something to do with the size of the clitoris. I was giving her a bath, and she asked me if I thought her clitoris was larger than average." Mommy laughs and imitates Anne's voice, "'Maybe all these years I've been ignoring my lesbian clitoris. What do think Ellen would say, Nonie? Do you think she'd like my clitoris?'"

"Well, that's just a stupid knee-jerk stereotype of lesbians as sexual aggressors," I inform my mother, "and I don't see why you think it's so funny!"

My mother, trained never to respond to pique with pique, turns to face the real me, not just my reflection. Using her high, truth-telling voice, she explains, "I guess it seemed funny to me because I'd started out fairly uncomfortable about washing another woman's crotch, and then there was Anne, making me go back and examine her clitoris for her. I'm sorry, honey. It seemed funny at the time."

All day long the Eugene stories continue: "It was very important that Dillie be spared night nursing so she could sleep—we all agreed on that." And: "I'd like you to come with me next time. I think you'd be good." Meanwhile my mother washes the dishes, sweeps the floors, does the laundry, and wants to go back.

Gwen, usually impossible to coax into a cuddle, leans back against Mommy's thigh and sucks the two middle fingers of her right hand. "I felt so guilty about staying away so long from Hal and the kids," my mother says, continuing to clean leaves from the swimming pool despite Gwen. "But I don't think they really need me."

She stops and smiles at me. "I think you've done a beautiful job. You're probably a much better mother than I am."

"See?" Gwen takes the fingers out of her mouth. "You're not the boss of me!"

I leave for Berkeley, telling Mommy to call if she really wants to go back to Eugene. For a couple of weeks I expect that call, but then Aunt Anne gets worse and is moved to a hospital. A week later she dies.

"Dillie still can't drive, you know," my mother says, breaking the news to me over the phone, "but she really wanted to go to Eugene and visit Anne in the hospital. Finally Dan, who was in bed with pneumonia, offered to get up and drive her. So Dillie brought Dan's pneumonia germs with her into Anne's hospital room and two days later Anne's lungs collapsed. I think that proves that we're the kind of family that not only believes in euthanasia, but actually practices it."

So, for the second time that year, my mother flies north for a funeral.

"A wonderful thing happened," she tells me afterwards, on

the way home from the airport.

"What?" I ask, imitating her tone.

"I was finally able to tell Phyllis how mad I've been at Dillie for scattering Mother's ashes under the Golden Gate after Mother told me so distinctly that she wanted them scattered on the Puget Sound. And guess what Phyll said? She said that Mother had always made it very clear to *her* that she wanted her ashes buried under the apple tree outside the Vashon chicken coop. So here I've been so mad at Dillie's disobedience when the real culprit all along was Mother's senility!"

I laugh. "How wonderful! How was Aunt Anne's funeral?"

"Oh, it was very nice." My mother smiles at me. "I think funerals are a lot more fun if you get to help plan them. Our big conflict was over a friend of Anne's who offered to sing. We all thought that would be nice, but Dillie was adamant that she didn't want to cry and she knew if there were singing she'd be undone."

At home I put on a record and make up the hide-a-bed, which my mother hates to see out during the day. Mommy beams as she identifies that song: *"Midnight Cowboy!"* Then she stops herself. "I'm sorry, honey. I've been so busy planning everybody's funeral music, and now here you are, the dutiful daughter, playing the very song I'd chosen for your dirge. Does that seem morbid?"

My stepfather comes home at lunch, full of the war stories from his job that I've refused to let him dump on me in my mother's absence (I'm very self-righteous in my rejection of other women's men). I make the kids their peanut butter and jelly sandwiches—Gwen's without the jelly—and hear Mommy apologize, "Oh, Hal, I'm sorry. I'm just so exhausted."

Later, I surreptitiously read the first line of my mother's diary entry: *This is ridiculous. I have to pull myself together. I can't lose another day moping over Anne's death.*

The diary lies open on the bathroom counter, and sure enough, I walk to the kitchen and find my mother staring out the window, her arms elbow-deep in dishwater and tears dribbling down her face.

"Having trouble wiping your eyes?" I suggest.

She laughs, rinses her arms, and blows her nose on a paper towel. "Did you ever see the movie called *The Member of the Wedding*?" she asks.

"I read the book by Carson McCullers."

"Did you? Well, I guess I always cry a little at the movies, but twice—once during that movie, once during *The Heart Is a Lonely Hunter*—I actually started sobbing in the theater."

"Both by Carson McCullers," I inform her.

Mommy nods. "That movie so exactly captured the way I felt about Anne and Dick's wedding," she goes on. "Nothing had been said, of course, but they both always treated me as somebody special, and I just assumed that I would move in with them after the honeymoon. Nothing ever felt as unfair as Mother ordering me to leave them alone.

"And then just now, when I was nursing Anne—" my mother's eyes fill up again, "I finally felt accepted. Anne and Dick let me be there, with them and— oh!—I just didn't want to have to give that up again."

My poor mother is sobbing and I put my arms around her. "You're out of your head," I say.

She squeezes me back. "I love you so much," she chokes.

I say "I love you too," but I'm thinking that my mother's breasts feel obscenely intimate pressed up against my midriff. This makes me feel like a jerk and then *I* start to cry.

The next Christmas Uncle Dick sends Mommy a card: *Dear Nonie, Inexpressible gratitude for all your help last spring. Dick Bulling*. The following spring another note announces that he's remarried—to a friend of Aunt Anne's. The second note is not, however, from Dick Bulling. It's from Aunt Phyllis, who adds: *Her name is Penny and I think Anne would have approved.*

"I'm pretty sure," Mommy tells me, "that this Penny is the same friend we met the time we visited Anne on the coast.

Penny's lover was in critical condition after a car crash, but poor Penny couldn't see him because he was married and his wife and children wouldn't let her into the hospital room. I think the lover finally died, but I don't know—that just seems like a nice thing to know about Dick Bulling's second wife."

I have a dream set in a big aristocratic mansion: my aunts and I romping amidst the ruins of family wealth after somebody's death. "It's funny," I tell them, "because Nonie was the youngest Dillon girl and you'd think she would outlive the others."

I speak brightly, cheerfully into my aunts' watchful stares, trying to shake them into shared laughter. Then I realize— Nonie wasn't just one of the Dillon girls, she was *my* mother. I didn't want *her* to die, and I wake myself up.

Mommy likes my dream. Dillie's dreams, she reports, are all about Cousin Carolyn. Dream after dream about Cousin Carolyn until finally in one she and Carolyn are birds: great gray geese, flocking south. Dillie is flapping exhaustedly in Carolyn's wake, just trying to keep up, when Goose Carolyn turns to her very kindly. "It's all right," she says. "I can fly alone now, and you can go home."

"Isn't that a nice dream?" my mother asks.

Five years later Aunt Dillie and Aunt Phyllis take a vacation together around the Puget Sound—a trip they nickname *The Sentimental Journey*—and Aunt Phyllis tries to apologize for flirting, etc., with Dillie's first husband back in the early days of that Early Depression marriage. Dillie, refusing to forgive, won't let Phyllis spell out the *etc.*

The real end of the story, though, comes in 1981 when I'm thirty and primping at home in front of my mother's bathroom mirror. I insist loudly that there must be some way to lose ten pounds in two hours. "Otherwise there's no way I can go to a wedding and be seen *fat* by people who went to high school with me!"

Gwen, the beloved bastard, is fourteen and using funny voices to recommend "cures" for my unsightly excess. "Well, Miz Chatfield, you *could* wear a pillow under your dress and pretend to be pregnant. Or what about painting bee stings all over you and explaining that the swelling is just an allergic reaction?"

It's a very comforting silliness—Gwen has become a very comforting silly person—and I'm thinking about how much I like her, when it strikes me, suddenly, positively, that Gwen's become a Dillon girl. Not all that surprising, except that I also realize she's learned how from *me*. And, as my mother says, that's very nice.

Yellow

Julia Alvarez

YOU WERE YELLOW. I was red, including pink and some lavenders. If the lavenders got too bluish, they were Tita's, our blue sister, who could also have green if she wanted. Our baby sister wasn't even born yet, and then she was mostly in white for a few years until she started learning her colors and wanted all of them for herself. We were ingrained in our colors; to this day, almost thirty years later, I see a sunset, and I think, yours.

Yellow, that was your color. Mami's right hand, the hand you got to hold. Yours were the top drawers with the pretty glass knobs, the left side of the closet that was closest to the mirror, the shoes with the little heels and bows, the desk with the pull out board because you were already in a serious grade, one year ahead, getting homework. I envied you those workbooks filled with upper and lower case alphabets, numbers you added until you came up with all the right answers. You'd trick me too, before I knew what you knew. Do you want six or half a dozen? A quarter or twenty-five cents? Sometimes I chose right by mistake. Mostly you got the bigger pieces, the larger parts, the warm yellow smiles that were already browning by the time I did something right.

You were yellow, older, more responsible. Allowed, or 'lowed, as you used to slang in our new English, to show a second language was no big deal to you. 'Lowed to hold babies because you wouldn't drop them and smash them the way everyone seemed to think I would. You knew, with a yellow smirk, where the crown was. "As plain as day," you'd say, though I looked and looked but couldn't see the little hole you said you could see in the skull. You also claimed to know where the North Star shone in the night sky. ("There! There!" There were dozens of *theres*.) How the baby got inside Mami's stomach. (Papi's thingamajig put it in there.) We snuck around to the backyard shack where Porfirio, the gardener with warts, slept, and watched through a crack in the wall as he wrestled with Blanca, the cook. "See," you said, "That's how the baby gets in there." You patted your yellow jersey stomach, trying to shrug off your shock with a bright, know-it-all smile.

Little yellow lies, fool's gold you gave me when I tried to hold you to the golden rule. You said that, no, you would not force Mami to make me invite you to my birthday party just because we were sisters, so there was no reason why you should have to invite me to your party when really everyone was going to be a year older than me. "Eleven months, you mean," I gloated; you glared, a bright yellow, blinding glare. You said those barrettes Tia Amelia brought me from Italy looked like bugs in my hair, so I gave them to you and you sacrificed yourself and wore them all the time. You made best friends with the cousin who was my age and who technically should have been paired with me. Little, yellow-polka-dot-bikini-type-takeovers, out and out white lies tarnishing to yellow—they were such low-grade untruths. Later, when I got mine, you told me you'd already gotten yours, and it turns out, years later, you confessed that it wasn't for another three years before you spotted, my color, red, on your yellow panties. I, the younger sister, got my period first!

Once, also, I got my hands on your yellow. His name was Alberto, and all through boarding school, you had a big crush on him. He was Cuban, dark-haired, not too tall. You and I had an ongoing disagreement about what made a handsome guy. Ironically, you claimed that fair, yellow-haired men didn't look masculine; I disagreed, enumerating some blonde hunks on the screen we'd both ogled. But you held fast to your theory.

Secretly, as with everything you said, I thought you were right, and I made an effort to re-orient my thinking. I looked hard at Alberto when he came to visit you; his dark black shiny hair, dark black shiny eyes and brows seemed too harsh for the tender regard I wanted turned on me by the world.

"You've got big eyes," Alberto said to me once. "Always looking, always looking. Can I help you find something?" I felt like curling a lip up in disgust, but instead I smiled.

Alberto Suarez, you would murmur sometimes, pressing your hands against the cold window as he walked away up the hill that took him back to our brother school. You made a little fog on the glass with your hot breath, and on it you wrote an A and an M. Alberto and Maury, you whispered. Mauricia Maria Suarez. You used your middle name only when you were signing yourself off, married. I looked through the fading A and the fading M at the dark-haired boy I could not blot out with my palm. His winter coat was unbuttoned, flapping open to show he could take the cold, exposing himself to death from pneumonia if not terminal cool. He wore a bright scarf around his neck that the wind dramatically blew behind him like a banner proclaiming his specialness. As he walked uphill by the one-way road that led to Boston, he'd turn a little to his left each time a car went by so we could see YELLOW written all over him, and that by itself was a powerful enough magnet.

One day you came over to my room for our weekly collect call home. When I was buzzed for a call on the hall phone, we both assumed it was Mami and Papi beating us to the draw. "Call me when you're done," you said. You were sitting on my bed, paging through my roommate's *Seventeen*, looking for a dress for the Christmas dance to which you meant to invite Alberto. Out in the hall when I picked up the phone, a strange male voice said, "Hi there!"

"Papi?" I asked, knowing it wasn't Papi, for sure.

"This is Alberto."

"Let me get Maury," I offered. I figured your roommate had you buzzed in my room.

"Can't you talk?" he asked.

"Yeah, I mean—"

"I called to talk to you." It was nowhere near your birthday, so there couldn't be a surprise party in store. It crossed my mind you were pregnant and had put Alberto up to telling your family. But I doubted you had exchanged anything more than a kiss with your heartthrob. After your lead over me in knowing about thingamajigs, you'd fallen way behind. Once we had that argument where you said that you didn't believe in sex unless a person were married. I wondered if you'd even French-kissed Alberto? Not that I'd done anything but a little hand holding and necking at summer camp dances, but I mean, I wasn't going to hold down my skirt if the wind was blowing.

I thought I'd make it easier on him to break whatever difficult news to me, "Is everything all right with Maury?" I tried to sound like you, the concerned, older sister.

"Why shouldn't everything be all right with her?"

"I just thought. . . ."

"Look," he went on, "There's an open mixer up here on Saturday—"

"Maury's got to go to Boston with her class this weekend." I was twirling that receiver cord around and around, as if the curl were my doing.

"But you'll be here, right?"

"Maury's got to go to Boston," I repeated as if one or the other of us wasn't getting the point. There was a long pause on the other end. Suddenly, it struck me, he was asking me to that mixer, behind your back! "I don't sneak around my sister," I added.

"Sneak?" Alberto scoffed. "Who's asking you to sneak? It's an open mixer. It's a free country. I'm inviting you to an open mixer in a free country. Give me a break!"

I was giving that cord a permanent the way I was twirling it around—struck dumb between vanity and guilt. "I'm not interested," I lied.

"Hey, if looks could talk, the looks you've been giving me at

139

the door—"

"Looks!"

He laughed. "Look, we're all adults, I'm an adult, your sister's an adult, you're an adult—"

I did so much want to be an adult before you were an adult, or maybe you were already an adult, and so I wanted to catch up. Anyhow, when Alberto said, "See you Saturday," I did not out and out refuse. I placed the receiver back gently on its cradle and walked pensively back to the room.

You looked up, surprised. "Didn't they want to talk to me?"

"Who?" I asked, guiltily.

"Mami and Papi, who else?"

"It was someone else," I offered vaguely, and you did ask, "Who?" but didn't wait for an answer as you held up the magazine. "What do you think of this one?"

That would have been the time to tell you, but I couldn't. I had already made up my mind walking back to the room; I wasn't going to the stupid mixer. Why hurt you with useless knowledge that would help poison you against me? Alberto's roving eye would land on someone else who would tell on him soon enough. Let your heart be broken by a stranger.

But by the time Saturday rolled around, I was more and more curious about what Alberto had in mind. A group from our school was going up, stag, to our brother school dance, and I figured I'd go along and see what exactly that creep would do. I added my name to the list and tagged along, all dressed up, pink on my lips, blush on my cheeks, a favorite wool dress we used to call a "tea dress" at school. But everywhere I looked as I walked, I saw yellow, in the cozy lit-up windows of the houses we passed and in the stars winking slyly as I cheated, wishing on each one. Yellow in the leaves on the autumn trees that canopied the sidewalk as we trudged up the hill under glowing street lamps that bathed me in a guilty olive light. Every once in a while, a car came from behind me on the road to Boston, and its light would beam a big yellow streak down my back.

Diamonds

Edith Chevat

M Y SISTER TIBBY was coming to see Mama, her first visit since my brother Alvin and I had put Mama in the nursing home. Tibby was the baby, the one who got whatever she wanted. I went to the bank, to my mother's vault. I wanted to be ready for Tibby's visit.

Someday, I had thought, I would come into what was rightly mine. Not money—there wasn't much of that and what there was would have to be divided three ways—but jewels. Jewels would be my legacy. Not that I would wear diamonds. I wasn't the kind, and I didn't go places where diamonds were necessary, but jewels would make amends. They were a covenant between us, security, like money in the bank.

I had never come to the vault alone, even though for twelve years, ever since my father died, I had been the co-signer. It was a precaution against the day when I would have to disperse my mother's legacy. I was the oldest, the only one who lived in New York so I was in charge. But even on that first day when I had come to sign the signature card, I had not seen the treasures my name guarded.

"It's none of your business," my mother said, "what I have and what I don't have. Someday, but not now."

So I had waited while she walked through the iron gates into the vault itself and then carried the little box to the examining room. In all the years since, I had heeded my mother's words: I had never come to see what someday would be mine.

In the tiny examining room, I took inventory: two diamond

cocktail rings; five U.S. savings bonds, one in each of the grandson's names; an Israeli bond for my daughter, Julie, the only granddaughter; a rhinestone bracelet watch; a canceled check for ten thousand dollars dated August 1929; three Kennedy silver dollars; a diamond and sapphire pendant on a silver chain; my father's citizenship papers; a pair of what looked like diamond shirt studs my father might have worn when he was rich, but which, after seeing the screw backs, I decided were earrings; my mother's passport, the one she used for her trip to Israel; a pocket watch; a mother-of-pearl pin watch, its case broken; a Waterman pen and pencil set still in its case, the pen the kind you filled.

Here it was—the treasure, the diamonds of my mother's stories. Here were the stones my mother had used to pave her way, the rocks that had held her place. Pawned, reclaimed, borrowed against, repossessed: they had paid for my brother's Bar Mitzvah, a catered affair before such affairs were commonplace; they had provided the down payment for the house my mother bought from Uncle Arthur, the house my grandmother owned that went to Arthur, sold when he and Aunt Bertha moved to Florida; they had paid for the car, the furs, the carpeting, the things that showed the world who my mother was, how refined she was.

I held the earrings in my hands. They did not look real; there was none of the sparkle, the fire and ice characteristic of diamonds, the setting more bronze than gold, old-fashioned rather than old-looking.

My mother always wanted diamonds; she wanted something she could count on. She wore her gold wedding ring and her gold watch. She kept the cameo at home, with her pearls, hidden in her underwear. Her jewels, the diamonds, she kept in the vault, arriving like royalty when the occasion demanded, a queen visiting her treasure house.

I never wanted diamonds. I craved my grandmother's candlesticks, the ones she brought from Europe. I hoped for a cameo my grandmother had given my mother when she became engaged. Sam had bought me a watch when we got married. A watch edged in diamond chips. Something valuable I could use. I never wore it.

"Someday," my mother always said, "the diamonds will be yours. Yours and Tibby's. Jewels go to the daughters."

"There's plenty of time," I'd say. It wasn't jewels I wanted.

I thought diamonds were cold like ice or glass. I did not want to wear a piece of rock around my neck. I did not want a chunk of glass sitting on my finger. Jade was something else. Jade had a way of connecting to its wearer, subtly changing with the change in blood and gland, a personal barometer. Rubies, too, had a special way. Or so I'd been told. I'd never had rubies; I'd never even seen them up close. I would not have minded rubies. Or opals, creamy smooth. Amber is what I had, glowing, warm, like the sun. And turquoise, the gem the Hopis think is sky. Lapis intrigued me, and jasper, carnelian and malachite, Bible stones whose names still held the power and glory of what once was. But diamonds! They always left me cold. Like my sister's smile.

Tibby had diamonds. My mother had given her a diamond wedding band for her twenty-fifth wedding anniversary. My mother had taken the ring off her own finger and handed it to her. Just like that, right in the middle of a family dinner. My mother always had a sense of timing; she knew how to get center stage.

"You'll get the cocktail rings," she'd said to me. "The necklace goes to Tibby. The cameo to Julie. It's not worth much; it's not good gold. Julie, my only granddaughter, should have it. For a remembrance. You'll get the cocktail rings and my Persian lamb coat."

She had not said anything about the earrings I held in my hand.

"I can't believe you don't want diamonds," Tibby used to say, her fingers flashing, her ears sparkling, her wrists ablaze. She used her diamonds like a price tag to show her worth. She was like my mother, always on show, trying to impress the neighbors, putting a value on how things looked, as if she was what she showed herself to be.

I remembered how I used to take lunch to school on Thursdays when my mother went to help my father at his chicken store. It was too much for my grandmother to give me lunch and watch Tibby and Alvin. Few children ate lunch in school, only the poor who had free lunch or those whose mothers worked. I ate fried egg sandwiches or salami on a roll. We did not have a thermos, so my mother gave me tea in a bottle, a clean scrubbed bottle that still said "Slivowitz, 100 proof." I remembered taking a swallow and hearing Mr. Pincus laugh. He whispered to another teacher and pointed in my direction. I turned around to see what could make teachers laugh. There were only children sitting at another table, eating. I took another bite of my sandwich and lifted the bottle to wash it down. "Having a little drink, huh?" I could still hear Mr. Pincus' voice; I still heard him laughing at me.

"I'm too old to eat in school," I told my mother. "They don't let you go to the toilet." That's when I began to eat lunch at home and wear a key around my neck.

On Thursdays, when my mother went to help my father, Alvin took lunch to school and I took care of Tibby. I watched she didn't fall and hurt herself. I watched she didn't run into the street and get killed. I took her to the bathroom. I told her to pull her underpants all the way down so they didn't get wet.

Tibby was the baby; she needed to be taken care of. She was weak. She had weak blood. She went to kindergarten and I had to take her home in the afternoon. I had to wait for her at three o'clock. She walked so slow. My friends called. "Hurry up, Millie," they said. I stood and waited for Tibby. Tibby—*Taible*—a little dove. My sister was chubby and pink, and cute. Everyone pinched her cheek, patted her head, gave her a squeeze.

On Thursdays I had to give Tibby lunch.

"I don't want bananas and cream," Tibby said, pushing her bowl away. I caught the bowl before it dropped off the table.

"I don't want bread and butter," she said, throwing her bread on the table so it landed butter side down, and I had to clean it up.

"I'm not going to school," she said, folding her arms across her chest, when it was time to leave.

I grabbed her arm. I pulled her off the chair. "Oh," she screamed. "Ow," she yelled.

"Crybaby," I said. "I didn't hurt you."

"I want Ma," she said. "I want Bubba. I don't want you."

"Let's go now," I said, afraid we'd be late.

"Crooked eyes!" she called. "Crooked eyes and crooked back, with a body like a sack."

I knew she was trying to provoke me. She wanted a scene; she wanted my grandmother to come and punish me; she wanted us to be late; she didn't want us to go to school.

"Stop it," I said. I shook her hard.

"Crooked eyes. Crooked eyes," she yelled. She looked like she was laughing. Slap. I hit her across the face. We stood, quiet, I waiting.

She kicked my shin. It hurt.

"Brat. Lousy brat," I yelled. I felt the anger rising in me. I wanted to stop her words. I didn't want a sister. I wanted to go to school.

She grabbed my schoolbooks and threw them on the floor. "Bookworm," she yelled.

I hit her. I hit her again. She kicked and screamed. She reached for the container of cream. She threw it on the floor, where it made a mess. She knocked down a chair and ran to the other side of the table. I went after her. She grabbed a fork; she meant to stab me. I picked up a knife. I meant to kill her.

"What's happening here?" Mrs. Sherman, our neighbor, stood in the doorway. She took the knife from me and the fork from my sister. "Wait until your mother finds out what happened here," she said.

I picked my books up from the floor. I didn't want to stay in this house. I took my sister's hand and pulled her into the hall.

I didn't ask what Mrs. Sherman would tell my mother. I was glad she came. I was glad she came before I killed my sister.

I picked up Tibby at the airport. She wore Aigner shoes, a linen suit—she was allergic to wool. She was always sickly. That's what protected her. Alvin had moved far away, but he'd never left home; he was still a little boy. Tibby had left long before when she was still a little girl. She had given up her health so she could keep herself. How could anyone make demands of a sick woman?

She wore gold chains around her neck, and her engagement ring flashed when she moved her hand. She would not agree to marry Bill until she had the ring on her finger. Two carats, square cut. "If you don't start out right," she told me, "there's no telling how you'll end up." Her bag looked like a Gucci. Was it real or imitation? I could never tell. Once I admired a ring she wore, gold with a little garnet in its rose shaped center.

"Here," she said, laughing, "It's yours."

I protested. I couldn't take something valuable like that, I said.

She laughed again. "Take it," she said. "You think it's real. Everybody does. It's not. People expect me to have the real thing because I have money, so I fool them. I mix the real with the fake and no one knows."

We drove to our old neighborhood, burnt out now, but our house still stood. My mother would have been proud. Tibby wanted to see the house of our childhood, she said, for old times' sake. She was not going to spend the night. She would not stay in our mother's apartment—she did not feel comfortable there—and I lived too far out on Long Island. She'd come to see our mother and the house where we grew up. She'd come to say goodbye.

"Have you been to the vault?" my sister asked. We were in my mother's apartment, in her kitchen. My mother liked things color coordinated: the wrought-iron chairs, white; the upholstery, orange; the tablecloth, orange and white checkered plastic; Fiberglas curtains, orange with a white and green design; the light fixture, Tiffany imitation, orange with varicolored fruits along the rim. The white walls held copper plaques, mementos from Israel. A picture of Golda Meir, cut from a newspaper and carefully framed, hung in the center of the dining area wall.

"Does she still have them?" Tibby asked, as if she were talking about old friends, as she spread paper towels over the tablecloth as if they were placemats, as if a plastic tablecloth needed placemats, her blood red nails gleaming. When it came to hands, Tibby was like my mother, her nails always polished. Tibby used to be a secretary, a receptionist really, until she married. I never understood how she could do the typing and filing and still keep those nails. Her nails were even longer now, a sign she didn't use her hands, a sign she was rich enough to have a maid. She still lived by the values she learned in childhood. "You can always tell a woman by her hands," my mother used to say. I used to hide mine, the cuticles ragged, the nails chipped. I used to be ashamed of my hands, hands that washed dishes and scrubbed floors, hands that refinished furniture and worked in the garden, hands that now filled the tea kettle and set it on the stove.

"They're magnificent," Tibby said.

"I guess," I said, my back still turned. "I haven't been to the vault yet." It was easier to lie with my back turned.

"I don't understand you," Tibby said. "Why don't you go and look? The vault's in your name too." She sounded disappointed as if I'd failed her, as if she'd expected something else.

"Why should I?" I asked, holding my hands above the kettle, as if to hurry up the boiling. "She's not dead yet." I hoped I didn't sound as touchy as I felt.

"That's not the point," said Tibby. "You have a responsibility. Besides, aren't you curious? Don't you want to see what you'll get?"

There was no point explaining I knew what I'd get, that it wasn't what I wanted. My grandmother's candlesticks, already promised to Tibby. My mother's cameo, pledged to Julie.

"I'd really like the earrings," Tibby said. "Don't get me wrong. I don't mean anything by it. Mama should live to be a hundred and twenty! But I've always wanted those earrings. I remember how fantastic they are, long. Were they two strands or only one? I can't remember."

Startled, I turned to look at my sister. Was this a trap? Was she trying to find me in a lie? There were no such earrings in the vault. Had there ever been? Had my mother sold them to pay for some emergency? Or were they but another of the myths that fed our fantasies, twisted into fact by time and repetition and Tibby's own desire?

I couldn't tell Tibby the earrings she described did not exist. She'd know I'd been to the vault. Even later, when the legacy would be claimed, she wouldn't believe me; she'd always think I'd taken the earrings for myself. I had trapped myself. That's what came of trying to play my mother's game, of trying to behave the way my sister would.

We can always share the studs, I thought, one for each of us. I smiled as I served the tea in the glass cups and saucers my mother had gotten at the movies: I imagined Tibby with one earring; I imagined how she'd feel not to get what she wanted.

"What are you smiling at?" she asked, as I handed her a paper napkin and a spoon.

"Nothing, really. Just remembering," I said. I wasn't really lying; I did remember.

"Oh, me too. I was sitting here remembering how Mama got the dishes. She used to take you with her to dish night so she could get an extra dish. She never took me."

I started to protest, then caught myself. You were a baby, I wanted to say, she couldn't take you. I watched as Tibby picked up her cup, put a napkin in the saucer to catch the drips. She was compulsively neat. Once, when Julie was in college, and Sam and I were at loose ends, we had decided to see Boston, and of course, we stayed with Tibby. How careful I'd been not to get crumbs on the floor or even on the table! I was afraid she'd start vacuuming while I sat there with my feet up in the air so she could get around me. It had not been a comfortable weekend. I was smoking then, and no sooner did I put my cigarette out, than she'd grab the ash tray, dump the contents down the garbage disposal, wash and rinse the ash tray and return it to the exact spot from which it had been taken. After that, I always made some excuse why we couldn't stay over.

"Do you remember all those dinners, the holidays and all the relatives?" she asked. I sat in the chair near the window, the one my mother always sat in. "Then things began to change," Tibby said. "After Bubba died. That was the first funeral I remember. Mama began to fight with Uncle Arthur. I remember they had a fight about the candlesticks, and about the money he owed her. It was after Bubba died. Then there was no one to hold the family together." She looked at me as if expecting confirmation.

"Do you remember when Mama finally bought the house? How angry you were! Even though you didn't live there anymore, you wrote a letter. You wanted us to move downstairs so it would really be a house. But Mama wouldn't move. All she did was take an extra room out of the back apartment so Alvin could have his own room, so he wouldn't have to sleep in the living room."

I remembered. I remembered that I had never had my own room. I always had to share with Tibby. Alvin got the extra room, Alvin who didn't care where he slept.

I remembered the fights. I remembered Aunt Bertha said my mother had the cameo so she should have the candlesticks. I remembered how my mother got the candlesticks, how Uncle Arthur made her buy them from Aunt Bertha's estate after Aunt Bertha died. My mother never spoke to him after that. He died alone in a hospital in Florida. "He lived like a dog, and he died like a dog," my mother said at his funeral. I remembered how my mother rented Bubba's apartment to a family with five children, refugees, and how my mother complained about them, the noise they made and the dirt. Then, years later, when the neighborhood changed and my father died, my mother lived there alone. She wouldn't move. She had lived there and she would die there, she said. Nobody died in that house, she said. But in the end, she'd moved to the apartment in the projects she disdained.

"Do you remember Alvin's Bar Mitzvah?" Tibby asked. "You wore a gown. I was so jealous."

A gown! The graduation dress I had made myself in sewing class, refurbished with pink ribbons, my mother's idea, to make it look different from what it was.

"And Mama with her diamonds and Bubba with her pearls."

I did not remember that.

"She was a tough old lady, Bubba. I was always a little bit afraid of her. She really kept the family together though. You've got to give her credit."

"I thought it was anger that kept the family together. Anger and arguments," I said, surprised at how strongly I felt, surprised I'd said as much as I had. It wasn't Bubba's dying that broke things up, or Uncle Arthur's moving to Florida. It was not having the house to go to. There has to be a center, a place for people to congregate. It was the place that had pulled us in, the people part of it, like furniture in a room. It was the place we had to leave before we could be free of the people.

"Family was not so important to you," Tibby said, dismissing my words. "You were always with your friends, trying out new things. Some of them were a little weird, or maybe it was because you took everything so seriously. Like the time you got religious and you would not go to the movies on Saturday, so I had to go with Alvin. And then suddenly you changed and asked to take me to the movies. How I envied you! You were so independent." She stood up and went to the sink to get a sponge.

I didn't know what to say. I didn't want to make nice, and I didn't want the pointless chatter we fell into just so we could avoid what we felt. So I said nothing.

I had always considered myself bound by tradition, unable to break the constrictions imposed by birth and class and time. I had envied Tibby, able to get what she needed without even asking. She was like my mother, concerned with things and their market value. I was like my father, who lost his money and pulled my mother down. My father who wanted to study Torah and do good works.

My mother had been ashamed of my father. She used to say she married the wrong man. "He fooled me," she said. "I thought he was a rich man. He gave me diamond earrings and a diamond necklace. He bought me a fur coat and a fox stole. But I was taken for a fool." She meant he lost his money; she was not a landlady.

It had been her idea for my father to get a store. She thought he could make a better living selling chickens than he could working in a shop where all they talked about was strikes and unions. She had a head for business. She was always thinking up ways to make money on the side where all it cost was time and work. It had been her idea to get a second store in a black neighborhood.

"You can pick up quite a bundle of change," I remembered, she told my father. "You have to go with the times," she said.

The people there shopped on Saturday, payday. They wanted cheaper cuts of meat, fryers and fowl instead of capons and pullets, lungs and soup bones, instead of flanken. They didn't need the meat kosher-killed.

"Someone has to sell to them," my mother said.

"But Shabbos," my father protested.

I listened from my bed, envisioning my father dressed for shul, my mother lighting the candles to welcome the Sabbath Queen, while we waited for my father to come from shul so we could eat the Shabbos meal.

"Someone has to do it," my mother said. "It might as well be us. God will forgive us. He knows we can't help it. He'll understand."

My mother knew about God. She knew He knew we came

from a refined family. He understood why my mother wanted to break the Sabbath.

So, on Saturdays, my father got up early and dressed in his Shabbos suit, but instead of shul, he went to the new store. In the afternoon, my mother dressed in her Shabbos dress. She wore high heeled shoes. She was vain about her legs. "Your legs show breeding," she told me. She dressed for Shabbos, but she went to help my father close up the store. "Otherwise, they'll rob him blind," she said.

One Saturday, in the summer when I was thirteen, I was sent to help my father at his store. Tibby had chicken pox and my mother had to stay and see she didn't scratch and end up with pock-marked skin.

It was a long walk straight down Livonia Avenue, under the El to Stone Avenue and then a few more blocks to Thatford. My mother thought the train was only for those who couldn't walk. "If your feet can't get you there," said my mother, "it's clear you don't need to go."

I liked the walk; it was an adventure, passing the poolroom and the stores and the movie theatre; walking over the bridge over the railroad tracks. I liked Brownsville with its tenements and children playing in the street, the women sitting on the stoops, the big library.

My father's store was small, stuck between a dry cleaner on one side and a corner drugstore on the other. A good location, my mother had said. Everyone needed a drugstore, if not to buy aspirins then to use the public phone. Coming to or from the drugstore a person could be tempted to buy a chicken or eggs. That's what my mother said. "Location is important. It's not everything, but it's important."

My father was alone in the store when I arrived. He smiled as if he were happy to see me. "You didn't have to come," he said. "I could have managed." He made it sound as if I had more important things to do. He made it sound as if I could leave, while all the time he stroked my arm or fingered the ribbon at the end of my braids.

He was always touching my hair or my arm, as if to prove I was real. It bothered me, those pokes. There was something crude about them. He never hugged me the way fathers in books did. He never kissed me or told me how to act or offered advice. It was clear he didn't know the finer ways.

My father's store was like my father, small and messy. He sold chickens, some cold cuts, and eggs when he could get them. He sold the chickens whole as they came from the slaughterer, entrails in, feathers still on. Only when somebody bought them, did he clean and dress them. His fingers were nimble but rough. He often tore the skin when he plucked the feathers.

I took a seat on an upended crate near the cash register ready to see that no one robbed my father blind. I sat and stared out through the plate glass windows at the people passing by. A customer came in, her shopping bag already bulging.

"How are you, Missus?" asked my father, leaning the broom against the wall. Quickly, without much thought, she picked a chicken from the few remaining.

"I'll have it ready in a minute," he said and took the chicken to the back to pluck the feathers. The woman waited near the doorway. She didn't look at me, nor I at her.

My mother was right, I thought. Anyone could come in, walk over to the register and take the money out. Then what could my father do? I was glad I was there to see that no one robbed him. It was clear my mother knew just how things were.

There were several customers, not many. My father sold three chickens and some eggs. He sold half of a long fat bologna to a man who took it unwrapped. My father cut the other half in two and placed them on the counter top as if inviting purchase. There were only two chickens left.

My father was getting ready to close up shop. He straightened the paper bags and began to sweep, sending feathers flying, bits of them stuck on his shoes, the edge of his bloodied apron swinging with the rhythm of his sweeps. Soon it would be time to leave.

"Do you want something before we go?" he called to me. "A soda, maybe?"

I would have liked a soda. I would have liked to sit at the drugstore counter sipping a cherry coke. I knew I shouldn't leave. I had been sent to stay and watch that no one robbed my father blind; I would not leave my post.

My father was a little man. He wore baggy pants and old-fashioned, high-laced shoes. My father had weak feet, my mother said. He lost all his money.

A boy came in, about Tibby's age but shorter and thinner. He looked older though, more than eight. He didn't walk but swaggered as if staking claim to whatever his feet touched. His shirt was held together by a safety pin; the bottom of his pants were rolled. I didn't see him look at me but I knew he saw me plain.

My father stopped his sweeping, his hands on the broom.

"Got any work today?" the boy demanded. He sounded as if he'd asked the question before. "Sweeping? Cleaning up?" His voice was tough; he sounded as if he were too good to sweep up dirt.

"Nothing for you," said my father. I sensed a tension I didn't understand. I put my hand on the cash register, then moved it quickly back onto my lap, afraid to call attention to where the money was.

"Nothing now," repeated my father. "You're late," he added, as if explaining.

"Okay, okay," said the boy. "Gimme a chicken, a good one. Get the feathers off good. And don'tcha tear the skin, hear?"

"Let's see your money," said my father, standing easy and relaxed, his hands still on the broom. Even I could see this scene had been played out before.

"It's here. It's here." The boy held out a fist closed tight around some bills crushed together. "Don'tcha trust me?" he laughed.

My father leaned the broom against the wall. He took a chicken from the counter, making a show of it, as if for some important customer. They didn't say a word, my father with his dirty hands, the boy in his shabby clothes. They looked the chicken over head to feet. Then, as if some unseen signal had passed between them, my father carried the bird to the back, a trophy in some contest I didn't understand.

I sat and did the job I'd been sent to do. I sat and thought how careful one must be of how one lived and whom one chose for friends and who one's parents were. Lost in thoughts of taste and form, I didn't pay attention to the boy who stood and waited.

Something broke my thoughts, a move no bigger than a blink. The boy still stood, his back relaxed against the counter, except that now he stared at me. There was something in his look: defiance, anger, hate, fear. I couldn't tell what it was. I sat up straight and looked again. Where once two pieces of bologna lay, only one now filled the space. Perhaps it had fallen; that might be what I thought I saw. I slipped down from the crate ready to track the missing piece.

My father was there beside me, one hand on my arm, his other clutching the neck of the freshly plucked chicken. "Okay," the boy said.

My father wrapped the chicken as it was, head and legs still attached. "Let's have the money," he said to the boy. He didn't count the coins and bills thrust into his palm, but handed it all to me, his eyes on the boy. It seemed the price had been agreed upon beforehand; it seemed this sale had happened more than once.

As the boy began to leave, the paper bag beneath his arm, the fragments of a smile across his lips, his eyes flickered past my face.

"But Pa," I began, concerned about the missing piece of wurst.

He did not allow me to continue. "It's time to go," he said. "We did enough for today. We'll leave a little early and take our time."

"But Pa," I tried again, "I think that boy took something. I think that boy's a thief." I was angry, as if, somehow, I'd failed

155

to do my job.

"It's all right," my father said. "Don't worry. I know his mother. They're very poor." I didn't see his face. He was busy emptying the cash register, stuffing bills and coins into the little sack my mother had made. He drew the strings together, twisting the whole upon itself, then stuffed his day's income into his pocket.

"It happens every week," he said. "You can forget it." He reached out to touch my arm. I knew he meant I shouldn't tell my mother.

He went to the back to change his clothes. It wouldn't do to let people know he worked on the Sabbath. He wore his Sabbath suit but he didn't change his shoes.

We walked home, hand in hand, with matching steps.

We came into the kitchen and there was Tibby, sitting on my mother's lap being fed tea from a spoon, as if she were a baby.

"You're home early," was all my mother said.

I watched as Tibby rubbed the sponge over the clean table. We had never understood each other. I used to think it was resentment that caused it, resentment and the anger we had felt as children, feelings we'd never lost. Now I knew it started long before. Tibby was my mother's girl and I, my father's girl.

"Maybe if I had some of your strength, I wouldn't have been so sick all these years. Maybe being sick was the only way I could get what I wanted." Tibby went on as if there hadn't been this long silence between us.

"Oh, Tibby," I said.

For a moment, quiet filled the room, as if even the air hung in balance. My sister, finally willing to share herself.

I reached out to take her hand.

Tibby's fingers touched my palm. She smiled, and gently moved her hand away. "It's too late now," she said, looking into her cup as if she could read the leaves. "We are what we are."

I got up and put my cup and saucer in the sink. I didn't offer to take Tibby's.

"I just remembered," Tibby said, looking up at me. "The bracelet watch. Do you remember it? My God! It would be worth a fortune if it were real. And the cocktail rings. They were her favorites. She used to wear them all the time." Tibby put her cup and saucer in the sink next to mine. She hadn't even pretended to drink her tea. "You really ought to look," she said. "The vault's in your name too."

She's not dead yet, I wanted to say again. It's too soon to divide the loot. I felt cold. The air more February than May, I thought, as I stood at the sink, side by side with my sister. A shiver passed through my bones. Inside, nothing moved. I was frozen, a solid block of ice. Nothing changes, I thought. The sides were drawn long ago. My mother and my sister, my father and I. We are what we were. Just more so.

My baby sister. Diamonds were all we had in common.

Funny Women

Shay Youngblood

M ISS TOM was not a pretty woman, she was handsome like a man. Tall, broad-shouldered, big-boned,
lean and lanky like a man. Her soft silver hair was cut short
and curled tight around her nut-brown, smooth and narrow
face. She had silver sideburns, thick eyebrows that almost met
across the top of her face, dark black eyes that could see through
almost anything, and a silver mustache, like a man. Kids, and
some grown folks, who didn't know Miss Tom were always
asking her if she was a man or a woman. Miss Tom was patient
with small children and strangers, so she would say in a deep,
husky voice:

"Don't judge a book by looking at the cover."

Her chest was flat as a man's, her hands were big, thick and
callused. But she had a woman's eyes, dark, black eyes that
held woman secrets, eyes that had seen miracles and reflected
love like only a woman can. Her walk was slow and deliberate
like she had somewhere to go, but wasn't in any hurry to get
there.

Me and Miss Tom were friends, good friends. She taught me
how to fish, throw a knife, carve a piece of wood, tame birds,
and believe in a world of impossibilities. She lived in a big,
white house next door to Miss Rosa. It was a nice old house
with long porches that wrapped around its sides and green
shutters; behind them, lace curtains whipped in the breeze.
She had lived there with Miss Lily for as long as I could remember. Miss Lily was real sick, in the hospital with a fever.

Big Mama said the doctors didn't know anything, so it was no surprise when they said Miss Tom couldn't visit Miss Lily because what she had might be catching.

When Miss Tom came by our house with a fishing rod over her shoulder headed for the river, I asked her if I could go. She nodded her head and waited under the chinaberry tree in the yard while I went in to ask Big Mama, who I knew would say yes.

I got my fishing pole and ran out. Big Mama stuck her head out the door and hollered at Miss Tom.

"Hey Tom, how you making out? I hear Miss Lily sick. You need anything?"

"I'm doing pretty good so far. Me and your youngun going to catch my supper and yours too I reckon." Miss Tom winked down at me.

"You tell Lily we all praying for her when you get chance to see her."

"Thank you. I appreciate your prayers and I'll tell her you praying for her. We all is. See you 'fore sundown."

"Tom, don't you drop my baby over in the river. She got some things to do round this house when she gets back. Y'all take care." Big Mama waved us on.

I put my hand in Miss Tom's, and she held it kind of light as if she might break it.

"I'm sorry about Miss Lily," I said and gave her hand a squeeze.

"Me too baby. You and me both," she said, squeezing back.

It was early in May and spring was in every strawberry bush, chinaberry tree and lime-colored leaf. The sky was crispy, deep blue and full of white fluffy clouds. The sun was so bright it hurt my eyes to look at anything white or shiny. Down by the river it was quiet, nobody around but us.

"What we got to catch with today?" I asked Miss Tom.

"We got a sardine, some Vienna sausages, and fresh bacon," she said, laughing that deep, rough laugh of hers. "These old crafty swimmers do like that fresh bacon." Then, after a while, like she remembered something terrible, the smile and the light in her face was pinched out like a flame.

I guessed Miss Tom was worried about Miss Lily. Her mind seemed to be miles off. I had thought she and Miss Lily were kin or sisters for the longest time, it was the only reasoning I could make out, them living together like that. When I asked Aunt Mae if they were sisters, she said:

"They sisters all right, but it ain't by blood."

I didn't know what she meant, so I left it alone then. I knew Miss Tom was different from other women, and not just because of her mustache and the mannish way she walked or the deep, rough way she talked. She was just different. I heard folks say she and Miss Lily were funny, but I never noticed anything funny about either one of them. They were serious women.

In silence, Miss Tom fed our hooks, and we threw the lines in. We leaned back into the shade of a pine tree on a soft bed of pine needles. After a while the sun caught us strong in the face. Miss Tom squinted directly into the sun, and when I looked up a few minutes later, tears were running down her face like twin rivers.

"Miss Tom, you all right?" I asked, taking her big, rough hand in mine, trying to give her some comfort.

She heaved a few times, like she would soon let out a shout, then she got up and walked to the edge of the river bank and stood there looking in. With her back to me, she breathed in deep a few times with her whole body, then calmed down easy and came back to sit next to me. She wiped her face with a clean white handkerchief, then blew her nose in it.

"I got a lot on my mind baby, but Miss Tom ain't gonna jump in yet. I needs to clear my head. Miss Juliette heavy on my mind."

"Who is Miss Juliette?" I asked. "You mean Miss Lily?"

"Miss Juliette is the most beautiful creature on God's green earth. She better get over this fever, we got things to do, we got plans. We going back to New Orleans. . ." Miss Tom said, like I wasn't even there.

She was real quiet for a few minutes, but I kept my eyes on her. I was real confused. I'd never heard tell of anybody around named Miss Juliette. Now, Miss Tom didn't talk much, said she didn't like to waste words saying nothing, but without warning, out of nowhere, without me even asking, she dived deep into a story simply because there was one that needed telling. She began in that deep, husky voice of hers that would've put me to sleep except the story kept me on the edge of those pine needles, and my eyes steady on Miss Tom.

"I growed up in a house wid six brothers on the banks of the Mississippi River. Six mens and me till Mama had Juliette. I member it like it was yesterday. . .the midwife coming in the middle of the night sending the boys out and making me boil water and tear up sheets. Way after a while I heard Mama in the bedroom hollering, grunting like her bowels wanna move, then I hear a baby crying. I peep behind the curtain in time to see the midwife hold up a ugly lil wrinkled up red baby.

"It was clear to be a white man's child, most probably Mr. Boone, who Mama kept house for. Mama called her Juliette after Mr. Boone's dead wife. It was a pretty name for such a ugly lil worm as that. My name rough, fit me like a glove, Tom. My grandmama's mama name me after her mama, Tomasina Louise Perry. That's what was wrote in the family Bible. But since I was little, the boys and Mama call me Tom, and treat me like I was a boy, no different from the other six. I believe sometimes even my Mama forgot.

"I was five years old when Juliette was born, but I was the one learn to bathe her, feed her and sit up all night wid her by the fire rocking wid her till she could sleep. She growed into such a pretty child. Long, black hair Mama kept in two plaits, so soft I would rub my face in it, taking hollow breaths of it, trying to take her in. She was a white man's child all right, her skin was white as Jesus Christ's. She was built slim, but strong and long-legged, and them eyes of hers was green and gold like cats' eyes. You look in em too deep and you was liable to be sucked in. She was strong-willed and we spoiled her rotten by giving her everything she thought she wanted. Yes m'am, she growed to be pretty as a picture. I was proud to walk the two miles into town wid her on my back to show her off. Folks who didn't know us ask me whose child she was. When I say she my sister, they fall out laughing like it wasn't possible. When she say I'm her sister, they laugh more, cause I looked like a boy even then. Even then I would've cut my arm to the sleeve to please her. When she was four, she demanded we call her Miss Juliette. The poor child thought she really was white, and to keep our precious Juliette happy, we called her Miss Juliette, Queen of the Mississippi, till she wasn't round to call no more.

"After Juliette was born, Mama had to go work in Mr. Boone's fields picking cotton. That left mostly me to take care of Miss Juliette. We slept in the same bed every night for sixteen years. For sixteen years we never spent a night apart. I never loved nobody like Miss Juliette, nobody. . ."

Miss Tom stopped suddenly. She looked up at the sun again and stared out at the water like she was blind. Finally she pulled a corncob pipe from the front pocket of her overalls and a pouch of sweet-smelling tobacco out of her back pocket. Without even looking down to see what her hand was doing, she pinched a bit of tobacco and stuffed it into the bowl of the pipe that was cradled in her other hand. She struck a match on the bottom of her boot, and for a few minutes was swallowed up in a cloud of sweet smoke. Miss Tom said some things to make me know she was way off somewhere. The next thing she said opened up a world of impossibles and never-even-dreamed-of ideas.

"It just seemed like we was always in love and loving one another. Sometimes I'd think about her being my blood sister and worry about going to hell for loving her that way. We started loving one another different the summer it was too hot to sleep. The summer the boys was all out possum hunting wid Uncle Trey and Mama was sleeping by Mr. Boone's house. I must've been thirteen, and Juliette was bout eight. It was dog awful hot and nobody was home 'cept us, so we figured it was safe to sleep naked. My lil sister turned to me in her sweet lil whispering voice and say, 'Tom, hold me to you like you do when it's cold. I'm scared.' 'It's too hot to be all hugged up, Miss Juliette. Go on to sleep,' I say to her kinda rough. Then I was sorry cause her feelings was hurt and she start to whining like a broke record, and I couldn't refuse her nothing. It was all in a natural move that I cradled up next to her lil body spoon fashion. Somehow in the middle of the night, we was laying face to face, me still holding her in my arms. By the moonlight she was almost too pretty to look at, like a angel. I member I closed my eyes and counted stars. Afterwhile I felt a soft something all over me, tingly kinda. I could feel the berries stand up on my bosom and then a nice easy rubbing on my nature. It felt so mighty wonderful I knowed it was a dream, so I kept my eyes shut tight trying to hang on to a good feeling. Can you blame me, Lord? I'd had so many bad dreams.

"Pretty soon I was moving against the softness, till I found relief. Behind my eyes was still a bunch of stars so I counted em till all the lights went out. I heard a whispering in my ear, then felt my hand being moved to a soft spot.

"'Tom, do me. Do me now, it's my turn.'

"I heard her whispering like cool air through the trees. She put my hand between her legs. She was laying on her back looking over at me, holding my hand on a spot as soft as goose feathers and melted down like butter. Then I loved her all over wid my eyes closed and I make out like it was a dream, so we wouldn't go to hell. I'd been having bad dreams. Since I was eight, my oldest brother had used me like a woman. The first time he did it to me, it hurt and I tried not to move so I wouldn't wake up lil Juliette, so I'd make out like I was having a bad dream, cause if it's a dream, you wake up, daylight come, and it's passed. Me and Juliette had good dreams together. The night me and Juliette start loving one another different, I make out like we was dreaming. She kept her eyes closed too. I give her a bath with my kisses all round her face and neck and the lil bumps on her bosom and all over the soft spot between her legs."

Miss Tom stopped again, and was quiet as the fish sleeping in the river. The sun poured down on us heavy, scorching between the branches. So quiet, I could hear birds singing and branches falling in the woods behind us. My line got a bite, but Miss Tom didn't even look up as I pulled the little wiggling baby fish out of the depths of the river. I unhooked it and without Miss Tom even telling me, I threw it back to its mama.

"Growing up in a four room shack on the Mississippi River in a house wid six men, I dreamed a lot. But after loving Juliette in that way, things was different. My brother didn't come to me no more. Juliette stopped that. She didn't make out like she was sleeping no more. When my brother come, she would kick him, bite him, scratch him, so he just quit and pretty soon left Mississippi to find a job out West. Juliette was jealous in a vicious kinda way, but she had a good heart. She wouldn't let no boys come round to court me. Not that they was tearing down the door, but some old men who was widowers wid children, and needed another hand on they farm, would come round looking me and Juliette over. She would put the dog on em.

"For sixteen years we slept in the same bed, loving one another like it was natural. Then Mama died of TB, and Uncle Reb and Aunt Taylee come to fetch Juliette. They said they only had room for her. Mr. Boone say me and the boys could stay on the land and work it.

"'You and the boys grown,' Aunt Taylee say to me. 'You can make it on your own. You near bout a old maid. Humph! At twenty-one years old you need to be married. If you fixed up some and shaved off that mustache you might look more like a woman.'

"Juliette's heart broke in two when I told her she had to go, but I promised I'd send for her. She cried all the way down the road. I cried late that night into a pillow filled wid the smell of her. After the funeral, and after Juliette left, me and Booker

T., my youngest brother, set out for New Orleans on a shrimp boat wid everything we own wrapped in a piece of newspaper tied wid string. I kept a lock of Juliette's hair in a lil bag wid some roots in it round my neck, and I touched it when I wanted to dream. After a week the only job I could find was washing dishes in a whorehouse. Booker T. got a job working on the shrimp boats the second day we was there. We rented a lil room in back of a stable yard and took turns sleeping on the lil cot they call a bed. Other times we'd sleep in a old raggedy chair wid the springs popping out. New Orleans was full of big, pretty houses and pretty mulatta women, though none could compare to Miss Juliette. Out the blue one day, Booker T. say:

"'Tom, I bet you down at the shrimp boats they don't know you from a man. Your lip hair and sideburns thicker than mine.'

"Don't you know they went for it? I got a job shrimping the very next day. Soon after that I got into a trade school for colored men, and me and Booker T. was living in a boarding house wid separate rooms. He was feeling his nature and took to drinking and bringing women to his room. All I worked for was Juliette, all I thought about was her sweet pink smile, black cloud hair and loving her soft lil body till daybreak. I almost had the money to send for her when me and Booker T. got a letter that froze my blood. Uncle Reb and Aunt Taylee was sending Juliette to school up North. She got a scholarship to a school in Canada, a teaching school. You could've knocked me over wid a feather.

"I was lonesome for a lot of years, but fate led me to meet a woman like me. She was a real woman though. She liked to wear fancy dresses, put on bright jewelry, dash herself wid loud perfume, and paint herself up. I was still doing men's work, and even after hours we went out wid me dressed like a man. She was named Ruth, but sometimes when we lay loving one another, I call her Juliette. Most times Ruth be so drunk she never member what I call her or what we did. The only way I could love her was if I membered Juliette, my eyes shut tight counting stars and dreaming, wid Juliette.

"It was twenty-two years before I heard from Juliette again. I got a letter in a handwriting that wasn't hers, begging me to come to her in Georgia, this very town, in the very house I live in today. The letter said she was sick and wanted to see me one last time 'fore she died, she said not to tell nobody else, I was the only one she wanted to see. The letter was signed, 'I will always love you, your gentle sister, Juliette.'

"I packed everything I owned in a suitcase like I did when I left Mississippi and never looked back. I left Ruth a lil piece of money and told her I was leaving and didn't know if I'd be back. She cried some and I hugged her one last time at the train station but I never looked back. All the way on the train I never once stopped thinking bout Juliette. Sometimes I'd wake up, and my face be wet from crying in my sleep.

"When I got to the address she wrote she lived at, I got a surprise. It was a big fine house for a colored woman, I figured she might work there. Indeed, a white woman met me at the door. I had on a new gray suit and stiff brim hat. I stood there wid my hat in my hand in a sweat.

"'Excuse me m'am,' I say. 'I'm looking for Miss Juliette Perry. This address she sent me say she live here.'

"The woman look me up and down in a friendly sort of way, kinda curious.

"'You Tom?' she ask me.

"'Yes'm.' I answer polite as you please.

"'I'm Lily. I been taking care of Juliette. She ain't well at all. I'm the one wrote to you. Why you dressed like that? You hiding from something?'

"'No m'am. This the way I have to live to find work. Only work a colored woman can get where I been is cooking, cleaning, washing, or whoring, and I ain't partial to none of them.'

"'You don't have to call me m'am, I ain't white,' she say, smiling at me.

"You could've bowled me over wid a dime. She had them light colored eyes, dark straight hair and white, white skin. She was young too. Couldn't have been more than twenty. She ask me to come in the house, took my hat and bag and led me to the kitchen.

"Juliette had been sick for more than a month. While we was sitting at the kitchen table, the woman tell me what happen in them twenty-two years that was missing. She say Juliette moved to New York when she finished school and started passing for white. She was teaching school up there, and Lily was one of her students. Lily was passing too. They kinda helped one another out and was soon living together. Juliette wanted to teach in the South, teach colored children to read and figure, and she got Lily to come wid her to study under a colored doctor to help heal coloreds. They was living here three years when Juliette was struck with this sickness.

"Then Lily showed her to me. My Juliette lay in a big, iron bed pale as a ghost and delicate like a dried-up flower withering amongst all them quilts and plump pillows. I walk up to the bed and whisper her name real low. Her eyes open and shut like bird wings. When she see me, her eyes light up the dark circles all round em. First thing she say is that she sorry for all these years gone.

"'Tom, I knowed you'd look just like you do.' Then she just look at me, us not talking for a long time. Finally she say:

"'You know, I ain't got much time, so I want you to come closer to me and listen.' I did like she wanted. I sat on the bed close to her and took her cool, dry hand in mine, and I heard Lily go out the room and close the door. Juliette sit up and speak stronger. She was still a beautiful creature. I tried to drink her up, swallow her whole wid remembering.

"'Tom, I wanna love you one last time before I go. I wanna love you wid my eyes open. I learned how to do that wid Lily, and I wanna give you something and take something of you before I go. And Tom, I want you to take care of Lily. She ain't got nothing and nobody in this world to claim her but me. This is my house, now it belong to the two of you. Promise me you'll do it Tom, promise me.'

"What could I do, 'cept like always?

167

"'Miss Juliette, I would die for you if I could.' She squeezed my hand wid a strength she didn't look to have.

"She didn't make love like a dying woman, but slow and natural, like a woman in love, and I loved her back wid everything in me till we was both wet wid loving and empty of all but love. After she fell asleep I got up and washed myself, then I bathed Juliette's body as if she was my sleeping child.

"When I went out to the kitchen to get a pitcher of drinking water, Lily was slumped over the table crying her eyes out.

"'Why? Why you have to love her like that? Ain't she sinned enough wid me? You her sister, and it just ain't right,' she wailed, like death was on her.

"She looked more like Juliette wid every tear that drop. I hadn't noticed so much before how much they look alike. Where Juliette was tall and lean, Lily was on the short side and kinda plump, but they could've passed for sisters and probably did when they was living up North like white women.

"'I love her as much as you do,' was all I could tell her.

"I put my arm round her and let her cry. That night I slept in the bed wid Juliette, and Lily slept on the floor next to Juliette's side. We went on like that till Juliette died, two weeks later, leaving us in mourning, loving her even into the grave. After the funeral, me and Lily stayed up all night talking about Miss Juliette. When it was time to turn the lights out, I took Miss Lily's hand and we went into Juliette's bedroom and lay down together, and we been sleeping in the same bed every night, ever since."

Miss Tom let out a cry so sharp, I dropped my fishing pole and it slid in the river. I took her big, rough hand in mine and felt my throat tighten up and tears fall.

"Miss Juliette, I can't lose you twice. Lord don't let her go..." Miss Tom said with grief deep in her heart.

We sat there crying on the banks of the Backbend River as the sun, a big red ball of fire, fell gently between the trees. Miss Tom seemed to come around after a while. She looked over at me through her tears.

"Lord forgive me for what this child have heard this evening, but you and me both know it's the truth. If you in heaven God, please spare me losing Miss Juliette a second time."

With not another word, Miss Tom got up, dusted off the seat of her overalls and started gathering up our stuff. She took my hand and whistled an old blues song as we walked home in the dark. Her telling me that story clicked the lock on our friendship and was never spoken of again, but that was the last time Miss Tom took me fishing. Like she predicted to Big Mama, my interests turned to boys and other young folks, but I never forgot Miss Tom or her story.

Miss Lily eventually got over her fever and continued to heal folks in the community. She and Miss Tom probably still live in that big, old white house on Sixth Avenue, loving each other with their eyes open.

Whatever Lola Wants

Cathy Cockrell

MAUREEN'S STANDING in a sleeveless yellow shift and bobby socks on a box in the living room, rotating on command.

"Turn," Grace says, through the pins she grips between her lips. June looks out through the bathroom door's open crack. She sees her older sister's skinny, rotating legs and the red hair that peeks out from under her armpit, as the right side comes around. Maureen's got hairs between her legs, too. At night she sits on her bed and preens them with a comb, sad and conceited.

"Turn," June hears again, from the toilet seat, where she sits painting her toes red with her sister's Maybelline. She wiggles her toes in front of her against the floor's background of white and black hexagonal tiles.

"Okay, turn," Grace mumbles. June stares at her nails. Maureen's answering sigh of impatience is so dramatic even June can hear it. Maureen has been pretending to be good, and it's hard for her to keep it up. "Right, Missy, that'll do."

The big toe is flat and tender still. June's quick brush stroke covers the purple bruise under the nail where an older girl, a bully, stomped on her toes. When June grabbed her foot, screaming, she dropped the quarter she had held in her fist. The girl scooped the coin up from the pavement and ran.

"Would you get the cart for me, Maureen?" Grace asks, but in her do-as-I-say tone. Grace is *not* their mother, only their godmother. Her cart for errands lives on a hook on the back of the kitchen door.

"But I thought you were gonna hem my dress! You're not gonna hem it?" Maureen protests.

"*Miss* Impatience! It'll be ready in time for mass Sunday."

"Mass my ass. I need it tomorrow," Maureen curses. June hears a fast smack against her sister's cheek.

"Where do you pick up language like that?" Grace hisses, as if her husband doesn't curse all the time. "What would your father do if he heard you? Your poor mother's turning in her grave!"

Maureen must be surprised herself; it must have fallen right out of her mouth like busted teeth. Maureen's been trying out all sorts of new expressions these days—so far only on her new crowd or June. No tears from Maureen. She's silent, as if penitent. She's probably biting her lip through. Tomorrow is Grace's day to visit homebound people from the parish, so big baddy Maureen plans to skip last period and meet her boyfriend Wilson and drive to Coney Island, to the boardwalk's air and space, to the wild rides, in the new yellow birthday shift she got in the mail from their father.

"Rush, rush, rush. What now, Maureen?" Grace says, instead of scolding her more. June's surprised and impressed. She never thought it possible to get so little punishment for cursing Grace. But Grace acts tiptoey toward Maureen these days, like she's holding her breath, worried for the girl, like she knows that Maureen stuffs her head in the pillow at night and cries.

All the toenails on the right foot and the second, fourth and big toes of the left are now shiny red. June jumps back to the little toe—the toe Grace used to call the baby pig that went "wee, wee, wee all the way home"— dips the brush into the bottle, and starts her stroke. Her hand wavers. She braces her arm at the elbow to steady it. She tries to breathe evenly.

"They told us the Cardinal might visit our school tomorrow," she hears Maureen tell Grace, and the brush swerves off the nail. There's sticky red polish on the skin. June tears a square

171

of toilet paper from the roll, daubs at the red smear, gets a fleck of white stuck on the toe. She drops the tissue and makes her forefinger and thumb into tiny pincers, hovers over the baby toe, swoops down on the white fleck as if to take it by surprise. Now there's a smear of red on the side of her toe and a finger-print on the toenail and red on her finger.

Stupid Maureen. Anymore, she's all lies. She'll make up any-thing on Wilson's account. He's a tall Negro, older than her; he comes to school in a green Chevrolet with tail fins to pick up Maureen, just Maureen, or Maureen and the crowd of dark-skinned girls she hangs around with these days. June remem-bers the first time she saw them together. On her way home from school that day, June showed her friend Dina the unlocked door of the Elysian Fields Funeral Parlor, next to the rectory. They went inside, scooted along the carpeted hallway, past the white-haired, hard-of-hearing caretaker who was forever bent over her knitting in her small office. They opened the double wooden doors to the chapel, walked softly to the front. They saw a coffin, its padded lining pink as a tongue, laid out in preparation for a wake. They stared at the sleeping corpse and read the dead man's name off the prayer cards. The room was cool and quiet. An electric candelabra mounted on the wall cast feeble yellowy fingers of light among the vacant folding chairs. When the two of them left the funeral parlor, hushed and excited, blinking back the sunlight, there was Maureen coming up the street. Her arm was hooked into the elbow of a tall dark dude with a thin mustache, and they walked with a pop to their step, both of them. June felt locked into place. She wanted to cry or die. "Sugar," she heard the guy call her sister. Maureen was looking at him with googoo eyes. His face had a soft look, too. Just then Maureen saw June and Dina. Her cheeks flushed pink.

"Yo there, sista. Slip me some skin," Maureen said, as she extended her pale, freckled white hand. Did Maureen know how ridiculous she was? June wanted to laugh in her face. She giggled; Dina did too.

"Whatchu doin' in there?" Wilson asked, pointed past them into the funeral parlor.

"Playin' with dem stiffs," Maureen said, before June could answer.

"*You* do, too," June protested. "You *love* them stiffs." Hypocrite Maureen! Before Maureen got airs and hairs and Wilson she used to go to the Elysian Fields with June. June remembered Maureen kissing the chalk-colored cheek of an old man, as if she knew him, with feeling. Once, they combed the hair of a little boy who'd died of pneumonia. Another time, they paid a solemn visit to the woman who had jumped from the roof of their apartment building, landed in the bottom of the air shaft beneath their window. That time Maureen looked disappointed, and she panicked when they discovered that the coffin was closed and buried under a pile of artificial flowers. Maureen pursed her face till the freckles over her lip bunched together, like something hard was stuck in her chest, like maybe she was remembering their mother. She touched the coffin. Her face seemed to form a question.

"'Cause she got messed up," June whispered. June was the one who'd heard the woman's low wail as she fell, and had seen her first, crumpled up at the bottom.

"Let her out," Maureen said, prayer-like. June tugged at Maureen's skirt, to get her to stop. Maureen turned on her. "You baby. You're too young! Think what it feels like in there. She can't breathe!" Maureen was fourteen then, not grown-up like she wanted to seem. What made her think she knew what the dead woman wanted or why she'd jumped? "She wants out," Maureen said.

"She *got* out," June whispered.

They'd both liked the Elysian Fields, liked how quiet and uncluttered it felt. They had gone there a number of times. Now Maureen didn't want her little sis to bring up their visits to the funeral parlor, June could see.

"This here's Wilson. Wilson T," Maureen said, to change the subject. "Wilson, this be my kid sister. And her friend Dina."

"I figured," Wilson nodded. He wore sunglasses and a hat with a narrow brim that he tipped at June and Dina. Maureen was wearing a blouse with a Peter Pan collar from Grace's closet. Only instead of tucked in neat, like their godmother would wear it, she had tied the ends together to reveal her belly and emphasize her breasts. It made June catch her breath, just to think what Grace would say if she could see Maureen now. How she'd love to tell!

Now Wilson surprised June: he took a few steps forward to the curb, to a green car with a rusted door. He opened the back door for Maureen, then looked at June and Dina, and at Maureen again, as if seeking her advice. June saw Maureen shrug her shoulders, and slip inside. June and Dina followed, onto the back seat patched with black electrical tape. For years Maureen had tried to lose June, wherever she went. The funeral parlor was one of the only places she'd ever let June catch up with her. This was another. There was another Negro in the front seat, smoking a thin cigarette.

"Hey, Bro," Maureen said offhandedly, like she wasn't a poor, white Irish Catholic girl pretending. June had never seen Bro or Wilson before. She wondered where Maureen met them. It smelled funny in the car. Wilson and his friend kept snickering, talking Negro and snickering. Wilson was reaching over the back of his seat to hold Maureen's hand; his friend fiddled with something on the front seat between them.

"So this's the little tomboy Maureen keep telling me about," said Wilson, pronouncing it "Mo-reen," talking loud for effect, or his friend's benefit. Bro nodded like it *was* for his benefit. June thought Wilson might be making fun. She felt hurt and ridiculed and abandoned. She kicked Dina in the foot, giggled, as if she wasn't hurt. The guys in the front snickered; Maureen snickered. June couldn't tell why any of them were laughing. Maybe Maureen was laughing at herself. She should be. June wanted to open the door and leave. Still, this was something, something intriguing. Wilson was Negro and worldly. He and his friend started crooning, like the doo-wop groups on the street corner, like the record: "Ain't that a shame," Maureen joined in with them.

"Hey, that's Pat Boone," June said triumphantly. But instead of being impressed, Wilson and Bro started snickering again.

"Who he?" Bro said, like Pat Boone didn't exist.

"Stupid," Maureen said to June. "It's Fats Domino. Pat Boone just steals his songs." Maureen had been studying up. June didn't know her anymore; she felt little and embarassed. Maureen had let her join this time, but she only wanted June for an audience, to see what she had, to be amazed. June felt like they'd set a trap for her to fall into, and she had. She despised her sister.

Wilson took something, a skinny cigarette, from the front seat by Bro, lit it, handed it back, and lit another for himself. Maureen took the cigarette, slipped it between her lips, and sucked. She passed it across to Dina. Technically, June noted, she had not given it to her. For this was reefer, she realized, the famous reefer.

June looked at her sister, who was holding her breath, swallowing smoke, and she couldn't match the girl she saw, the hard, cool way she was acting, with the little girl with asthma, who'd fought to breathe and almost died in the night. Or the one who still combed her hairs down there like they were a prize. Or the one who only last week got caught on the inside of Grace's bed, where she'd fallen asleep, with the sleeping body of Scotty, Grace's husband, on the outside. She had been terrified to cross over him and had to be coaxed across by Grace. Now she was acting so opposite.

June hears Grace say "Let me get my perm then, Maureen, and I'll hem it soon's I get back. It's nice to look beautiful for the Cardinal." Grace should know better than to believe Maureen's Cardinal story. Wouldn't every Catholic in the neighborhood have been talking about it if it were true? But what hooks Grace, what Maureen has counted on, is the idea that Maureen would decide to wear a smart new dress, on purpose, for the visit of a high Catholic dignitary. Grace is so pleased she forgets her common sense, forgets what Maureen is like. Now what if Grace makes June wear a prissy dress to school for the Cardinal's "visit"?

June screws the top back on the toenail polish, wiggles her piggies to air them. Beyond the bathroom door she can hear Grace's voice. She hears the front door shut, then Maureen talking to herself in a Negro voice in the other room, like she's rehearsing. June had better skedaddle. She leaves the bathroom, scoots around the ironing board set up in the hallway, goes into Grace and Scotty's room, and presses the door shut.

It is cool and peaceful here. The door is solid. She feels safe. The walls are pale blue, like the inside of an ocean liner, she imagines. There's a dressing table with a low stool and a big round mirror. On the dressing table there's a single jar of Revlon body lotion and a hard pink comb planted neatly in the bristles of an up-turned brush with a pink handle that has "Grace" written on it in gold cursive. There's a small spider plant in the window and two soft pink slippers waiting by the head of the bed for Grace's two perfectly scrubbed pink feet.

June turns on the radio. It's the hit parade program, "Today and Yesterday." Eddie Fisher is singing one of last year's hits. "Oh, My Papa!" the announcer breaks in, "a 1954 chartbuster!" June lies on her back, her legs extended above her to examine her work. Maureen opens the bedroom door.

Get out! June wants to hiss. But she doesn't, and Maureen plops down on the end of the bed and heaves a sigh, looking dreamy, her head cocked to one side, her jaw tense and moving slightly, back and forth so that the blue vein in her temple pops in and out. June clenches her back jaw, too, and closes her eyes tight, as if to sleep. When she opens them again, her sister's watching her, and an advertisement for Instant Swan's Down Cake is ending on the radio.

"I'm thirsty," Maureen says finally, just as several strong downbeats lead into a new song.

"Shhh," says June, but it's too late. She's missed the announcer saying, over the music, who the group is. June likes to see if she can guess the songs and the groups, but this one she doesn't recognize. She glowers at her sister as Maureen lays down on her belly, dangling her feet above Grace's pillow, her chin propped on her palms at the foot of the bed. June sees the curved base of Maureen's breast through the armhole of her slip. Maureen smirks. June looks away. She knows Maureen likes it that she looks. Maureen is vain and a lazy bones. Fifteen years old and she won't hem her own dress.

"I wanna soda. Go on," the Princess says. "I'll listen for de dope on the next one." June rotates, her back to Maureen. She rolls slowly off the bed and leaves. She's eleven already and she's still Maureen's slave. The radio's the only sound. Thank God Scotty's still out on his bender, June thinks. But as she passes the couch she sees it isn't true. He's come in, and there's all six feet of him—his knees pulled in tight against his chest, his big black shoes pressing into the far arm of the couch. Scotty's head looks big, like the head of one of those giant stuffed bears at a Coney Island game booth. Strings of hair fan out onto Maureen's precious shift, crumpled under his head. June feels a surge of hate for all of them.

The refrigerator door swings open, blocking the light from the window over the sink. June twists on the red light bulb at the back of the fridge and sees a bottle of Dr. Pepper on the bottom shelf. She gets two glasses from the drainer, and the bottle opener and the bottle. She hears static from the other room—Maureen moving the dial, landing on "Whatever Lola Wants." Maureen is Lola, June thinks, and whatever Lola wants Lola gets. June closes the refrigerator door, quietly so Fe-Fi-Fo-Fum won't wake. That's what she calls him sometimes. June and Maureen's dad left them for Grace to raise, after their mom died. She wonders if he would have done it if Grace had been married to Scotty at the time. She doesn't want to believe he would have.

When June comes back in the bedroom, she sees that Maureen has switched ends. She has her head on Grace's pillow now, is reaching again to impatiently twist the dial of the radio on the night table. The bottom of her feet are black with dirt. June feels like telling Grace. But Grace hates dirt, and then she'd be mad at June for not cleaning the floor better. June sets down the Dr. Pepper and glasses by the radio.

"Why'd you change it? Who's that singing now?"

"You don't know? LaVerne Baker," Maureen says haughtily, so that June knows that LaVerne Baker must be Negro. Maureen acts like the new Miss Queen of Negro Facts.

"Thanks," June says. She's furious and not sure why. "Stop looking. There was only one bottle. You have to share." June pours the Dr. Pepper into two glasses, eyeing them carefully so the soda comes up even. If Maureen gets less, she'll be mad. "Scotty be sleepin' on your shift," she taunts.

"Don't be funny, June Lacey Lynch."

June shrugs, scoots her fanny up onto the bed. Her feet dangle over the side, and she pumps them fast like she's riding a bike, till the red toes make a blur. She takes a gulp of soda. "See for yourself."

Maureen's jaw has closed up. It looks tight and puffed like a bullfrog's. Her eyes are green and beady. "Let me see!" June's noticed that even though Maureen's cool at school, and changing race, she isn't cool once she gets home; she's scared. She never goes inside if she knows Scotty's there and no one else; she sits on the steps and waits. Now June watches Maureen wriggle into a big flannel work shirt that hung on the chair back, the one Grace wears for cleaning. The curved bottom of the shirt hangs almost to her knees. Maureen opens the door and stands in the doorway, hands on her hips, her head craned forward to see if what June says is true. The backs of her knees are blue with veins. Her legs are pale and bowed under the shirt. She might have breasts now, and a daddy-o, but she still has frog legs.

June jumps down off the bed and stands behind Maureen. She can see past her sister into the front room. She sees Scotty open his eyes and squeeze them shut and open them again. If she didn't know he was drunk, she'd think he was teasing. He looks surprised to see his oldest goddaughter glowering at him from across the room, like she's about to boss him. Only Grace has ever told him to do anything and gotten away with it, June remembers. And then only once or twice. Anyone else, he'll smack. June sees his black tie-up shoes, the size of boats, float from the end of the couch to the floor, sees him raise himself to his elbow, then sit up. Maybe he'll make them popcorn, June thinks quickly, hopefully. It's her favorite thing that Scotty does for them. He's in his ribbed undershirt and his boxer shorts that open as he moves. You can see black hair inside. He's big and muscular. He has a tattoo of a flag on his left bicep. The shift lays crumpled on the pillow where his head was.

"My shift! My birthday present from my dad!" Maureen protests. June sees Scotty weave forward sloppily from the waist, then back into the couch. He's drunker than she imagined. She should never have opened her mouth. She sees him stand up. He's coming toward their doorway. He places a hand on each of Maureen's shoulders, curling his fingers. They're so big that when he squeezes he leaves marks, even when he doesn't mean to. They're close to June, too. She can see his nails.

"Don't talk to Scotty like that," Scotty growls, like he's talking about someone else. "*I'm* 'dad' now. Don't you boss your dad." He has Maureen by the shoulders. He is shaking her back and forth, back and forth, like the piggy bank on June's bureau in the old apartment, when she shook the pennies out. One time she broke it trying.

June stands frozen behind Maureen, and since she's glad to be out of his immediate line of vision, she's glad it's Maureen and not her, she thinks guiltily. "Turn around, Maureen," she wants to say. She wants to see her sister's face, her hazel-green eyes, and know she's all right. But he's got hold of Maureen. Maureen pulls loose, tries to kick him, misses. June's glad she missed, or he'd go wild.

"You, who the fuck you think you are?" he curses, and reaches. Maureen ducks and runs across the living room, backs

179

against the wall by the radiator and the open window, cornered. June remembers the way the woman looked at the bottom of the air shaft, bent funny and staring straight up at them. She pictures Maureen like that, looking up from the bottom at Scotty, slicing him with bottle-green eyes as he stares down and starts to realize what he's done.

Whatever has held June frozen breaks, and she rushes past Scotty. He takes a swipe at her, too, but misses. June throws herself toward the wall where Maureen is and reaches out with her right, strong hand, yanking her sister out of the corner. Maureen lurches like a ragdoll, almost losing her balance; her mouth hits the edge of the radiator. There is blood. Scotty stands large and idiot-like in the center of the room. He sees the blood, and something seems to click. He pauses, like a balloon losing air, just long enough for the two of them to rush past him out the door, down the stairs and out the building's front door. They clatter up the steps of the apartment building across the street, exactly opposite. A grimy old man is sitting on the top step. He sees the blood and mutters. They bang on the door of the first apartment on the left and Pearl, their friend PeeWee's mother, opens it.

"Good God," she says, and takes them in. She holds the towel from her shoulder to Maureen's face till it soaks up the blood coming out between her lips and down her chin and onto her collar. Pearl makes Maureen open her mouth, and she looks. The lip is split but no teeth have come loose. "What happened?" she says, and before June can answer she hears her sister say "I fell on the radiator."

June looks at Maureen to see if she is going to say more, and Maureen looks at June like "shut your trap," like Scotty will get her if they tell. Pearl sets them down in the front room by her plants and windows. She's in the middle of making a cake, she says. "Now you girls just make yourselves to home. You're welcome here anytime." When she leaves the room, Maureen starts to cry. "I hate his guts," she keeps saying, between blubbers.

They sit together in the chair by the window, June counting

the number of disciples in the wall picture of the Last Supper while Maureen pulls herself together. "My shift," Maureen says, and June wants to say forget the stupid shift. But she knows it's more. June doesn't say what she wants to say, just strokes Maureen's head. She's been stroking Maureen's head since forever, it seems. She's the one who got help the times Maureen had asthma attacks at night; she's the one who saved Maureen's life.

"You'll be okay," June says automatically, like she did those other times, but she's not sure she believes it anymore. She feels that Maureen, like their mom, like their real dad, will go away. June looks out the window and sees Grace coming up the cracked sidewalk in her tight, new perm curls, her shopping cart with groceries rolling behind her.

"Come on, Maureen, there's Grace." She remembers to yell "thanks" back into the apartment as they leave. The geezer's still sitting on the steps, and he looks curious, but June doesn't say anything. Let him ask Pearl if he wants.

"This place—just a nasty spot," she hears him mutter behind her as they start across the street. Maureen has gotten some of her spring back; she keeps up. Scotty's gone when they get upstairs, but June can see the signs of his visit. It wasn't a dream: there are cigarette butts in the ashtray by the couch.

"What happened to you?" Grace exclaims, when she stops inspecting her perm in the mirror and notices Maureen's red eyes and fat lip. Grace hates disorder, and June thinks it's more this than Maureen's condition, exactly, that has excited Grace.

"I fell on the radiator," Maureen says for the second time.

"What were you doing by the radiator?"

"I dunno." Maureen looks trapped. June has never heard a rule "no playing near the radiators," but now it will be added to the list of official rules.

"You two should stay away from the radiators," Grace admonishes, then sits, motions Maureen up on the couch next to her. "God is punishing you for cursing at me," she tells Maureen. The next thing, it seems to June, Grace has the shift on her lap and a needle and thread between her lips, like Maureen wanted in the first place. Grace's needle moves swiftly around the hem, and every so often Grace leaves the needle in the cloth, reaches to Maureen's head to stroke it. June sits on the matching stuffed chair. Since Maureen has lied about what happened she can't say anything like "thanks" to June for rescuing her. She only pays attention to Grace. June now remembers exactly how much she'd been resenting Maureen before everything happened. She gets up to leave.

"Where are you going, young lady?"

"Out," June says.

"Would you mind putting those things away while I do this?" Grace gestures toward the shopping cart.

June drags the squeaky-wheeled thing into the kitchen, squeezes the groceries, bag and all, onto the shelf. Grace will get mad when she sees, but June doesn't care. She hangs the cart on the back of the door, then goes out the door, shutting it behind her on the apartment.

June takes the stairs by twos, up through the building. She goes fast by the Lipowitz's, hoping to avoid Mrs. The bolt on the door to the roof is fastened. June pulls it back and steps into the breeze and light. Her milk crate stands against the chimney where she's left it. June lifts the crate from the wall and sets it in the center of the tar paper. She sits up on the crate, her feet pulled up against her, arms clutching her shins. When *she's* fifteen, she thinks, she's not wearing a yucky shift or becoming Negro like Maureen. But like her sister she's gonna do something exciting before she dies. She's going to escape this nasty spot. For sure, she's going to live before she dies.

Far below are the sounds of cars, of kids playing stickball, of someone's mom calling. June could tell exactly which mom it is, if she were to listen, but she doesn't. She remembers something else, far away, when she was practically a baby. Her mom was still alive. Her dad was there, too. They were on a car trip. They stopped at a playground. She sat in a swing. Her dad took the swing from behind, pulled it back and let it go, and she sailed back and forth, back and forth, her mother's encouraging face in front, her father pushing from behind. She went higher than her mother and father, even, to the top of the world.

Later, on the same trip, she was in a rowboat on a lake and her dad let her hold the fishing pole. He sat on the seat beside her. Maureen and mom were on the bank. He sang that one he always sang: "Get up there, mule, here comes a lock; we'll make Rome 'bout six o'clock." She felt a jerk at the end of the line. She shrieked with excitement and felt his hand over hers.

"Whoa there!" he said—to her or the fish, she didn't know. He cranked the reel saying "whoa there!" Then a fish wriggled in the air—brown and black and quick, slick with water. He pulled the rod back till the fish was in the boat.

"Lookee, Ramona! My baby's caught her first fish!" he kept exclaiming across the water. He took the fish off the hook. She could hear it thumping inside the basket. He kissed her cheek, his stubble prickly against her skin. "My baby's first fish!"

Whenever June comes up to the roof she lands back in that day. Her dad and her mom and Maureen. No Grace and, especially, no Scotty. How it might be again someday. Not a picture, even, just the pieces, a feeling: everybody likes her, no one bothers at her, no one yells or hits, or lies, or cries. Her body feels strong and she is running through the sky. All around there's air and light and space, and she's running through the sky.

My Sister, My Eye

Linda Ostreicher

I F IT'S TRUE the body knows more about itself than it lets on, that could be why I always craved a sister. A subtle physical signal may have been scrambled last spring, inspiring me to invite Cathy to live with me.

Everyone thought it was a fine idea. My cousin and I were both unmarried, both nearly thirty. Her parents hoped I could find her a husband among the fun-loving singles they assumed I knew; they couldn't imagine a daughter choosing to leave home for crowded Manhattan except to enjoy a daring social life.

On her first morning in Manhattan, Cathy left me a message in soap on the bathroom mirror, just like lovers do in movies: "See you tonite! Have a nice day!" Housekeeping is not my strong point before breakfast, but grouchiness is. I scrubbed the soap off the mirror and polished the glass. It had been a long time since I'd seen myself so clearly so close up. There were fine hairs growing from the familiar mole in the middle of my forehead. I didn't know if they were one of the seven warning signs of cancer. The mole felt tender when I touched it.

I found a magnifying mirror and took a closer look. The hairs were a shade darker than the down on my cheeks. Two fine tracks branched down from the mole, one toward each eyebrow. I forced a smile that dug the lines from my nose to mouth a little deeper. I promised my face a treat of some kind later, maybe a new moisturizer. There was only time to wash it now, in my daily race to work. This was one of the slow weeks at the office. The month's copy had been printed and proofed; the artist was pasting it up. All I had on my desk was a pile of manuscripts to read.

I work for a magazine called *Love's Deep Secrets*. It's not racy, though the cover always shows a pretty girl whose neckline is slipping down to meet a banner headline promising she'll reveal much more inside. The catch that keeps us in business is that when she does, she's in such bad shape that her good looks don't help at all. She drinks too much, gets batted around by her husband, and falls prey to ugly villains who reduce her to sorrow and shame. There isn't even a moral to her story. A heroine's sin might be a reader's own bad luck, so our audience might take it personally if we pointed fingers at anyone. She picks herself up and starts again, more wary, with new self-respect.

Our writers are professionals, the unsigned stories are fiction, but *Love's Deep Secrets* presents itself as truth. Fans see the grainy photos of dowdy women and homely men, they see their own troubles in smudged type on cheap paper, and they take the stories as a kind of news, easy to read and very local. When something huge and bad happens to them in real life, they remember they saw it first in *Love's Deep Secrets*; when it's all over, they try to make the best of a bad thing by writing it down and offering it to us for publication.

A former nurse sent us her life story in installments scribbled in pencil on paper napkins. She lost her medical license for drinking on the job to forget a bully she followed around the country for fifteen years. The day I noticed my mole growing hairs, her story was cancer. She had three months to live and hoped her story was worth two hundred and eighty dollars. That was the fee a Milwaukee quack was asking, to cure her by recoloring her aura.

I sent her a rejection card and a free magazine. My eyes hurt from reading her story; pencil gets blurry on napkin paper, and her writing was shaky anyway.

Something seemed to be wrong with my vision. It was like

the squat hot dog you can see if you point your forefingers at each other and move them together in front of your eyes: the hot dog's two ends are your fingertips, overlapping when they come too close to get into focus. I didn't see hot dogs, just ghosts of the edges of things straight ahead of me. They flickered, dead in the center of my vision, like things glimpsed from the corner of your eye.

My cousin was a teacher of special children. I knew some of her pupils had trouble seeing things normally, so I thought Cathy might have heard of ways to help eyes working the way mine were. That night I asked her if any of her students had wandering eyes.

"Sure, a lot of them can't concentrate. They're always looking around."

"I meant literally, two eyes looking in different directions."

"That's convergence. I don't do that; it takes physical therapy. I just do emotionally disturbed, slow learners, hyperactives—no muscle problems."

"Could you tell if I have convergence trouble?"

Cathy was putting pieces of candy from different bags into nests of cellophane grass in miniature baskets. She knocked a basket over, spilling jellybeans into her lap. "That's a cause of dyslexia. You're always reading, you can't have convergence problems. You don't even wear glasses."

"Would you look, just in case? My eyes have been giving me so much trouble."

I faced my cousin, avoiding her eyes because I hardly knew her. I looked at the barrettes holding her hair on either side of her head. It looked to me as if she had a nose above her nose, a phantom nose that ended at the upturned tip of her real one. When she shook her head, I saw a blonde halo follow her light brown hair. She looked like a doll or a saint. My eyes were fine, she said. I remembered her as a good child, while I'd tended to be grumpy.

I poked in one of her little baskets and found a chocolate egg wrapped in gold foil. "Are these for your classes?"

She nodded.

I buried the egg back under the jelly beans, sourballs, and marshmallow chicks. "Can I help fill them?" I asked.

Cathy looked surprised, but she assigned me the ribbons. I can tie a fancy bow, and soon we had a real assembly-line process going. I laid a patch of grass, she layered on the candy, I tied a pink or blue bow on the handle, and she topped off each full basket with a small rabbit made of pom-poms.

This was how we had played with her dolls when we were kids. She had half a dozen identical Barbies, and we'd dress them all, one step at a time: tops, skirts, jewelry, handbags, shoes. Then I'd feel cheated because there was nothing to do with the dressed-up dolls.

When we played at my house, we played my way. For years my dolls had acted out an endless serial based on *Little Women*. Having no real sisters, I tried to disappear into the world of four sisters in a book. To make their Victorian costumes, I stole towels and napkins, my mother's old lacy slips, my father's silk ties. I looted the boxes of my own outgrown clothes on their way to the Salvation Army. My parents were too busy making their candy store support us to notice my pilfering or the dolls' strange wardrobe.

The dolls were a mixed, anonymous group, none as glamorous as Barbie, but in costume they became fairly striking. I couldn't sew much, but with glue and pins and strategic draping, I got an exotic effect that looked historical enough for me. I also built houses of cardboard walls, furnished with cut-up boxes. These were even flimsier than the clothes, but I lavished curtains, rugs, and tassels over all the rough edges, which is what I thought the sisters themselves would have done.

When Cathy came to play, my houses caved in. The doll clothes fell apart in her hands. I made her wait to play until I had dressed the sisters myself. When it came to the good part, the acting of my favorite scenes, my cousin changed everything; she had never read the book. She put modern words in the dolls' mouths, talk of radios and cars. The plot, the dolls, the houses all looked shabby to me while she was there.

Every time she came, I looked forward to playing with her: I wanted to hear someone else speak the dolls' words so I could answer them. I wanted to see the dolls move by a power that wasn't my hands.

But after each visit, I hated Cathy for spoiling my game. I hated the dolls for not being my sisters or even Little Women. I threw them against the wall. I banged their heads on the floor. Then I was Jo, the sister with the terrible temper; then I was the gentle sister, Beth, to soothe the abused dolls, tucking them into boxes, closing their mindless eyes.

Cathy had a shocking pink case, round and zippered like a miniature suitcase. Under its lid was Barbie's frilly bedroom. She also had a black patent leather case, which unfastened with a twist of a clasp of the kind that closes ladies' purses. This opened to become Barbie's closet.

It was all so neat. The outfits slid on snugly; everything had accessories you could mix or match. Cathy was proud of her Barbie collection. She had no urge to sew funny-looking dresses that resembled nothing worn today. She let me drape Barbie's muffler around her like a shawl over her nightgown, with her six-inch bride's veil trailing from her waist and a necklace wobbling on her hair. Cathy allowed everything, but she thought it was silly: the nightgown wasn't a long dress; the necklace wasn't a crown.

For her, the play was in putting together outfits that made sense in the modern world. Dolls were for dressing. You dressed them, maybe paraded them down a runway like models, but you didn't expect them to live afterwards. You just changed their clothes.

"What happens to your kids?" I asked Cathy, after we filled the last Easter basket. "Do they ever go back to regular classes?"

"Once in a while, but it takes years, usually."

"Then what?"

"Then I get more kids."

"I meant, then what for the kids?"

"Whatever regular kids do." She shrugged. "They grow up, I guess."

Cathy was easy to live with. At first she acted as if a mother was going to turn up to take care of her, but she soon got the hang of helping to clean up, and she got very involved with my cookbooks. She'd never cooked at home; my kitchen became her lab. She baked cookies for her classes and made dinner for us every night, sometimes for her brother and his wife as well.

They came over often: she adored Larry and admired Joyce. He lapped up Cathy's cooking and loving attention; Joyce had to keep reminding him to watch his weight, for the sake of his heart, which is delicate. There was something warm and comfortable about the three of them together, tumbling over each other's sore points like kittens, landing harmlessly on their feet. They talked about concrete things: the new fall line of sportswear at Larry's showroom, Joyce's recipe for homemade hair dyes.

Because I felt awkward hovering around Cathy's family dinners, I began taking yoga classes after work. I'd had my eyes checked, and the diagnosis was overwork and tension. Yoga helped me to loosen up and it featured a few exercises specifically for eyes. Still my vision remained disturbed.

While I watched my cousin mumble over a lesson plan, brilliant rays shot from the lamp over her head. One night when I came home to find Cathy, Larry and Joyce playing Monopoly, their edges looked too distinct and the space between them appeared intensely empty. The depth of the scene was exaggerated, like colored slides you look at through a stereoscope that adds a fake dimension to flat film. I wondered if this was related to what happened in yoga class, when a muscle would suddenly give way and I'd realize how easy I could feel if it would stay that way. When this happened to my eyes muscles, I'd see more clearly, in richer colors.

Cathy preferred aerobics to yoga. She started bringing home friends from her new Manhattan class, healthy people who looked ordinary but broke into rapid sit-ups on the living room carpet on any excuse at all.

One night, Cathy was doing sit-ups, rhythmically as a wind-shield wiper. Another woman, flat on her side, was raising and lowering her leg like a scissors blade. A third woman lay face down, holding her feet in her hands, arching like a person bound on a wheel each time she pulled her ankles up to meet the back of her head. Not to be outdone, I touched my toes and stayed there, attempting to pull my head to my knees. My upside-down sight suddenly doubled and I watched six women perform motions that could fit right into an animated triptych of Hell. I closed my eyes, breathed deeply, and saw a red blur cut by a few lines. I straightened up so fast I got dizzy.

Later, my magnifying mirror clarified things: the mole on my forehead had tiny lids that I could now open and shut at will. Behind them, something dark glistened. It was smaller than a match head, but it was unmistakably an eye.

I cut bangs in my hair that night, to conceal the eye. I learned that the shooting rays of light, the false depth and the double vision were growing pains of the tiny eye as it learned to coordinate with the other two. When the side effects bothered me, I could shut the new eye while the other two stayed open. It was harder than winking, but easier than wiggling my ears, which I still can't do.

It seemed time for a new step. I prowled health food stores and occult bookstores. Yoga had opened my third eye, but my yoga teacher was no theoretician. I knew this was something high on the psychic scale, and I wanted expert guidance on how to use it.

I tried polarity experts, naturopaths, shiatsu masseurs, but they all spoke in vague generalities. I could tell none of them had ever seen a real third eye.

My friend Alison invited me to hear a spirit guide who spoke through a therapist specializing in affirmations. My friend promised that Jeffrey—the therapist—was perceptive himself, but that the spirit guide had uncannily described several people attending a recent session. They called it a class, not a seance.

The process was called "channeling," which reminded me of TV channels, and gave the whole thing an aura of technical competence. One Sunday, I followed Alison to Jeffrey's class.

He was only a few years older than us and looked a little like my cousin Larry, although Jeffrey had a much better haircut. He seemed very gentle during the first part of the class, while people affirmed good things about themselves. Then we all held hands and closed our eyes and chanted his invitation to his spirit guide. My third eye forgot to close and watched him change like a comic impersonator. His shoulders squared, his jaw jutted forward, and his voice took on a Cockney accent.

"'Ogwash," he said, when I asked him what he thought about the possibilities of a third eye. "Ain't no sight outside the inner vision. Them special effects are so much claptrap and balderdash. Lead you right off the path, they will. Why, there's only one way through and that's through the valley of everyday life, watching the road unwind under yer feet, 'earing the wax grow in yer ears. All you need to know is, blow out if yer lungs is full, breathe in if they're empty."

I asked him to open his eyes and look at my forehead. He looked, closed his eyes again and hummed a low note. "It's a spot, a bit of a blemish you've got. Flesh and its weaknesses, that's all that is. You've got to learn to tell spiritual things, like a third eye, from material matters, like that spot you've got."

For the rest of the class, I silently fumed at Jeffrey. A good actor with a knack for an accent, that's all he was. After all, why would a spirit, finally free of the flesh, come back to it to tell strangers things they already knew about themselves? Why wasn't it out in heaven or Nirvana? And why should being dead be educational, anyway? How would a spirit know any more than Jeffrey, himself an obviously expert fraud who couldn't even recognize a genuine psychic organ when it stared him in the face?

Maybe I would have abandoned the spiritual path anyway, but I was firmly detoured to the medical model by my next symptom: a killer headache. For a whole weekend my scalp

191

felt like a girdle forcing a giant knuckle through the front of my head. Cathy made me see her doctor, who she said was very good and used to want to marry her mother.

My cousin didn't know about my eye. I made the doctor promise not to tell her, because it sounded so crazy. This convinced him that I was rational enough to merit a serious examination and all the latest, highest-tech tests. He thought my series of vision problems was intriguing.

When my tests were ready, he wouldn't give me the report over the phone. "You'll be better off hearing it here," he insisted. When I got to his office, he actually came out from behind his desk and sat beside me. "I'm going to ask you to agree not to broadcast this," he began.

I nodded.

"If my guess is right, and I can't think of any other way to explain your tests and history, it's fairly sensational."

"Good news?" I doubted that, but "sensational" is usually positive. It seemed too strong to describe good health in someone like me, who felt basically well.

"Newspapers might pick it up. They've done it before."

"What are you talking about?"

He hedged and hinted and showed pictures of his trip through my skull until I had no doubt that he meant I had a twin in my head. My third eye was hers. We were Siamese twins, joined at the front of our brains. She'd waited, dormant, all these years to suddenly blossom on my forehead, hooking into the network that passed her sense perceptions to my brain.

I had a million questions for the doctor. What if it was her brain we were using, not mine? In the scan, that cloudy image of a shrimp curled over my eyebrow—could it really be my sister? Was she my age? Was she alive? How did she eat? What would she do now?

I was damn lucky, he told me. The few recorded times this had happened before, the undeveloped twin was lodged deep inside the other's body, tangled in delicate tissues and vessels that made removal risky. But my twin was easy, right under the surface, and could come out as neatly as a corn.

"But why can't she stay?"

She could die at any moment, releasing fatal toxins straight into my blood. Why, she was like a tumor—the sooner gone the better, and my headaches had only just begun. I probably wasn't seeing through her eye at all; chances were the visions I saw came from her pressure on the sense receptors of my brain.

I put off scheduling surgery, claiming my right to a second opinion. He made me promise to tell no one but my immediate family and the second doctor.

I'd waited too long for a sister to give her up now. I took her for a walk through Central Park, parting my bangs so she could see. I felt like a pregnant woman, bearing a double measure of life, but even better; this one didn't have to leave me.

Except that now she was stirring, starting with her eye. She might spring from my head like the goddess Athena, fully formed, though tiny as a doll. I could carry her anywhere, inside or out of me, whichever she chose.

We were tired and hungry. We went home and slept. We took aspirins for our headache so we could enjoy each other's company without distraction.

On Sunday, I realized Cathy had been gone all weekend.

We were reading a letter to "Dear Abby" from a nurse recovering from cancer. I told my sister about the nurse who wrote to me on paper napkins: maybe this letter was hers and she would live! Abby congratulated the nurse and reminded us all that every day is a priceless gift won from death itself.

This reminded me that Abby had her own twin sister, Ann Landers. Could my sister and I form a working team? Could I read proof aloud to her, while she searched the printed page for errors? I was trying to read two columns of the newspaper at once, one with her eye, one with mine, when Cathy came in.

"You went home?" I asked. She sometimes spent the night at her parents' house. She was crying, I saw now. "Is it your folks? One of your kids at school? You lost your job?"

She shook her head, unable to speak until I hit on it. "A

man?" She wailed and poured out details in no particular order. He was married, he loved her, he gave her a marionette from Paris with human hair and china fingers, he gave her a ticket to Hawaii and they were going there together, his son was sick, his son was better, he bought a new house for her, now his wife moved into it, he couldn't leave his family, he was so good, he gave her two tickets to Hawaii and told her to take a friend along to help her forget him.

There was so much she'd had to hide from everyone, especially her family. She was almost happy it was over and she could let out some of the secrets she'd been carrying in her head.

Her story was just like those I read at work every day, but it was different hearing it from Cathy, having known her all my life. For one thing, I went to Hawaii with her a few weeks later. I had had a loss too, by then.

First, my headaches stopped; then the eye went dark. I have such a small scar on my forehead, it will soon disappear into the other lines around it.

I had thought it would be like an abortion to kill my sister, more wrenching because she'd been with me so long and was my exact twin. It didn't seem fair for me to have a whole body and a lifetime, when all she had was that one small eye, so late to open. And she was so vulnerable, I feared dust and sand would fly into her only functioning part. "Watch it," I warned her when the wind blew, when my impatient doctor phoned.

Her first tear felt like a pinpoint of sweat. Then the headaches stopped; then everything else stopped.

My doctor says some growths are reabsorbed by the body. No one knows how, but in cancer it's called remission. He also says he's only human, and the shrimp we saw in the scan may have been a flaw in the film itself. The evidence in my body is all gone now.

But I feel her with me all the time. She gives me the strength to comfort Cathy, who bounced back well enough in Hawaii but sometimes gets discouraged. "I want a child so badly," she says. "I know every way to help it grow, and it all goes to other people's kids. Think what I could do with one who was mine all the time, who wasn't even a slow learner."

"You could have it alone. . ."

But she wants it to have more, not less, than she had. That means two parents and at least one brother or sister, and probably a dozen Barbie dolls.

I can see her point—having a sister did wonders for me. I don't feel different from people who aren't lonely, anymore. It could be that it was my sister who was always lonely. Sometimes I think I have her brain; sometimes I know it's mine. She could be in every cell of me, or riding through my blood and I'll drop dead tomorrow when she clots.

Now that I don't have to protect my sister from the pressure, I'm learning to stand on my head. They say it does wonders for the circulation.

There have turned out to be so many ways to look at things.

A Family Game

Wendy Ann Ryden

NADINE FELT PRETTY damn good this Sunday afternoon, sitting with her sister Loisa, drinking beer and waiting for the game to begin. The sun on her shoulders and lap felt good and warm on her bones and the slight breeze dried the sweat that formed under her Tom Seaver Day cap.

"Baseball just like the way you think it oughta be," she laughed suddenly and turned toward Loisa, raising her Big Beer in a toast.

Loisa turned too and winked, the two looking at each other happily, clear gray eyes meeting clear gray eyes. Nadine bared her silver-capped grin that her daughter, Maisy, had paid for, despite the child's annoyance that her mother had not chosen the more expensive enamel-colored fillings.

The sisters had arrived at Shea ahead of time to watch the players warm up. Nadine liked the way that Number 17, who wasn't bad looking, "far as white folk go," straddled his legs and stretched. She watched him do the splits as she looked through the tiny set of plastic field glasses she had got by sending away the coupons on the back of the Toasty-O's cereal box. Loisa told her it was shameful, an old thing like her, looking like that, but she quieted down when Nadine let her have a peek too.

The box seat section where they sat was speckled with vacant corporate seats gone to waste. There was nothing particularly important about this game, so no company big shots were around.

"Coming just to say they come," Loisa scowled condescendingly.

"That's right," Nadine agreed. "Following baseball the same way they read about goings on in South America; so's they can make conversation if need be. No passion. It's sin, folks' lack of genuine feelings."

But, in a different way, Nadine and Loisa were real proud of their half a box too, even though it had to be a secret pride. Neither of them had a great deal of money, and they stretched the allowance the children gave them by eating beans and stew made from goat legs bought at the Jamaican market, keeping the heat turned down and their old coats on indoors (when the children weren't around) in order to save enough money for the two seats. Sometimes they just plain lied about how much cash they had left at the end of each month. They felt guilty about how they spent the money they were supposed to be using for their necessaries, because none of the family knew about the secret seats. All anyone knew was that after their husbands had died, the two women became fans and went to a lot of games, a harmless enough activity for two old widows who lived close enough to the stadium. Thrifty as the two sisters always seemed to be, no one would believe that they purchased anything but the cheapest seats.

And today any guilt they felt disappeared in the joy of watching their favorite player, Number 1, courageously shag flies in the outfield, always practicing, never giving up.

"A damned shame he don't play more often, the way he give heart and soul of hisself. Why, it's sin that he don't play more often," Nadine would complain. She had actually written a letter to the manager, expressing her thoughts on the subject, only at the last minute she didn't send it on account of Loisa convinced her too many of the words were probably spelled wrong.

"Besides," Loisa had accused, "his wife probably think you sweet on him. I think so, too, the way you look with those glasses."

It wasn't that she had anything against the other little fellows who "platooned" (as the sportscasters called it) in center field, and maybe she didn't know all there was to know about how to play the game, relative newcomers as she and Loisa were, but one thing seemed pretty clear: at any one time those Mets had only three black players on the field, and more often than not, it was just that right fielder, lanky as a yearling, who hit home runs when he had a mind to. It was that fact that rankled Nadine, not what Loisa thought at all, and she wished her sister would learn to know her thoughts a little better. The thing with the toy binoculars, she was just fooling.

The other black player they admired so was that fine young pitcher. "So young, it hard to believe he that good," Loisa would smack her lips in respect. Nadine had a particular soft feeling for him, especially when those so-called experts were being critical, because he reminded her of her youngest, Ulysses. Shy and sweet, Ulysses, whom she had later in her years, had enlisted with the Marines a while back, "hoping to become a good man," he had told Nadine, in all seriousness, and it had made her sad to think he didn't already know he was one. He was probably, like a lot of people, just a little lonely.

She reached down between her skirted thighs to cover the movement of popping a beer can. Between them was the old handbag Loisa had saved from her daughter Jonelle's trash can, perfect for smuggling in a six pack of Rheingold and ice. While Loisa carried the small purse, Nadine, like a mama bird faking a broken wing, passed by security carrying a large beach bag, overstuffed with Cracker Jacks and roasted peanuts. The guard would fall for it every time: squeeze the decoy, trying to find the something forbidden, while Loisa sailed in free. "So easy to fool 'the Man'," Nadine smirked, imitating her lawyer son Lloyd's slang. Loisa was a little less certain. But why would anybody want to turn them in? They weren't some smart-alecky kids causing disturbance. They were two nice old colored ladies—might even be a bit senile— minding their own selves. Still, Loisa liked it when Nadine acted secret-like, bending over, showing a mouthful of silver, hiding the can between her legs as she poured the pale gold liquid, before sitting upright to hand over the cool drink, and smooth her white wool hair back under her cap.

Nadine was also in charge of choosing the pretzel the sisters treated themselves to on the walk from the subway to the stadium. It was a little game, testing Nadine's psychic capabilities, to see if she could figure out which vendor had the hottest coals. Sometimes she guessed wrong: the pretzel would be cold and mealy, and then Loisa'd let her know about it. But most times Nadine was right on the money. They'd walk side by side with their twisted lover's knot of dough, pulling it apart like a wishbone to allow the steam to escape, picking off the extra crystals of salt, and by agreement, finishing it before they entered the stadium.

Now the announcer was calling for everyone to stand for the the national anthem, and Loisa and Nadine obliged, joining in singing, not because they felt particularly patriotic, but because they loved to sing. Their voices were untuned, but clear, and when they sang together the rest of the world fell away, along with fifty years, making them children again, singing their praises in the old colored church in Fayetteville. Having parted during their middle years, each to the business of raising families, Nadine and Loisa, in widowhood, were together once again.

The Mets took the field, and the game began. This was where they were at their best, where Nadine and Loisa could offer the most support. They could run to the warning track with the outfielders, jump high with the shortstop anticipating the unanticipated hop, stretch long at first base to coax the ball into the glove half a heartbeat before the runner's foot hit the bag. As serious as young animals at play, somehow their concentration came easily.

The first batter began with a high chopper that the shortstop bounded up beautifully to grab. It wasn't easy, only looked that way, and Nadine sighed over the close one and wiped her forehead with a napkin. She was soft and plump and needed to spread her legs apart to allow the breeze to catch underneath her skirt. Loisa was more wiry than her older sister and wasn't too affected by the heat. She had always been on the thin side, except for the pot of belly flesh that in the comfort of older age had begun to accumulate. Nadine patted it now, like a Buddha's tummy.

"From all them Big Beers you put away," she chuckled approvingly.

Loisa elbowed her. "Mind the game, now," she said curtly, but gently wiped some perspiration from the back of Nadine's neck.

The next batter did get a base hit, and Loisa curled her lip at Nadine, and Nadine knew that she was right: she hadn't been paying attention. So she made it up to her with an infield fly followed by two strikes and a foul tip right into the catcher's mitt.

"Hallelujah," said Loisa. "We redeemed." And they split another ice-cold Rheingold to celebrate and prepare for the bottom half of the inning.

All skills require practice, even when there's talent, and the offensive game presented a problem. Oh, they weren't bad by any stretch, but what with the competition being fiercer than mosquitoes in a swamp, consistency was difficult. They started off looking fine with a couple of hits, but the cleanup batter, Number 26, he had a mind of his own.

"Just like my Lloyd, that mind of his own," Nadine shook her head in remembrance. "Can't say it's hurt him none in this world, but it drove me to the Devil sometime."

A power hitter like that, twice as likely to strike out as hit a home run. That was the deal; that was the risk. Today they reached a compromise: no strike-out, no home run, but an off-the-fence double that drove in two runs. Nadine grinned.

"Don't I know it, just like Lloyd."

The two sisters had had a little trouble convincing Nadine's lawyer son to let them live alone. They had finally made a bargain and agreed not to live too far away and to have dinner with the children twice a week.

They were pleased about getting those two runs in so early in the game, but it took a lot out of them, so the next two batters struck out. If they had more endurance, and if the fifth and sixth positions weren't changing so often, they might have been able to keep the streak going, but for right now it was okay.

"It be confusing," Nadine scratched her head in disappointment.

"Oh, you give up too easy, that's all," Loisa chided. "You get comfortable real quick." But it was hard to be mad when the going was good and she gently mopped the rivulets of sweat from Nadine's fat bosom.

But the powers that be were strong, and over the next few innings they could get no more runs, the pitcher being a wily one, outsmarting them with curve balls when they expected fast, keeping the ball inside and jamming the batters. Nadine thought about thinking mean about the pitcher, but Loisa told her it wasn't right, she had better get that right out of her mind, and besides no good would come of it. It was a devil's lure to try to get her to waste herself. "You better off having another hot dog, keep your energy up." So Loisa got both of them two more dogs and a damp paper towel from the lavatory to hold up against Nadine's neck, hoping to cool down her blood.

But in the seventh inning, at two crucial junctures, they lost control, giving up a walk and then a home run that barely made it, tipping the left fielder's glove. It might not have been so bad if they could have done a little more with the bat, but in this case the two mistakes tied the game up good. Next the pitcher gave up a base hit and then the manager came out and told the young Number 16 he'd have to leave, and Nadine and Loisa felt pretty bad about it, knowing he wasn't entirely to blame. Loisa didn't say it but Nadine knew she was thinking that if they hadn't killed the rally in the first inning, hadn't got complacent with limited success, or whatever it was that happened to them, that poor young pitcher might still be in the game. After all he allowed the same number of runs as the other team's pitcher and that boy was still in. Now chances were he wouldn't get the win. But not if they could help it.

Nadine spread her legs wider to brace herself and focused her clear gray eyes on the playing field. Loisa held her hand tight and leaned forward in concentration. The batter got a piece of one and Nadine followed the ball, moving with the shortstop to scoop it up (she winced, feeling what it was like to have to stoop down so low), run to second for the force, and then fire it hard to first for the double play. Loisa was right there, stretching with that Number 17 to save the throw and make the play. "Honey, you cookin' now!" Nadine beamed at her sister, and Loisa's face nearly split with a prideful grin.

The lump in Nadine's throat got a little smaller, but they still had to break the tie, and it was near the bottom of the order. She felt sure they could hold on defensively, but they needed some runs, and she had a sick kind of feeling that if they didn't get them in the seventh inning and wear down the relief staff, hell, after enough time they might get tired and make a mistake in the field. That could happen to anyone, and it wouldn't be the mistake that would cost them the game. It would depend on what they did now in this inning. As the sisters stood for the seventh inning stretch, Nadine broke out in a terrible sweat, like the beginning of the Change, and she could barely croak out the lyrics, "Take me out to the ball game," as she and Loisa swayed with arms around one anothers' shoulders, singing their nervous tenor and soprano.

The Diamond-Vision camera spun around the field looking for interesting sights to display on the stadium's big screen, and a lot of people waved and jumped up and down, but some acted nonchalant because the rumor is that if you look like you don't care the crew is more apt to swing the camera around your way. So, maybe because Nadine and Loisa were genuinely not thinking about getting on TV and were genuinely thinking about matters at hand, sure enough, the camera spotted them. And because they were trained to look at the screen even though they weren't *really* looking, they each eventually saw what was going on, saw the image of the two of them, arm in arm, holding on tight, singing into the sky, getting themselves ready for what they had to do. They couldn't contain their pleasure at being television stars, though, and their wide lips gradually peeled back from their teeth in satisfaction. But they kept looking straight ahead, singing sweet and out of key, exhibiting near perfect control, not letting on they knew they were on the closed circuit. The crowd frenzied, trying to stick waving arms and hands in front of the sisters' faces.

Nadine was feeling confident but still uncomfortably warm. When the first batter stood up at the plate, Loisa took some ice out of the Rheingold bag and began rubbing it on Nadine's back and neck. The ice melted on Nadine as if it had been dropped on a griddle, and she felt the cool sweet river travel down her back, droplets converging in the crack at the base of her spine. Even at this critical moment, Loisa couldn't help but think what a handsome woman her sister was, plump as a purple plum and as full of juice, despite the years of tribulation. Admiring Nadine made her feel strong and gentle all at once.

They watched the first batter like two hawks on a mouse, and he slipped one right through the hole between center and right field. That's it, Loisa thought, strategy *and* power. She thanked the Lord these Mets' pitchers could hit because the reliever was up next, and damn if he didn't slap one fair on the left field line. Enough action to make the other team yank their pitcher. Loisa and Nadine were glad that he hadn't lasted much longer than their own fellow. But when he came out, both Loisa and Nadine took a moment to privately acknowledge that he had done a good job, since they knew it was his due. They relaxed a bit while the new pitcher warmed up, feeling a surge of victory that made them wish for some wood to knock on.

Loisa began attending to Nadine like a trainer to a boxer in between rounds. She took some more ice from the bag and began rubbing it on Nadine's chest until it glistened. Then she leaned forward and blew on the spot while she worked on Nadine's back with a hanky she had dipped in the melted ice water. When she was satisfied that Nadine wasn't in any more danger of boiling over, Loisa leaned back, absently dropping her arm across her sister's shoulders, and tried to focus on the game.

"Mama! What are you doing here?"

It was Nadine's surprised Lloyd, standing next to Loisa's Jonelle, who was holding a melting Dixie cup, looking more grim than surprised. Loisa and Nadine had never thought about this statistical possibility, and now they realized they had been foolish not to.

"You see us on the TV?" Nadine asked, figuring what did she have to lose?

"What?"

"We was on the TV a little while ago."

"You two children enjoying the game?" Loisa added, her hands carefully folded over her little gut.

"What TV are you talking about?" Lloyd asked, trying to follow the logic.

. Suddenly Jonelle leaned forward and grabbed her mother and aunt tightly by the forearms. She whispered fiercely, "We didn't see you on no TV. Lloyd and I was sitting with Lynette and Calvin in the mezzanine when we heard a bunch of drunk punks laughing and carrying on about two old black lesbians feeling up on one another. Lloyd looked down front to see what was going on, and he saw *you* two."

Nadine and Loisa didn't get a chance to respond because Lloyd resumed his line of questioning.

"Mama, just how the hell did you get box seats?" He stopped as an idea occurred to him. "You two sneak on down here from up top?" He winked slyly, approvingly.

"Shoot," Nadine chortled huskily, seizing the opportunity. "No need to be broadcastin'."

"Why were those kids talking about lesbians?" Jonelle started and then got sidetracked when she saw the purse. "What's that

old thing doing here? Mama, you need money for a new pock-
etbook?"

But there was no way to stand in an aisle for so long without
blocking somebody's vision, and pretty soon the catcallers
started hollering for down in front. Lloyd and Jonelle reluctantly
went back to their wife and husband, respectively, Lloyd calling
over his shoulder that they'd be back for them.

"Caught," swallowed Loisa.

"Like rats," Nadine agreed.

"Guilty."

"As sin."

Nadine sat with her legs clamped together in a way unnatural
for a big woman, looking like an oversized chicken in a too-small
wire cage. She stared out at the field, but she wasn't seeing
what was there. The sweat beaded like the blood on Christ's
forehead, and Loisa didn't wipe it away. For some reason, Loisa
was thinking about Rooster Wallace, a boy from back home.
Fifteen years old she was, and trying to be a good girl, changing
her drawers and washing the hard to reach spots like everybody
said to, and then Rooster comes along and tells her how she's
giving him the blue balls, and what was she going to do about
it? Somebody says this, somebody says that. That was all outside. But what about the soft inside? The soft inside, too delicate
to stand up to the light of day. . .

Before either Nadine or Loisa had a chance, the man at the
plate fanned out: one, two, three, and the spell was broken.
The disappointment of the crowd brought them back to the
game, and the sisters watched, loyally and helplessly, the next
batter fly out, and the next batter do something else that
amounted to nothing, and then the inning was over. The teams
changed sides.

They didn't talk about what had happened. But they both
knew that just as a pitcher sometimes can't get it back after a
home run is hit, the rest of the game would pass them by, as
though they were watching it on TV. Nadine hoped it would
end quickly, mercifully, and that she and Loisa could sneak out

before Lloyd and Jonelle found them again. The crowd smelled gamey as a wolf; the gaudy orange and blue stadium was making her dizzy.

"I wish," Nadine broke her silent frustration, "these Mets'd picked some nice lookin' colors. 'Stead of this old Brooklyn Dodger blue, this New York Giant orange."

"Compromise," Loisa had started looking through the cereal box glasses again. "Just ain't very satisfying, sometimes."

Nadine leaned back in her chair, her knees opening a little. She looked at Loisa's belly, protruding as though it concealed something. "We outta beers for today," she sighed. "All our joy gone."

"Next time," Loisa said simply, focusing the glasses.

"Yeah, that's right. Next time."

About the Authors

Julia Alvarez is a poet and fiction writer. Born in New York City, she spent her early childhood in the Dominican Republic, the homeland of her parents. She is the second of four sisters, the first three born eleven months apart. She has taught English and creative writing at various schools and universities and is currently Assistant Professor at Middlebury College. Her publications include *Homecoming* (Grove Press, 1984) and *The Housekeeping Book* (Vermont Arts Council, 1984). She recently completed a collection of short fiction, *Small Change*.

Edith Chevat lives in New York City, where she was born. Her fiction has been published in *Sojourner*, *Other Voices*, *Country Women*, and *Broomstick*.

Cathy Cockrell was born in 1951 and has a younger sister and brother. Family is a common theme in the stories in her second book, *A Simple Fact* (Hanging Loose Press, 1987). "Whatever Lola Wants" is part of a longer work-in-progress about a pre-Stonewall working-class lesbian. Cockrell lives in San Francisco.

Terri de la Peña lives in her hometown, Santa Monica, California. Her father was a descendant of a land-grant family, and her mother is a native of Mexico. She has an older brother and sister and two younger sisters. Her stories "Once a Friend" and "A Saturday in August" were jointly awarded third prize in the University of California at Irvine's Chicano Literary Competition in 1986. Her novel-in-progress, *Margins*, focuses on parental and sibling relationships and issues of sexuality within an urban Chicano family.

Fay Myenne Ng's short fiction has been published in *Harper's, The PEN Syndicated Fiction Project, The American Voice, The Crescent Review, Calyx,* and *The City Lights Review,* and anthologized in *The Pushcart Prize XII: Best of the Small Presses.* She has received the D.H. Lawrence Fellowship and a Bunting Institute Fellowship from Radcliffe College.

Linda Ostreicher has lived in and around New York City for most of her life, as has her older sister. Despite this proximity, they maintain their fairly close relationship almost entirely by phone. This means that, in person, they usually surprise each other with slight changes in appearance that have accumulated over time.

Marianne Paul grew up along the St. Lawrence River. Her father worked in a factory, her mother as a housewife. There were five children in her family—three girls and two boys—and she was the second youngest. From her father, she inherited a strong work ethic: the ability to stay with a story until it is finished, and the stubbornness to be a writer in spite of the difficulties of the profession. From her mother, she inherited the vision to dream, and the audacity to think she can accomplish whatever she sets out to accomplish. She now lives in Kitchener, Ontario.

Dawn Raffel grew up in Milwaukee, Wisconsin and now lives in New York City, where she works as a writer and magazine editor. Many of her stories center on the relationship between sisters; her relationship with her own sister has had a profound influence on her.

Jean Roberta was born in the United States in the 1950's and is the oldest of three sisters (no brothers). She moved to Canada with her family as a teenager in the 1960's and has been a Canadian citizen since the 1970's. She is divorced with a daughter. She lives in Saskatchewan, where she has spent the last few years working on a Master's degree in English.

Wendy Ann Ryden was born in New Jersey. She is a feminist writer who believes in the magic of fiction to influence and transform. She is also a new student to the old art of belly dance. She and her sister are devoted Mets fans—but don't eat hot dogs on their visits to Shea Stadium, since Wendy is a vegetarian and animal rights activist.

Bárbara Selfridge once taught school in Puerto Rico, and has done waitressing and newspaper pasteup in Oakland, California. Her stories have appeared in *The Caribbean Writer, Sojourner, Five Fingers Review, Other Voices*, and *Unholy Alliances* (Cleis Press, 1988). She has been honored by a writing fellowship at the Fine Arts Work Center in Provincetown and participation in the 1989 Poets & Writers exchange program.

Donna Weir was born in St. Catherine, Jamaica and migrated to the United States at seventeen. She has written poetry since she was eleven. She is currently pursuing a B.A. in English at Hunter College and hopes to embark on a lifelong career of learning, writing, teaching, and performing in the tradition of African women. "Gal Pickney" is her first published story that deals directly with Jamaican immigrants: their culture/language, their struggles to make it in "dis man's country," and the often explosive conflicts that exist between the older heads and the younger, more Americanized generation. She gives credit to her mother Daisy for being the inspiration behind her writing, her survival, her very life, and to her sister Lavern for breathing life into the character Shirley.

Budge Wilson was born in Nova Scotia, Canada, in 1927. She has one older sister and is married with two daughters. Budge worked as a teacher, freelance artist, photographer, editor, and fitness instructor before starting to write in 1978. Her adult writing has won seven awards, and she has published five children's books, with three forthcoming.

Shay Youngblood was born in Columbus, Georgia to a family of loving, old, Black women. Her short stories and poetry have appeared in *Essence*, *Catalyst*, *Conditions* magazines and The Greenfield Review Press anthology, *The Stories We Hold Secret*. A collection of her short fiction, *The Big Mama Stories* (Firebrand Books, 1989) was adapted for the theater in a full-length play titled, *Shakin' the Mess Outta Misery*. She is at work on a novel set in Paris. She says: "I was raised an only child by seven mothers. In my chosen family I now have many sisters."

About the Editor

Paula Martinac was born in Pittsburgh in 1954, the youngest of three sisters, and now lives in Brooklyn, New York. For the last eight years, she has worked in lesbian and feminist publishing. A fiction writer, her short stories have appeared in *Conditions*, *Focus*, and *Sinister Wisdom*, and are featured in *Voyages Out #1* (Seal Press, 1989). She is a member of the editorial collective of *Conditions* magazine and the coordinator of a lesbian and gay reading series in New York City.

Attic Press

Fiction

ISBN Prefix: 0 946211

WILDISH THINGS: An Anthology of New Irish Women's Writing
Ailbhe Smyth (ed) 73 6 £7.95 (pb) / 74 4 £15.95 (hb)

The Bray House Eilís Ní Dhuibhne 96 5 £5.95

Blood And Water Eilís Ní Dhuibhne 54 X £4.95 (pb) / 53 1 £10.00 (hb)

The Awkward Girl Mary Rose Callaghan 95 7 £5.95

Night Train To Mother Ronit Lentin 72 8 £5.95 (pb) / 80 9 £12.95 (hb)

Stars In The Daytime Evelyn Conlon 78 7 £4.95

Different Kinds Of Love Leland Bardwell 34 5 £3.95 (pb) / 35 3 £10.00 (hb)

There We Have Been Leland Bardwell 81 7 £3.95

My Head Is Opening Evelyn Conlon 32 9 £3.95 (pb) / 33 7 £10.00(hb)

Changelings Melissa Murray 41 8 £4.95 (pb) / 42 6 £10.00 (hb)